E.R. PU
STRANGE ENDING

ERNEST ROBERTSON PUNSHON was born in London in 1872.

At the age of fourteen he started life in an office. His employers soon informed him that he would never make a really satisfactory clerk, and he, agreeing, spent the next few years wandering about Canada and the United States, endeavouring without great success to earn a living in any occupation that offered. Returning home by way of working a passage on a cattle boat, he began to write. He contributed to many magazines and periodicals, wrote plays, and published nearly fifty novels, among which his detective stories proved the most popular and enduring.

He died in 1956.

The Bobby Owen Mysteries

1. Information Received
2. Death among the Sunbathers
3. Crossword Mystery
4. Mystery Villa
5. Death of a Beauty Queen
6. Death Comes to Cambers
7. The Bath Mysteries
8. Mystery of Mr. Jessop
9. The Dusky Hour
10. Dictator's Way
11. Comes a Stranger
12. Suspects – Nine
13. Murder Abroad
14. Four Strange Women
15. Ten Star Clues
16. The Dark Garden
17. Diabolic Candelabra
18. The Conqueror Inn
19. Night's Cloak
20. Secrets Can't be Kept
21. There's a Reason for Everything
22. It Might Lead Anywhere
23. Helen Passes By
24. Music Tells All
25. The House of Godwinsson
26. So Many Doors
27. Everybody Always Tells
28. The Secret Search
29. The Golden Dagger
30. The Attending Truth
31. Strange Ending
32. Brought to Light
33. Dark is the Clue
34. Triple Quest
35. Six Were Present

E.R. PUNSHON

STRANGE ENDING

With an introduction
by Curtis Evans

DEAN STREET PRESS

Published by Dean Street Press 2017

Copyright © 1950, 1953 E.R. Punshon

Introduction copyright © 2017 Curtis Evans

Published by licence, issued under the
UK Orphan Works Licensing Scheme.

First published in 1953 by Victor Gollancz

Cover by DSP

ISBN 978 1 911579 05 2

www.deanstreetpress.co.uk

Detective Stories, the Detection Club and Death:
The Final Years of E. R. Punshon

> ... but, they dead,
> Death has so many doors to let out life,
> I will not long survive them.
>
> *The Custom of the Country* (c. 1619-23; 1647)
> JOHN FLETCHER AND PHILLIP MASSINGER

WHEN IN 1949 E.R. Punshon published *So Many Doors*, his twenty-sixth Bobby Owen detective novel, the Englishman was seventy-seven years old, with nearly a half-century of published novels behind him and a comparatively scant seven years of life and letters remaining before him. 1901, the year of the appearance of Punshon's first novel, *Earth's Great Lord*, saw the death of Queen Victoria, the long reigning granddaughter of King George III for whom a regal age of European global dominion has been named; while 1949, a year during which a convalescent Europe was still bleakly recovering from a world war that had reduced much of its civilization to ashes and rubble, saw the testing by the USSR of its first atomic bomb and the proclamation of the formation of the People's Republic of China. The world was changing with a fearsome fleetness that not merely old men who had first glimpsed light in the Victorian era were finding hard to follow.

Rapidly changing too was the craft of crime and mystery fiction that E.R. Punshon had long practiced (this admittedly a minor thing compared to unsettling phenomena like armed revolution and atom splitting). Like the once seemingly imperishable British Empire, the hegemony of the between-the-wars "Golden Age" clue-puzzle detective novel was breaking asunder, under pressure from increasingly popular rival forms of mystery fiction, such as hard-boiled, noir, psychological suspense and espionage. Already stalked by Raymond Chandler's famous gumshoe, Philip Marlowe, as well as ill-humored and hard-drinking would-be Marlowe doppelgangers like Mickey Spillane's brutish Mike Hammer, Punshon's well-born English policeman Bobby Owen, along with other of his surviving gentlemanly detective colleagues from the era of classic crime fiction, soon found himself in the sights of no less deadly a professional killer than James Bond. Agent 007's creator, Ian Fleming, who cited as his literary influences Raymond Chandler, Dashiell Hammett, Eric Ambler and Graham Greene, published his first Bond spy novel, *Casino Royale*, in the United Kingdom in 1953, where it enjoyed immediate popular and critical success. In the United States, where the novel appeared in 1954, the same year as Raymond Chandler's much-lauded *The Long Goodbye*, *Time* magazine wryly declared that "Bond . . . might well be [Philip] Marlowe's younger brother, except that he never takes coffee for a bracer, just one large martini laced with vodka."

Upon the publication of *So Many Doors* in the UK and the US (in the latter country it would prove the last Punshon mystery published during the author's lifetime), crime fiction reviewers deemed the novel and its author representatives of a vanished era. "The twenties were the plotter's heyday (consider Freeman Wills Crofts, J.J. Connington, Dorothy L. Sayers)," observed the Democratic-Socialist *London Tribune* in its review of the "well-plotted" and "studiously told" *So Many Doors*, "and to the twenties, in spirit at least, belongs Mr. Punshon." In the United States, Anthony Boucher, dean of American mystery critics, allowed in the *New York Times Book Review* that the narration of *So Many Doors* was "leisurely"; yet, after noting the seventeenth-century English stage derivation of the novel's title, he approvingly added that there "is something Elizabethan, even Jacobean, about the obscure destinies that drive [Punshon's] obsessed and tormented characters, and about the frightful violence that concludes the story." Punshon, it seemed, still had something to say in the harried and hectic atomic age, when crime fiction reviewers and readers alike seemed increasingly to believe that brevity was the soul of death.

* * * * *

To his death in 1956 E.R. Punshon maintained a loyal following in the United Kingdom among readers who staunchly adhered to the strict standard of fair play puzzle plotting associated with Golden Age detective fiction. During the Fifties the aging but seemingly indefatigable author, who still lived quietly with his wife Sarah at their house at 23 Nimrod Road, Streatham, produced, through the medium of his prestigious longtime publisher Victor Gollancz, nine new mystery titles-- *Everybody Always Tells* (1950), *The Secret Search* (1951), The Golden Dagger (1951), *The Attending Truth* (1952), *Strange Ending* (1953), *Brought to Light* (1954), *Dark Is the Clue* (1955), *Triple Quest* (1955) and *Six Were Present* (1956)— that detailed the final criminal investigations of his longtime series police detective, Bobby Owen, now risen to the august rank of Commander (unattached), Metropolitan Police. Additionally Punshon continued to remain active in his cherished Detection Club, a London-based social organization of distinguished detective novelists, in which the author had been inducted, along with Anthony Gilbert and Gladys Mitchell, in 1933, three years after the Club's founding, joining such luminaries from the crime writing world as G.K. Chesterton, Dorothy L. Sayers, Agatha Christie, E.C. Bentley, Anthony Berkeley, R. Austin Freeman and Freeman Wills Crofts.

Like other British institutions the Detection Club from 1939 to 1945 bore the bitter burdens of war, including the devastating Nazi air raids known collectively as "the Blitz." When the Club revived its meetings and annual dinners in 1946, it became immediately apparent that time had wrought cruel changes with its membership. On seeing his brother and sister detective novelists again at the Club premises after the long interval of war years, John Dickson Carr, a comparative stripling at the age of forty, recalled that he had been "shocked" by their appearance, which he had found decidedly "greyer and more worn."

By 1946 eight of the original twenty-eight Detection Club members, including G.K. Chesterton, R. Austin Freeman and Helen Simpson, had passed away and many other members were now elderly and inactive. Several more members would expire over the next few years. Even the formerly quite engaged Freeman Wills Crofts and John Rhode (Cecil John Charles Street), now in their sixties and living in the country, became markedly less involved with Club affairs, as did an increasingly infirm Henry Wade (the landed baronet Henry Lancelot Aubrey-Fletcher). For his part, John Dickson Carr, deeming British life under postwar conditions and the governance of the Labour party intolerable, would in 1948 depart for his native United States. Besides Punshon, only Christie, John Rhode and Henry Wade, among original members, and Anthony Gilbert, Gladys Mitchell, Margery Allingham, John Dickson Carr, Nicholas Blake, Christopher Bush and E.C.R. Lorac, among the smaller number of Thirties inductees, remained substantially active as crime writers into the 1950s. Of these Lorac and Wade, like Punshon, would not survive the decade, and another, John Rhode, would barely outlast it.

Clearly some new blood was badly needed. During Punshon's remaining span of life the aged and ailing Detection Club received transfusions, so to speak, from seventeen new members. Although with the deaths of Baroness Emma Orczy and A.E.W. Mason (in 1947 and 1948 respectively), Punshon became the oldest surviving member of the Detection Club, the author, who served as Club treasurer between 1946 and 1949, during the postwar years remained extensively involved in Club affairs, actively participating in hearty debates concerning prospective new members, like Christianna Brand, Michael Innes, Michael Gilbert, Elizabeth Ferrars and Julian Symons, as to whether or not they practiced fair play and sufficiently respected the King's (later Queen's) English, the Club's chief requirements for induction. (These debates are chronicled in detail in my CADS booklet *Was Corinne's Murder Clued? The Detection Club and Fair Play, 1930-1953*.)

In 1949 Punshon found himself at odds over the matter of new enrollments with the man who unquestionably was the Club's crankiest and most cantankerous member: Anthony Berkeley, famed author of *The Poisoned Chocolates Case* (1928) and, under the pseudonym Francis Iles, of *Malice Aforethought* (1931) and *Before the Fact* (1932), three of the best regarded British crime novels from the Golden Age. In April Berkeley wrote a provocative letter to Punshon in which he claimed that as the Club's "First Freeman" he possessed blanket veto power over prospective members, despite the fact that he no longer served on the membership committee. During the early days of the Detection Club, Berkeley had observed at a meeting that the Club had two "Freemans" as members (R. Austin Freeman and Freeman Wills Crofts), and he pronounced that as the person who had originally suggested forming the Club he would be its "First Freeman." To this suggestion everyone else had laughingly assented, taking the office as a joke; yet now, nearly two decades later, it seemed that Berkeley had not been joking.

Incensed by Berkeley's gambit and the rude language in which he had couched it, Punshon wrote Sayers, enclosing his antagonist's "offensive" letter (which evidently has not survived) and warning that "[Berkeley] intends to make some sort of fuss." Punshon speculated that "possibly it is better to take no notice [of the letter], except perhaps as regards the absurd claim of his to hold some special position as what he calls 'First Freeman.' I have a vague idea that once before he put forward a claim to be a permanent member of the [membership] committee on the same ground." He noted dryly that while he had forborne responding to the specifics of Berkeley's letter, he had sent the notoriously tightfisted "First Freeman" a reminder that his annual membership fee was due, to which he had received no reply.

"Bother AB!" responded Sayers in a letter to Punshon that she composed the day after receiving his missive. "I do wish he was not so rude and silly." She entirely concurred with Punshon's recollection of the once comical but now rather annoying office of First Freeman and added resignedly: "If he tries to make a fuss at the meeting, the committee will have to cope; but I hope he will have more sense. I am sorry he should have written to you so impertinently."

By the summer of 1949 the First Freeman's irksome machinations had been checked--but only, Punshon feared, for the moment. With considerable skepticism Punshon wrote Sayers, "I gather the reconciliation with Anthony Berkeley is now complete and the hatchet well and truly buried. Until dug up again." Sayers, who soon would succeed E.C. Bentley as President of the Detection Club, advised members to tread carefully around Berkeley's tender sensibilities. "Let a (more or less) sleeping Berkeley lie," she urged. Nevertheless Sayers agreed with Punshon that the Club members would have to keep Berkeley off the membership committee, because were he to be on it the Club would "never get any new member . . . he turns them all down on sight." She lamented that "Berkeley is a difficult man to work with."

Sayers found working with Punshon, whose detective fiction she had enthusiastically promoted as a book reviewer for the *Sunday Times* between 1933 and 1935, to be an altogether more pleasant experience. Surviving correspondence between the two authors suggests that Punshon was, along with Anthony Gilbert (Lucy Beatrice Malleson), the Detection Club member with whom Sayers got along most amicably at this time. The two communicated fairly frequently during the postwar years, chatting not only about Detection Club matters, but more personal affairs as well.

As treasurer of the Detection Club, Punshon gave his attention to matters large--such as any taxes the Club might have to pay to a revenue-hungry British government ("we have to remember that we may be dropped on by the Income tax people")—and matters small. As an example of the latter, Punshon advised Sayers in December 1948 that the Club should give a "small Christmas present" to Mrs. Buchanan, caretaker of the Club premises at 12 Kingly Street, Soho. ("A room and loo in a clergy house," Christianna Brand bluntly recalled of the locale.) Although payment for services was included with the rent, Punshon pointed out that "services included are very often badly neglected and so far as I have noticed in this case they have been quite well carried out and the room always seemed neat and tidy." "[E]ven in this sordid age," he reflected with characteristic gentle irony, "a few thanks and expressions of satisfaction . . . often please as much as gifts—at any rate if accompanied by a gift." A few days later Sayers gave Mrs. Buchanan a £1 Christmas tip (about £32 today).

Sadly, Punshon suffered a serious setback to his health in August 1949, not long after a busy summer that saw the English publication of *So Many Doors*, his nettlesome skirmish with Anthony Berkeley and the annual Detection Club dinner at the Hotel Café Royal, Piccadilly. (Recorded treasurer Punshon of the latter event: "L87/9/9—Miss Gilbert paid L6/9/4 for after dinner drinks. I gave the head waiter L1. Total 95/9/1. Great success.") After writing Freeman Wills Crofts and John Rhode to inform them about the Berkeley brouhaha, Punshon went into hospital for an operation. In September Sayers wrote Punshon that she was pleased to hear from his wife that he was "making a really good convalescence," adding: "We will miss you greatly at the October meeting, but of course you must have a good long holiday and get quite fit."

By early November Punshon, recuperating at Christopher Bush's house, Little Horsepen, near Rye in East Sussex, was able to report that he was "very much better," though the same month he resigned as Detection Club treasurer. (Christopher Bush succeeded him to the office.) Later that month Punshon wrote Sayers from Bournemouth, where he was taking a "long rest." He wished her good fortune with the recently published Penguin paperback edition of her translation of Dante's *Inferno*, remarking, "I don't know any translation of Dante except the old one [1805] by [Henry Francis] Cary, and that was a fairly pedestrian performance." He also heaped praise on Penguin's ambitious paperback publishing scheme, deeming it a "very praiseworthy attempt to turn us into a nation of book buyers instead of borrowers. A Real Revolution—if they can bring it off." Punshon had particular reason to applaud Penguin's effort, as the previous year the company had issued a pair of 1930s Bobby Owen mystery titles as paperbacks. (Three more titles would follow in the next half-dozen years.)

Punshon remained active in Detection Club affairs in 1950, though he urged that Michael Gilbert be tapped to replace him on the membership committee. "Would [Anthony Berkeley] take the suggestion as an insult," he sarcastically queried Sayers, obviously still smarting over the events of the previous year. Punshon also participated in evaluations of the work of proposed new member Julian Symons (1912-1994), one of Britain's new wave of consciously self-styled "crime writers." Of Symons's recent *Bland Beginning* (1949), a novel based, as was Punshon's own *Comes a Stranger* (1938), on the Thomas J. Wise literary forgery scandal, Punshon wrote Sayers, "On the whole I should be inclined to say 'yes,' even though I think the character drawing deplorable and the construction and final explanation a bit shaky. But he does manage to produce a readable story and it is certainly an intelligent and clever book."

By 1952, Punshon's health had declined to the point where he felt unable to attend the Detection Club's annual dinner. "[A]s they used to say in the war, the situation on the (health) front has deteriorated," he mordantly wrote Sayers, adding ominously that he had scheduled an "appointment with a specialist." The next year, however, both he and his wife, now octogenarians, managed to make it to the dinner, much to the pleasure of Sayers, who promised, "you shan't be bothered with the [initiation] ceremony at all—there will be plenty of people to carry candles." Sayers promised the Punshons good seats at the High Table to hear philosopher Bertrand Russell speak, and in a contemporary letter Christianna Brand somewhat cattily reported observing Mrs. Punshon sitting "terribly close to the speakers so as not to miss a word, and sound asleep."

Sometime in the 1950s an increasingly fragile Punshon took a dreadful tumble down the landing steps at the Detection Club premises at Kingly Street, an event Christianna Brand vividly recollected many years later in 1979, with what seems rather callous amusement on her part:

> My last memory, or the most abiding one, of the club room
> in the clergy house, was of an evening when two members

were initiated there instead of at the annual dinner [possibly Glyn Carr and Roy Vickers, 1955 initiates]. As they left, they stepped over the body of an elderly gentleman lying with his head in a pool of blood, just outside the door.... dear old Mr. Punshon, E.R. Punshon, tottering up the stone stair steps upon his private business, had fallen all the way down again and severely lacerated his scalp. My [physician] husband, groaning, dealt with all but the gore, which remained in a slowly congealing pool upon the clergy house floor.... However, Miss Sayers had, predictably, just the right guest for such an event, a small, brisk lady, delighted to cope. She came out on the landing and stood for a moment peering down at the unlovely mess. Not myself one to delight in hospital matters, I hovered ineffectively as much as possible in the rear. She made up her mind. "Well, I think we can manage *that* all right. Can you find me a tablespoon?"

The club room was unaccountably lacking in tablespoons. I went out and diffidently offered a large fork. "A fork? Oh, well . . ." She bent again and studied the pool of gore. "I think we can manage," she said again, cheerfully. "It's splendidly clotted."

I returned once more to the club room and closed the door; and I can only report that when it opened again, not a sign remained of any blood, anywhere. "I thought," said my husband as we took our departure before even worse might befall, "that in your oath you foreswore vampires." "She was only a *guest*," I said apologetically.

"Dear old Mr. Punshon," no vampire he, passed through a door to death in his 84th year on 23 October 1956, four years after his elder brother, Robert Halket Punshon. On 25 January 1957 the widowed Sarah Punshon presented Dorothy L. Sayers with a copy of her husband's thirty-fifth and final Bobby Owen mystery, the charmingly retrospective *Six Were Present*. "He would like to think that you had one," wrote Sarah, warmly thanking Sayers "for your appreciation of my husband's work during his writing life" and wistfully adding that she would miss her "occasional visits to the club evenings." Sayers obligingly invited Sarah to the next Detection Club dinner as her guest, but Sarah died in May, having survived her longtime spouse by merely seven months. Sayers herself would not outlast the year. As Christianna Brand rather flippantly reports, Sayers was discovered, just a week before Christmas, collapsed dead "at the foot of the stairs in her house surrounded by bereaved cats." Having ascended and descended the stairs after a busy day of shopping, Sayers had discovered her own door to death.

* * * * *

Dorothy L. Sayers's literary reputation has risen ever higher in the years since her demise, with modern authorities like the esteemed late crime writer P.D. James particularly lauding Sayers's ambitious penultimate Peter Wimsey mystery, *Gaudy Night*--a novel E.R. Punshon himself had lavishly praised in his review column in the *Manchester Guardian*--as not only a great detective novel but a great novel, with no delimiting qualification. Although he was one of Sayers's favorite crime writers, Punshon was not so fortunate with his own reputation, with his work falling into unmerited neglect for more than a half-century after his death. With the reprinting by Dean Street Press of Punshon's complete set of Bobby Owen mystery investigations—chronicled in 35 novels, five short stories and a radio play—this long period of neglect now happily has ended, however, allowing a major writer from the Golden Age of detective fiction a golden opportunity to receive, six decades after his death, his full and lasting due.

Short Stories by E.R. Punshon

FIVE BOBBY OWEN detective short stories complement E.R. Punshon's 35 Bobby Owen detective novels, and these short stories are reprinted, one to a volume, with the new Dean Street Press editions of Punshon's *The Attending Truth, Strange Ending, Brought to Light, Dark Is the Clue* and *Triple Quest*.

Although Punshon's Bobby Owen detective novels appeared over nearly a quarter-century, between 1933 and 1956, the publication of the Bobby Owen short stories was much more concentrated, with the first one, "A Study in the Obvious," appearing in the London *Evening Standard* on 23 August 1936 and the remaining four, "Making Sure," "Good Beginning," "Three Sovereigns" and "Find the Lady," in the *Evening Standard* in 1950, on, respectively, 15 February, 1 August, 17 October and 21 December.

"A Study in the Obvious" appeared as part of an *Evening Standard* series devoted to "famous detectives of fiction," edited by Dorothy L. Sayers. Besides Bobby Owen, fictional detectives included in "Detective Cavalcade" were Sherlock Holmes, Sexton Blake, Raffles, Eugene Valmont, Father Brown, the "Man in the Corner," Max Carrados, Dr. Thorndyke, Dr. Priestley, Dr. Hailey, Hercule Poirot, Reggie Fortune, Philip Trent, Albert Campion, Lord Peter Wimsey, Roger Sheringham, Ludovic Travers, Mrs. Bradley, Mr. Pepper, Mr. Reeder, Mr. Pinkerton, Chief Constable Sir Clinton Driffield, Inspector French, Superintendent Wilson, Inspector Head, Uncle Abner, Trevis Tarrant, Charlie Chan and Ellery Queen.

As editor of the series Dorothy L. Sayers warned Gladys Mitchell, who was contributing an original Mrs. Bradley short story, that the *Evening Standard* "will probably say they want it as short as possible and as cheap a possible! Don't let them screw you down to 4000 words, because I know they are prepared to go to 6000 words or thereabouts. . . . I have almost broken their hearts by pointing out to them that all the older people, like Conan Doyle and Austin Freeman, run out to something like 10,000 [words] and their columns will be frightfully congested."

In her *Evening Standard* introduction to "A Study in the Obvious," (2814 words) Sayers wrote:

> E.R. Punshon's detective novels are distinguished by two things: a delicate, sub-acid humour and a fine vein of romantic feeling. They fall into two groups—the stories about Inspector Carter and Detective-Sergeant Bell, and

the more recent series about Superintendent Mitchell and Detective-Sergeant Bobby Owen.

In this short story . . . Owen—that nobly-born and Oxford-bred young policeman—appears alone, exploiting his characteristic vein of inspired common sense.

The crime here is a trivial one; those who like to see serious crimes handled with delicate emotional perception should make a point of reading some of the novels, such as "Mystery Villa" and "Death of a Beauty Queen."

"A Study in the Obvious," which appeared the same year as *The Bath Mysteries*, a Punshon detective novel that delved into Sergeant Bobby Owen's aristocratic family background, is Bobby Owen's origin story, showing how he came to be a policeman. Though light, the tale is one of considerable charm that should delight Bobby Owen fans.

The later *Evening Standard* stories are shorter affairs, though they are all murder investigations. "Good Beginning" and "Find the Lady" take us back to earlier years in Bobby Owen's police career, when he held the ranks of, respectively, constable and sergeant. "Making Sure" and "Three Sovereigns" capture something of that quality of what American mystery critic Anthony Boucher called "the obscure destinies that drive [Punshon's] obsessed and tormented characters," which so impressed Dorothy L. Sayers about Punshon's novels.

Curtis Evans

CHAPTER I
RE-OPENING A CASE

COMMANDER BOBBY OWEN, C.I.D., Scotland Yard, had suggested to his wife, Olive, that they should take an evening stroll together. This had surprised Olive very much. For, in this respect at least, she was well aware she had married a man of extremes, one who knew no golden mean between sprawling in an arm-chair at home, most likely with his feet on another chair unless she were on the look-out, and doing six miles or so round the park in the hour before breakfast, all in the sacred name of keeping fit.

She asked no questions though, since, as Bobby spent his life both in asking questions and answering them, they were things she tended to avoid. Now they had reached Mayfair Crescent, once upon a time so fashionable, so exclusively the home of the great, that even the crossing-sweeper at the corner had a cachet of his own and was apt to refuse mere coppers with a bow of such mingled dignity and reproach as seldom failed to achieve a transmutation into silver. But its glory had fled, as is inconstant glory's habit, and in place of former magnificence the Crescent now consisted of gaps where stray bombs had fallen, a private hotel, two mansions still in the 'stately homes of England' class, others turned into single-room apartment houses, three in a row devoted to the needs of the overflow from the Ministry of Priorities, and others that had been converted into blocks of highly rented flats.

Of these last was No. 7, once the residence of a Duke, then of a wealthy brewer, whose intrusion into those then sacred precincts had been an omen of the decadence to come, and now reconstructed to provide nine more or less convenient, and much more rather than less expensive, 'residential flats-de-luxe', to quote the agent for the property.

Opposite No. 7's front door was a pillar-box, and by it stood a girl, gazing up at No. 7 with an odd intensity of gaze as though she were putting to it a question she had little hope would receive an answer.

"See that girl?" Bobby asked.

"Why?" asked Olive, for indeed there was little chance of not seeing her, since she was so directly in front of them and so near.

A policeman came up from behind.

"That's her, sir," he said in passing, and then, without looking and crossing the road, disappeared down a side street opposite.

"Pretty girl," remarked Bobby.

"Is she?" asked Olive with some doubt. "She looks worried, as if she had lost her boy and was wondering how to get him back, instead of being sensible about it, getting another, and never noticing the difference."

"Don't be cynical," Bobby rebuked her, for cynicism was a reproach Olive sometimes hurled at him—not without effect.

The girl turned away from the pillar-box and came towards them. She was tall, fair, and young, her face pale and peaked, a certain light grace of movement visible in her walk and bearing. She certainly had claims to be called pretty, in spite of the signs of nervous strain Olive had remarked, though perhaps she was no more so than every young girl considers her birthright. Her best features were her complexion, which owed much to God and little to artifice, and her nose, which managed somehow to add a touch of piquancy to her face. Indeed, she did occasionally, when regarding herself in the mirror, murmur 'tip tilted like the petals of a flower', though she could not have told you where the line came from. She was wearing a neat little coat and skirt, 'utility' Olive decided, and she went by them with a hurried, uneven step, as though suddenly remembering some pressing errand.

"Who is she?" Olive asked, and she asked the question uneasily, as if already she had received some subtle warning of impending tragedy.

"A young lady who seems curiously interested in Number Seven Mayfair Crescent," Bobby explained. "Number Seven Mayfair Crescent mean anything to you?"

"I don't think so," Olive said. "Why?"

"Remember what the papers called the Banquet Murder or the Chef Crime or things like that?"

"Oh, that," Olive exclaimed. "The one nothing was ever found out about. Months ago, wasn't it?"

"Yes. It was while I was in the U.S. over that atom-bomb scare that fizzled out like a damp squib. No clues in the Mayfair Crescent affair. Nothing to go on. A wash-out as far as the investigation went. I've been going through the dossier again. I didn't see what else could have been done. Man found dead in the first floor front flat at Number Seven. Name of Hugh Newton. Probably he had more names than one. He always paid, rent included, in cash. No bank account, and some of his underclothing marked 'H. A.', not H. N. Nasty death. Mean sort of end. First he had been knocked out. Must have been a tremendous blow given with all his force by an exceptionally powerful man. Either by accident or design a cushion cover had been torn open and the poor devil's mouth filled with feathers. It rather looked as if the feathers had been deliberately rammed as far down as they would go, but you can't be sure, because before our chaps got there the caretaker, a man named Marks, had tried to clear the feathers away. An unconscious man with his mouth full of feathers wouldn't have had much chance of surviving anyhow, and this one didn't."

"Weren't there any friends or relatives?"

"None that we could hear of, and none came forward," Bobby answered. "Somewhere or another there may be people wondering why they never hear now of a friend or relation with the initials 'H. N.'. We may get an inquiry in time. There are men like that. They cut themselves off entirely from their past and live in the heart of London as the old hermits used to live in the Thebiad. Of course, sometimes they are just hiding."

"Criminals?" Olive asked.

"Well, not as a rule," Bobby answered. They had moved on now, and were walking slowly the length of the Crescent. "If they are, it is more often not from us but from their pals they've double-crossed. The double-crosser is always in danger, and if there isn't much honour among thieves, there's a very lively sense of what's likely to happen to you if you turn informer. Or it may be their families they are hiding from—especially their wives."

"Good gracious," said Olive, incredulous and astonished.

"Or again merely a morbid love of solitude. Anyhow, London is full of such minor mysteries. Nothing to show what the explanation was in this case. Not that Hugh Newton can have been entirely without outside connections. He had been expecting a visitor. The table was laid for two, and there was a most elaborate meal in course of preparation."

"What was it?" Olive asked, interested.

"Oh, I don't know exactly, it's all there in the reports," Bobby told her. "But the care taken over it did rather suggest the expected visitor was someone it was advisable for some reason to treat extra well. Did I say he was wearing a chef's cap and apron? But I doubt if our people would have paid much attention, only for Johnny Staples."

"Who is he?"

"He's the *Daily Announcer's* crime expert and also their cookery editor. Queer mixture—cookery and crime. No accounting for tastes, though. The *Announcer* being a cultural paper, he signs as 'Lucullus', and what he says, goes. Whacking sale of his articles in book form."

"I know," Olive admitted dispiritedly, for often these articles soared to elysian heights she felt she could never climb, not at least till wine became less expensive and butter more plentiful.

"Johnny did rather lay it on thick," Bobby continued, "but he did come along to us to insist it was a line our chaps ought to follow up. Someone known to the Food and Wine Society, or something like that. He said there weren't a dozen men in England, outside the professionals, who could live up to that dinner on their own. It was tried, but got us nowhere. No professional chef missing, and there are so many first-class amateurs there wasn't much chance there. Astonishing number of men fancy themselves as cooks, and really good at it, too."

"I wish all men did," said Olive, and gazed wistfully at the stars above.

"No robbery," Bobby went on unheedingly. "Money and some jewellery left untouched. At the time it was thought two people must have been concerned, even though it looked as if only one guest was expected. A man—no woman could have knocked the poor devil out the way he was. A good straight left right in the middle of the face. A tremendous blow, must have been a whacking big chap who landed it. Expert opinion. There was even some idea of rounding up all the known swell boxers. Came to nothing. But the idea of killing by pushing feathers down your throat looks more like a woman."

"Ugh," said Olive and complained: "Why always put it down to a woman when it's something specially nasty?"

"Because," Bobby explained, "when women are, they generally rather specially are."

Olive tried to unravel this remark so far at least as to be able to decide whether it was meant in a complimentary sense or not. As it was the utterance of a husband, she came to the conclusion that most likely it wasn't. But not being sure, she thought it would be as well to change the subject, and she asked:

"What has it all got to do with that girl you were making eyes at just now?"

"I wasn't," protested Bobby. "I never do—anyhow, not when my wife's there. Things have been happening. As no claimant turned up for Mr Newton's goods and chattels, the Crown took over, stored the furniture, used what ready cash there was—not much—to pay expenses and fees, and then released the flat. There have been two breakings-in since the murder. The first immediately afterwards, and a very thorough job was done, ransacking the place. Nothing taken as far as is known, except oddly enough a pile of travel agent's advertisements, and a lot of postcards of continental resorts. Suggested, of course, that Hugh Newton liked to go abroad, but that wasn't much help either. The second time was soon after new people had moved in—a Mr Pyne and his wife and daughter. Pyne is a Civil Servant—Ministry of Priorities. The two women were out one evening, and when they got back they couldn't get in. Our people were called, climbed in at the back, and found Mr Pyne tied up in a corner, most uncomfortably, with a sheet thrown over him so he couldn't see what was going on. Once again the place had been ransacked and nothing taken, except two wrist-watches.

An odd feature is that both were returned anonymously through the post a few days later. So it does look as if the flat were still an object of interest to someone for some reason."

"Morbid attraction of the scene of a murder," Olive suggested.

"Might be," Bobby agreed, but with some doubt. "There are often staring crowds for days after a murder, but I don't know that I've ever heard of it leading to breakings-in—two of them at that. Now there's the girl you saw by the pillar-box. Chap on the beat reported noticing her hanging about. He had been warned to keep an eye on the place, just in case of any more breakings-in. The D.D.I. passed the report to me. Then she was found on the stairs outside the flat and no explanation, except some vague story about looking for a Mr Smith."

"Who found her?" Olive asked.

"Mrs Marks. She has the basement flat with her husband at a reduced rate on condition of keeping the stairs clean and so on. The husband looks after the boiler and does odd jobs after he gets home from work—he is a packer with one of the big stores. And then there's Mr Jasper Jordan, who is beginning to try to make himself unpleasant, as is, I gather, his chief aim and desire in life."

"Oh, that man," Olive exclaimed, bristling visibly. "That silly paper you brought home—*Freedom's Bugle Call*, didn't it call itself?"

"That's it," Bobby agreed. "Organ of the Mayfair Nihilist Group, which, besides, doesn't exist unless one man can be a group. I don't know why Jordan is interested, but he does seem to think, and even to say, that Commander Owen is an incompetent nincompoop who owes his promotion solely to influence: he's found out that for my sins I went to one of the sacred nine as well as Oxford—the whole bag of tricks, in fact; and, as a kind of head-piece, with a distant cousin of sorts in the House of Lords—at least, he would be if he ever went near the place. Which, of course, he never does."

"What's the sacred nine?" asked Olive. "Aren't they the Muses or something?"

"In this case," Bobby explained, "they are the nine Public Schools, which are so far above all others that those who have been to them never tread the common earth again. Unless, of course, they join the police, and then they jolly well have to."

"Oh," said Olive, suitably impressed.

"All of which means," Bobby continued, "that, in Mr Jasper Jordan's opinion, Commander Bobby Owen came up by the back stairs instead of by the hard way, as he himself thinks he did. So I want to drop in for a chat and see if I can find out if there's anything behind this sudden and rather vicious interest in me. But I've had a hint not to take any notice of it officially. All the same, I can't help thinking there's something behind it all. If I take you with me, no one can say it was in any way official, just a mild protest by a private citizen out for an evening stroll."

"Me as a camouflage?" asked Olive, rather doubtfully.

"Well, you could put it that way," Bobby admitted. "I wouldn't. But it will stop him writing to Centre to demand what it means and how dare the police, etc., etc. Also there's another report that a young woman, the one we've just seen, has been visiting Jordan as well as hanging about the flat where this Banquet Murder, as they call it, took place. It all seems to add up to there being some connection between the flat, the continuing interest in it as shown by two breakings-in, the murder of the man, Hugh Newton, and Mr Jasper Jordan."

"What you mean," Olive said resignedly, "is that you're off again."

"Well," Bobby answered, "it's not too good when murderers get away with it. My job to see they don't."

CHAPTER II
AN ENEMY OF SOCIETY

WEST KING STREET, into which Bobby and Olive now turned, was one of tall, narrow, business-like Victorian houses with no nonsense about them, built for plain, business-like Victorians with no nonsense about them. Unfortunately, tall and narrow as they were, built before 'c. h. w.' and bathrooms had become necessities or slaves of the basement as rare as slaves of the lamp, they were now degenerating, with the slow inevitability of history, into slums, so that a district once of such prim respectability was already neither prim nor respectable. Half-way along, over the basement of one such house, a large sign announced:

J. Jordan and Co.,
Printers and Publishers,
Freedom's Bugle Call.
Central Bureau Mayfair Nihilist Group,
Discussion Circle. Evenings. 8 p.m.
You are welcome. Admission free.

A faint glimmer visible through the fanlight of the area door suggested also that possibly some of these numerous activities were now in progress.

"Well, here we are," Bobby said. "Come along."

"Are you going down there?" Olive asked, viewing with distaste the murky descent offered by extremely dirty stone steps into a darkness murkier still, and illumined so very feebly by that glimmer barely penetrating through the immemorial dirt of the fanlight. "Suppose there's a meeting?"

"Well, it says 'Admission Free', so that's all right," Bobby answered, and led the way. "But according to our chaps, there never is any meeting. They seem to regard that as rather suspicious. I think that's a swill bucket there, so don't put your foot in it. Personally, I am inclined to think that there's rather an unnecessary amount of interest being taken in Mr Jordan. Nothing more likely to please him. My own idea is that he is just a harmless eccentric who sees himself as a David challenging the Goliath of Authority. But you never know. He may be in the black market or the brains of one of these gangs that are giving such a lot of trouble just now. I want to form my own opinion, and I want to make my visit as unofficial as possible."

"Am I a wife or a camouflage?" demanded Olive, and then said, and loudly: "Oh, dear."

"I told you to look out for that bucket, but I think it's only ash, not swill," Bobby said, and knocked at the door with some vigour.

It was opened at once, a flood of light streamed out, and an angry voice demanded:

"Who the hell's there? What do you want?"

"Well, my name is Owen," Bobby answered, and then what he was saying was drowned in a roar of beautifully mingled delight, anger, and surprise.

"It's the raid," the roar proclaimed, becoming articulate. "Come in, come in by all means, and we'll thrash this out if I have to take it to the House of Lords, I'll get it raised in Parliament. I'll—but where's the rest of your gang?"

"What gang?" Bobby asked, slightly bewildered by this reception. "What are you talking about?" He turned to Olive. "Mr Jasper Jordan, who is agin authority just as the American preacher was agin sin. Mr Jordan, my wife, Mrs Bobby Owen."

Mr Jordan, silent now, retreated down a dirty stone passage into a large room opening from it. Bobby and Olive followed. Over his shoulder Mr Jordan mumbled in a voice heavy with disappointment:

"I made sure it was the raid I got word of."

"Sorry," Bobby said apologetically.

The room they entered had probably once been the kitchen. Now it had been transformed into half-sitting-room, half-office. The furniture was an odd accumulation gathered apparently more or less haphazard. There were various chairs, all in different states of decrepitude, an old roll-top desk in one corner, a tumble-down sofa that once no doubt had graced a Victorian drawing-room but now sagged on three rickety pegs, and an old biscuit-tin. On an occasional table near the window stood a brand-new typewriter, which at present prices must have cost £50 or so, and on the floor near, was the aspidistra it seemed to have displaced. One side of the room was entirely covered by shelves, crowded with books, the lucky ones, that is, for on the floor beneath were piled many others that either had been ejected from the shelves or had never been so fortunate as to find a place there. Making a swift expert calculation, based on the thickness of the dust lying about, Olive decided that it must be between three and five years since the room had last been swept, and her eyes went instinctively in search of a broom with which to start operations.

"Well, if it's not a raid, what is it?" asked Mr Jordan, his voice rather subdued now, but still strong and deep.

He was a short, broad man, almost a dwarf indeed, and very nearly as broad as he was tall, with arms so long he could probably, if required, have rivalled Rob Roy's legendary power of fastening his stockings below his knees without stooping, and with a face of a fascinating grotesque ugliness few women could resist. His flat little nose with wide, hairy nostrils, his enormous mouth with black irregular teeth, several of them missing, his ears that stood out like handles, the cast in his left eye, a sprinkling of warts here and there—all made up a picture that sometimes attracted comment from rude small boys, who, however, were apt to flee in terror even if he did no more than turn upon them the full force of his astonishing and hideous scowl.

Before Bobby could reply to Jordan's question the door opened and there appeared the tall, fair girl of the pillar-box. She was carrying a tray on which were two cups, a jug of cocoa, and some biscuits. She nearly dropped it when she saw Bobby and Olive, but recovered at no worse cost than the slopping of some of the cocoa on tray and floor. Bobby said, "Good evening," Olive produced a friendly smile, Jordan said, or rather shouted, "Come in, come in, girl." She, however, responding neither to greeting, to smile, nor to invitation, vanished with extreme, silent speed. Mr Jordan turned angrily upon Bobby, and with every appearance of deep and genuine indignation exclaimed:

"There you are. Bullying again. Bullying the public. Can't help it. That's you all the time."

"Who? Me?" asked Bobby, slightly astonished at this accusation.

"You," repeated Jordan firmly. "Look at the way that girl ran at the sight of you. That shows. And I suppose you called off your raid? Eh?"

"Never heard of any raid," Bobby asserted, and Jordan snorted his disbelief. "I probably should have though, if anything of the sort had ever even been thought of. And surely you don't want to pretend that saying 'Good evening' is bullying?"

"Of course it is," declared Jordan stoutly, "when it's you police, puppets of authority that you are. There was to be a raid. That's certain. I had information, and my information is always good. Only you've called it off and come along yourself? Why?" demanded Jordan, looking very fierce indeed. "Why? I demand an answer."

"Oh, well, Mr Jordan," Bobby answered, his tone almost as mild as the other's had been fierce, "you've been taking a great deal of personal interest in me just lately. Very uncomplimentary interest, too. Every week I get a copy of *Freedom's Bugle Call*. More than personal at times. So, as my wife and I were taking a stroll this evening, I thought we might as well call in and ask what it was all about."

"Murder," said Jordan briefly.

"At Number Seven Mayfair Crescent?"

"That's right."

"Why," demanded Bobby, "this sudden interest in something that happened three or four months ago?"

"I am always fair, strictly fair," pronounced Jordan with obvious sincerity. "I felt it only right to give you your chance. You had it. You have failed. I decided it was time for me to intervene. I ask: Is it, or is it not, your duty to protect life and property? I ask: Is letting a murderer go free through sheer bungling incompetence compatible with the proper performance of that duty? Is—?"

"Hold hard," Bobby interrupted, feeling it was time to check this flow of invective. "Tell me. Do you know anything that might help?"

"I do not, not my affair. Up to you, not me. If I did know something, it wouldn't be any good telling you. You would only bungle it."

"Were you acquainted with Mr Newton?"

"Never heard of him till he was murdered. All my concern is to expose the neglect, the incompetence—"

"Yes, yes, never mind that just now," Bobby interrupted again. "I'm still inclined to think there's something behind this sudden outburst of interest in a crime half-forgotten by now. Except by us. We never forget."

"Perfect elephants, aren't you?" sneered Jordan. "Only elephants are supposed to be intelligent."

"A young lady has been noticed," Bobby went on, "showing a good deal of apparent interest in the flat where the murder took place. Other people seem interested, too. Two breakings-in have been reported. And now the young lady turns up here. Any connection, do you think?"

"Smart, aren't you?" growled Jordan. "In a silly sort of way," he added hurriedly, as it occurred to him that 'smart' and 'gross incompetence' did not fit too well. "Probably got it into your head now that she's the murderer. What on earth could she have to do with it?"

"That's what I want to know—what I mean to know," Bobby told him, and this time put into his voice that note of hard determination he could employ at times and that so often had its effect.

"Oh, well," Jordan growled, "people come to me. They know I'm always there. They know I'm not easily frightened. They know I'm the enemy of all bullying officials; all stupid, blundering, brutal authority. An enemy of a society organized to uphold its own tyranny. What right has any man to give orders to another? Let us act together if we must, freely and willingly, like the brethren we were meant to be, not with halters round our necks and the other end of the rope in the hands of—of—"—and now came a glare too full of scorn, of indignation, and of hate, for words to be found to match it—"of officials."

"The simple anarchist creed," Bobby remarked. "Have you many members?"

"Every living man or woman is a potential member, and will join us as soon as they understand," Jordan retorted. "That's why ultimate triumph is certain in the undeviating logic of history. Except the trained, tamed puppets of Governments, such as police and bureaucrats, every human being resents being ordered about. It is an insult to our humanity. Brother helping brother. There lies salvation. Master ordering slaves. There lies the last damnation."

"Dear me," said Bobby.

"How very interesting," said Olive, whose presence the two men had almost forgotten where she had seated herself inconspicuously in a corner.

And it was her comment that was the most effective. Mr Jordan almost choked.

"Interesting," he gasped, "the salvation of man, and it's very interesting," and he took out a large red handkerchief and wiped his forehead. "That's women," he muttered darkly.

Bobby went to the door and called:

"Young lady, are you there? Could you let us have a word with you, please?"

Jordan bounced forward indignantly and instantly.

"Here," he shouted, "who do you think you are?"

His evident intention was to push Bobby away from the door and shout a warning to the girl to pay no attention to Bobby's request. But Bobby, six feet of him and near a hundred and eighty pounds of bone and muscle, did not come easily into the displaced-person category. He stood stolidly, amiably, immovably, in the door-way, his air one of bland surprise.

"What's the matter?" he asked.

"You've no business, you've no right," Jordan spluttered, and choked into silence as he tried to express clearly what it was he so strongly felt Bobby had 'no business', 'no right' to do.

But already it was too late. In answer to Bobby's summons the girl emerged timidly from another room, farther down the long stone passage and came towards him. He stood back to allow her to enter. Jordan went back sulkily to where he had been standing before. Olive greeted the new-comer with another friendly smile and pulled forward a chair for her. Bobby said, "Oh, good evening," and Jordan said still more sulkily:

"You shouldn't have paid him any attention. Like his impudence."

"Won't you introduce us?" Bobby asked Jordan, and to the girl he said, when Jordan only scowled: "My name's Owen—Bobby Owen, employed at Scotland Yard."

"Don't let him frighten you," Olive said. "He's my husband. I'll see he behaves."

"I always do," Bobby protested, hurt.

"Tell him to shut up," Jordan growled. "Don't say a word. You never know with these fellows. He's got no right to ask questions."

"Oh, yes I have," Bobby retorted. "The right to ask questions is one of the natural rights of man—I'm sure Thomas Paine would agree." He was consulting his note-book. He found the entry he wanted. "Oh, yes," he said. "Miss Doreen Caine, Flat B, Seventy-two, The Terrace, Chelsea. Occupation. Cookery Instructor. Is that correct?"

CHAPTER III
AN INSTRUCTOR OF COOKERY

EVEN OLIVE looked surprised, used as she was to Bobby's way of keeping back information till he judged there had come the appropriate moment to disclose it. The thus suddenly identified Doreen gasped and looked inclined to drop through the floor, if only that had been practicable. Jordan once more opened the black cavern of his mouth to the fullest extent. Olive, the first to recover, gave Doreen another smile and made another little gesture of invitation.

"Just professional swank," she explained. "Sort of thing that doesn't impress any wife."

"I never swank," protested Bobby. "Ruin you in the force, swanking."

Doreen, wary eyes on Bobby, whom she evidently suspected of being liable to produce at any moment an even more startling rabbit out of his hat, but encouraged by Olive's smile, slipped across to her and felt safer. Jordan demanded angrily:

"How the devil did you know?"

"Shall we say—sheer incompetence?" suggested Bobby in his silkiest tone, and then, changing it again, he added briskly: "Oh, come, Mr Jordan, be your age, as the Americans say. Did you really think that if you suddenly started being—shall we say, 'impolite'?—to us chaps in the C.I.D., and to me in particular, and if at the same time a young lady had been remarked taking a good deal of interest in the scene of a recent murder, no one was going to sit up and take notice? Things don't happen without cause, you know. So I thought it might be as well to find out who the young lady was. Quite simple. She was followed home."

"Outrageous," Jordan roared. "I'll take that up. Compromising. A man following a girl! No woman's reputation safe!"

"Not a man," Bobby said, and went on to Doreen: "Remember a quiet little woman who got out of the 'bus when you did one night and asked if you were going her way and could she come with you, because she was so nervous at night? You said, yes, of course, and you lived in The Terrace, and was that anywhere near where she wanted? So she walked along with you a little way and then you parted, and she was very grateful. Sergeant Kitty Yates in official life, and one of the best of our women C.I.D. helpers. Of course, once we knew the street where you lived, it was easy to find out the number, and your name and occupation, and so on—that you lived alone with an invalid mother, for instance, and worked as a teacher of cookery."

"Disgraceful," Jordan boomed once more. "The lowest kind of spying. You'll hear more of this. No one's private life is safe."

"No one's," Bobby agreed grimly, "when it's murder."

There was a silence then as that word seemed to sink into the consciousness of them all. Even Jordan seemed to hesitate. Doreen had become very pale and was trembling a little. Olive patted her hand reassuringly.

"I'd tell him everything if I were you," she said. "He only wants to help."

"How I earn what they are pleased to call a salary," Bobby explained, his voice a little bitter as he pronounced this last word. "Pittance," he corrected himself. "That's the proper word." Abruptly he turned to Jordan, thinking it well to allow Doreen more time to recover, so scared was she still looking. "I imagine," he said to that gentleman, "you know that holding back information in a case of murder can be regarded very seriously?"

Jordan yawned ostentatiously, once again exposing that enormous dark fascinating cavern of a mouth which, on occasion, to various small boys, had seemed as if it could serve no other purpose than that of swallowing them alive.

"And I imagine," Jordan said when he had finished yawning, a process Bobby had watched with some interest, "that most of the time you manage to get paid for by the hard-pressed taxpayer, you spend in teaching your grandmother how to suck eggs?"

"When she seems to need it," Bobby answered, though feeling that this was one up to Jordan. "Of course, you know too that some of the things you've said about me come pretty near being actionable?"

Jordan produced a smile that was even more startling, more surprisingly hideous, than his scowl.

"Try that on if you want to," he said. "Hasn't all your careful snooping informed you that I'm a barrister? Passed all my exams pretty near the top. Special commendations. What was the good with a mug like mine? Imagine me addressing a jury," and suddenly Bobby felt very sorry for him.

"Oh, well," Bobby said awkwardly.

"Oh, what a shame," exclaimed Olive.

"Not at all, perfectly natural," thundered Jordan, and Olive had the impression that only by the narrowest of margins had she escaped having a handy book hurled at her head.

Bobby somewhat hurriedly turned to Doreen. He said:

"Before I start asking questions, I always explain there's no compulsion to answer. You have a perfect right to refuse. Or to ask for a lawyer to be present. Well, it happens that there is one here—an exceedingly aggressive one, too," Bobby added, thinking he might as well try to get a little of his own back—total failure, Jordan merely nodded in agreement and looked pleased. "Only," Bobby went on, "if you do refuse—well, there are other ways of getting necessary information."

"Threats," interposed Jordan delightedly. "Pressure. I take a note."

"To begin with," continued Bobby, ignoring this, "it does seem, doesn't it? as if you must have some strong reason for being interested in Mr Hugh Newton's murder. Do you care to tell me what it is?"

Doreen looked at Jordan, who shook his head violently and produced another scowl. Then she looked at Olive, who gave her an encouraging smile and the faintest possible nod. Doreen said:

"I suppose I thought he was going to ask me to marry him."

"Do you mean you were engaged?" Bobby asked quickly, and at the same time remembered that in some of the reports on the case he had recently been reading mention was made of stories that various unidentified and unidentifiable ladies had been known to visit the dead man's flat at hours at which social calls are not often made.

True, Doreen hardly looked as if she came in that category, and then such visits to flats occupied by men living alone are too common for them to open up any very fruitful line of inquiry. Doreen had not yet answered Bobby's question. She had become a little red, and she seemed to be hesitating. But her voice was steady as she said now:

"No. No. But you always know. Don't you?" she appealed to Olive.

"Of course," Olive agreed. "You may have to help sometimes," she added meditatively. "Get them in a corner or something. What I did."

"Who's swanking now?" Bobby demanded, and went on to Doreen: "Well, then, you must have known something about him. You never came forward, though a public appeal was made for information."

"I didn't know anything," protested Doreen. "I didn't even know it was him at first. I only knew him as Hugh. He never told me where he lived. We only met in public-houses."

"In public-houses?" Bobby repeated incredulously, for Doreen had hardly the air of a frequenter of those generally admirably conducted institutions. "That's rather extraordinary, isn't it?"

"I don't suppose you believe her," Jordan put in. "I do. I know a liar when I meet one. Even the way they hold their hands shows it."

"Was it any one public-house in particular?" Bobby asked, again ignoring Jordan's intervention.

"I don't think so. No. It was almost always different. The first time was at 'The Rose and Crown' at the corner in the High St. They do a good-class trade in luncheons and dinners—banquets sometimes. I go there to plan their menus and make suggestions. They pay rather well. Mr Groom—he's the landlord—brought Hugh into the kitchen one night. He said it was a gentleman who had enjoyed his dinner so much he wanted to congratulate me. We talked cooking. He really knew about it. He was waiting for me when I left. He said there were some points he wanted to ask me about. We walked home together. He talked about getting me a chef's job with one of the big hotels. When I asked him his name he just said it was Hugh."

"Did he say he was in the hotel business? Or how he was going to set about getting you a job of that sort?"

"I told him I wasn't very sure I wanted it. Not yet. It's not the cooking itself. I could deal with that. But there's a big staff you have to manage. A lot of them men. You would have to be a lot older, elderly," and her tone did not indicate any great desire for this to happen too soon.

"The murder was in all the papers," Bobby said. "Headlines. They called it the Good Dinner Murder, Murder of Amateur Chef. So on. The menu was talked about. All very elaborate. I forget what it was exactly. What the French call *haute cuisine*. You didn't see any connection? The dead man's first name was given as Hugh."

"I don't read the papers much," Doreen said. "I haven't time," and Bobby noticed that she had put her hands out of sight, behind her back.

"Had you told anyone?" Bobby asked. "Your mother for instance?"

"Oh, no," Doreen answered quickly. "I wouldn't. Not till I was sure," and now her hands came back into sight again. "Mother says I must marry some day and I must never let her stop me, but I won't, never, unless it's someone who'll let me have her, too. I'll never say anything till I know it'll be all right about her."

Olive interposed, suddenly and quietly:

"Bobby," she said. "We must be off home. That's enough for to-night. You can talk to Doreen another time if you have to. But that's enough for now."

"Oh, well, all right," Bobby consented at once, for he, too, had seen that Doreen was trembling on the brink of a breakdown, and than that there was nothing he dreaded more when he was trying to question a woman. It gave her automatically an opportunity to recover, to think out something fresh. It was almost, he felt, as if a boxer had the right to retire to his corner any time he wanted to, and to stay there as long as he wished. Unfair, in Bobby's opinion. So now, at Olive's warning, he turned to Jordan, who had been looking on with ferocious disapproval, but evidently not quite sure when or how to intervene. Waiting, perhaps, for something to be said that he could somehow twist into a real grievance or indiscretion. To him, Bobby now said: "This raid of yours, Mr Jordan. What made you think there was going to be one? Guilty conscience?"

This last suggestion was received with evident disapproval, and it was a moment or two before Jordan managed to control himself sufficiently to growl:

"I had information. My information is always good, first class. Always. Your semi-imbeciles round here have got it into their thick heads that I'm a communist, and they think communists keep stacks of bombs in their back kitchens. They keep something much more dangerous: ideas—silly ideas for gullible fools. For nine people out of ten, that is. But ideas all the same. Me a communist indeed." Jordan snarled his contempt. "Me! The enemy of all organized society, another word for tyranny.

The more tightly organized, like communism, the more the need to fight it."

"Interesting," Bobby remarked, having noticed how much that particular—and well-meant—comment from Olive had annoyed him, and, then, while Jordan was still struggling for words to express himself concerning it, Bobby nodded him a 'good night', and to Doreen he said: "Well, good night, Miss Caine, or rather it should be *au revoir*, I think."

CHAPTER IV
MEET MR PYNE

OUTSIDE, WALKING away, both Olive and Bobby were silent for some time. It was Olive who spoke first, saying, half to herself:

"What a strange man."

"He's had a raw deal," Bobby said. "He's gone sour on it. No wonder, not many wouldn't. First-class brain in a body like that. Hard luck. Only if you go sour you may go a long way and a bad way. No telling."

"You knew about him before, didn't you?" Olive asked.

"Well, I've heard about him off and on for years," Bobby admitted. "He was suspected at one time of being a receiver of stolen goods. No real evidence. I expect he enjoys dropping dark hints about himself. The Mayfair Trouble Maker, they call him. It's been rather a wonder how he's managed to get away with the stuff he prints in that rag of his, *Freedom's Bugle Call,* without getting hauled into the Law Courts. I suppose, if he's a barrister, he knows just how far to go."

"Did you know about Miss Caine being there?"

"Oh, well, we do try to keep our eyes open," Bobby explained. "Especially when there's a murder case still open in the background. Rather a nasty murder, too. Feathers. You remember I said I thought there was a bit of a feminine touch about it?"

"Bobby!" Olive exclaimed, startled by something in his voice. "You aren't thinking of the Caine child surely?"

"Only keeping an open mind," Bobby answered. "You've got to consider everything. She's a simple type, of course, one of those gentle, timid, shy little things, entirely ruthless, entirely unscrupulous, stopping at nothing to get whatever it is they're after. Generally a man, but not always."

"Oh, Bobby," protested Olive, entirely shocked for her part.

"Oh, I've met 'em," Bobby assured her. "It's the very devil when you do. Iron painted to look like a lath. Question is—what does she want? On the face of it, to clear up the death of the man she expected to marry. Is that all, I wonder? Or is there something else—something different? Clear she meant to get things going again. Probably thought we had forgotten all about it, which we hadn't. She hears of Jordan and his reputation as a professional trouble-maker—enemy of society, as he calls himself. So she trots off to him, and he promises he'll set the pot boiling again. Just his cup of tea."

"You're getting quite kitcheny, too," Olive remarked, and Bobby looked at her sharply.

"You've noticed that," he said. "I've a sort of vague idea that it is all mixed up with all this interest in cooking. What has cooking to do with murder? I don't know. Anyhow, I'm going to put you on the next 'bus for home, and then I'm going to call at the first-floor flat, Number Seven, Mayfair Crescent, now occupied by a Mr Peter Pyne, of the Ministry of Priorities. A bit late for a call but not too late."

"Meaning, I suppose," Olive said sadly, "that you're off again, full cry."

"It does," Bobby agreed. "Yes, it does, and I do not think the end will be yet," and when he had seen Olive safely on her 'bus he went back to the Crescent.

There his knock at Mr. Pyne's flat was answered by a dried-up little man, very neatly dressed, peering up suspiciously at Bobby through pince-nez he seemed to have some difficulty in keeping in position. He held one hand in the pocket of his coat, and with the other hand held the door half-closed.

"Mr Pyne?" Bobby asked. "My name is Owen. I'm an officer of police. C.I.D. Scotland Yard. Could I have a few minutes chat with you?"

"I am inclined to think," Mr Pyne answered in a careful, precise, extremely cultivated voice, "it would be more satisfactory if you could provide me with some evidence of your identity. You may be aware that I have been the victim recently of incidents of an unpleasant character involving considerable inconvenience of a personal nature. I do not wish to be involved again in similar circumstances."

"Of course not," Bobby agreed. "Very wise to take every precaution. Will you ring up our local people—or dial 999 if you like. I left word I might be calling here. You see, there have been fresh developments."

"Indeed," said Mr Pyne in his slow, precise tones. "I will act on your valued suggestion. I trust you will not consider me discourteous if, while taking such action, I leave you—er—so to say—on the door-mat."

"Not at all," Bobby said, beginning to feel slightly amused by this precise little bureaucrat and by the careful formality of his language.

The door closed. It opened again. Mr Pyne appeared standing invitingly aside to permit Bobby's entry.

"I am happy to inform you," he announced, "that the response to my inquiry was wholly satisfactory."

He led the way into a large room—converted flats have generally the advantage of space—comfortably if somewhat sparsely furnished in the favourite style of the present day with a good deal of chromium and an abundance of straight lines. One or two reproductions of modern pictures hung on the walls, and the whole apartment looked as if nothing in it was or ever could be out of place. Bobby's first impression, indeed, was that Mr Pyne had produced not so much a home from home as an office away from the office. He would have felt little surprise if at any moment there had entered a serious-looking young woman in spectacles, armed with note-book and pencil, ready to take down Mr Pyne's letters. Mr Pyne was now indicating a chair, delicately balanced on shining metal legs, that at first sight Bobby hardly thought was big enough to hold him. However, he lowered himself into it successfully, though carefully, and said:

"Oh, by the way, Mr Pyne, if you don't mind the question, I noticed you kept one hand in your coat pocket all the time you were talking to me, and I thought there was rather a bulge there, too. The sort of bulge I've seen before. I'm just wondering."

Mr Pyne looked slightly disconcerted. He almost blushed. Bobby told himself the little man would probably have done so had he had red blood in his veins instead of red ink, as Bobby was most unfairly inclined to suspect. With some hesitation Mr Pyne produced from the indicated pocket a small automatic—a point two-two. He said:

"I am inclined to presume that your observation has reference to this. I referred before to an unpleasant experience I had recently, one against the repetition of which I have felt it desirable to take precautions."

"Do you mind," Bobby interrupted, "pointing it away from me? I'm rather nervous about firearms."

"Oh, certainly, certainly," Mr Pyne said, "but I assure you it is quite safe, as the safety catch is on—at least, that was my impression," he added doubtfully.

By this time the little automatic—a sufficiently lethal weapon at such close quarters—was once again pointing directly at Bobby's stomach. He rose, and very gently and very, very firmly took the thing from the surprised hands of Mr Pyne, slipped the safety catch into the position it had not occupied before, and put it on the mantelpiece.

"Safer there," he remarked and resumed his seat. "Have you a certificate for it?"

"A certificate? Is that a necessary requisite?"

"It is," Bobby assured him. "You should apply for one at once. At present you are liable to a fine and to confiscation of the pistol."

"I will take the appropriate measures without delay," Mr Pyne promised. "It is far from my desire or intention to in any way infringe upon regulations that are no doubt most desirable but of which I was unaware, though that, of course, is in no way an alleviation of such an offence. Most undesirable in my case, considering the position I occupy at the Ministry of Priorities."

"Naturally," Bobby agreed. "I've been reading over what you told us about the attack made on you. I'm sorry, but it does seem that we've not managed to make much progress. Of course, it's almost certain there's some connection with the murder that happened here."

"We had no cognizance of that occurrence," Mr Pyne said. "When the estate agent communicated to us the intelligence that he now had a commodious flat he could place at our disposal he made no mention of that somewhat unpleasant fact. Ever since our return from the remote district in the North to which the Ministry was evacuated during the war we had been searching for accommodation. We were only too glad to hear of anything at all. It was only after we moved in that we learned of the events you refer to. But as I remarked to Mrs Pyne: 'Better a flat cum murder than no flat at all'."

"Yes, indeed," agreed Bobby. "You think that one of those in the attack on you was a woman?"

"That is the case," Mr Pyne agreed in his turn. "It is in fact not open to reasonable doubt."

"Can you add any details about her—age, appearance, tone of voice, blonde or brunette, anything at all?" Bobby asked. "The fact is we are getting interested in one woman we've heard of. If we could identify her, it would be a great help. Give us what we want—a line to follow. Her voice, for instance, could you tell it again?"

"I fear," Mr Pyne replied, "my answer must be in the negative. What happened was of so hurried and precipitate a nature that my recollections are not so clear and orderly as I could wish. When I proceeded to open the door, subsequent to hearing a knock, my first impression was that the man standing there was a member of one of the coloured races. He was, in fact, wearing a mask. Before I was fully aware I received a violent and unexpected blow on what I believe is known in certain circles as the solar nexus."

"Plexus," murmured Bobby.

"I note the correction," Mr Pyne said gravely, and took out a small pocket diary, in which he apparently did note it. "The next thing I knew," he continued, "was that I was supine on the floor and that a young lady of considerable weight was sitting on me. I judged she was young from her form. Of her weight I had ample cause to form a fairly accurate estimate. I could not see her face, as her back was to me, and besides she was heavily veiled. I heard her say: 'Hurry up, or the little devil will be passing out for keeps.' The expression 'little devil' undoubtedly referred to myself."

"Oh, undoubtedly," Bobby said; and wondered if he had been entirely mistaken in thinking that Mr Pyne's last words had been accompanied by what had looked exceedingly like a self-satisfied smirk.

"As you know," Mr Pyne continued, "I was then fastened up and rolled into a corner, where my wife and daughter found me on their return home. A most unpleasant and even humiliating experience, but one that I have to admit has proved to possess certain compensatory features."

"Indeed," Bobby exclaimed, very surprised. "In what way?"

"One, who like yourself," Mr Pyne explained, putting the tips of his fingers together, "lives the exciting and always varied existence of a member of the detective force—"

"What? What did you say?" interrupted Bobby, as there flashed before his mind so many memories of interminable hours spent waiting and watching for something that never happened, or taking endless statements from people with nothing to say and incapable of saying it, of writing reports that no one ever read, of searching for clues that didn't exist, of laboriously following up others that slowly but surely faded away, "Eleven months, three weeks, six days in every year of boring routine, that's police work," he told himself indignantly, and all unheeding, Mr Pyne continued, his finger-tips still pressed together, his even, cultivated voice flowing smoothly on:

"—you must find it difficult to appreciate how welcome is any break in the extreme regularity of routine so necessary to the smooth working of so important a Ministry as that to which I have the honour to be attached. I found myself in fact an object of interest and even perhaps of some envy to my colleagues, none of whom had ever experienced anything of the kind. I was even brought temporarily into a more intimate relation with the Minister himself. He sent for me, ostensibly to discuss a memorandum I had submitted a month or two earlier and that I had reason to know had been marked 'For further consideration'. Following the customary procedure, it had then been relegated to one of the pigeon-holes from which memoranda emerge but rarely. However, it was now upon his desk again, though it was chiefly my recent experience on which our conversation turned. Whether I made good use of the opportunity offered to urge the adoption of the proposals I had put forward I am not sure. I understand, though, that my memorandum has now been returned to its original pigeon-hole, and I have received what may be called a certain limited promotion in that I now occupy a larger room provided with a carpet of greater extent and of demonstrably superior quality."

CHAPTER V
THE BANNER TRAVEL AGENCY

"No luck—except for one doubtful and probably irrelevant detail," Bobby said in answer to Olive's inquiring look when he arrived home, fortunately not far distant from Mayfair Crescent. "There was just a chance I might get a lead, more especially about the woman who was mixed up in the last break-in at the murder flat—the one I mean when the new tenant was knocked out and tied up. He's a man named Pyne, Peter Pyne, a Civil Servant. He hadn't anything useful to say." Bobby sat down in a rather dispirited way and began to exchange his outdoor shoes for bedroom slippers. He remained dangling one discarded shoe in his hands, brooding intently over the bedroom slippers. Abruptly he said: "Jekyll and Hyde."

"What do you mean?" demanded Olive, startled.

"Mr Peter Pyne," Bobby explained, resuming the operation his lapse into what had come to be known as 'the Owen trance' had momentarily suspended. "Dr Jekyll, the prim, precise, routine-bound little bureaucrat. Mr Hyde, the reckless adventurer, quite in his element when mixed up with gangsters, mysterious ladies, answering knocks at the door with a pistol in his pocket, fully prepared to shoot it out if necessary in the best Wild West style. I gather it's all brought him a bit of prestige in his Ministry, even earned him the notice of the Minister himself."

"Oh," said Olive, suitably impressed, for though Ministers come and go like the passing dream, none the less are they, while there, very much there indeed. And Olive, well knowing all this, said, "Oh," again.

"He's even got a bigger and better carpet," Bobby told her, he also suitably impressed.

"What for?" Olive asked, for this to her was a new aspect of favour from on high.

"It's an outward and visible sign of an inward official grace," Bobby told her.

"Don't be irreverent," Olive rebuked him severely.

"I don't," Bobby continued, letting this admonition pass him by, "altogether like it. So far I appear to have collected an odd little man who seems to have gone sour and calls himself an enemy of society. Another odd little man who seems to have let a new taste of adventure rather go to his head. And two young women who may be the same young woman or may never have heard of each other. In the whole business there are just two very faint connecting links."

"You mean cookery?" Olive asked. "Every one's interested in cooking, more or less. What's the other link?"

"Serve you right not to tell you," Bobby said severely, "if you haven't seen it for yourself. Haven't you? Dear, dear." He shook his head, dropped his dangling shoe on the floor with a thud, began to pull on the bedroom slippers, and said. "Don't you remember the only thing reported missing from these breakings-in was a bundle of travel-agency circulars?"

"What about it?" Olive asked. "Plenty of people go abroad, and plenty of people like to think about going, even if they can't afford."

"Yes, but it also means Mr Hugh Newton might have had his name on some travel agency's list. That was tried out. Nothing doing. But Newton seems to have been a bit of a gourmet. I'm thinking of sending one of my chaps to see if any of these advertised tours makes a point of extra good feeding. Some of the Air Lines do. And the Wine and Food Society do something of the sort, I think. A kind of gastronomic tour is what I mean. If we draw lucky, which is the merest off-chance, we might get identification. And once we have some idea of the dead man's background, we may be able to guess at the motive behind the murder."

"I thought you always said motive didn't matter," Olive interjected.

"It doesn't as proof of fact," Bobby agreed. "But it almost always points in the right direction." He stood up and yawned. "Time for bed," he said. "I don't suppose I shall get a wink of sleep," he added sadly, "worrying about those two girls, one of 'em, Doreen Caine, wanting to set it all going again because she thought it had come to a full stop, which it hadn't." Bobby paused to emphasize this, for his professional pride had been a little hurt by the suggestion that any case ever did come to a full stop before it had been satisfactorily cleared up. "The other girl, unidentified so far," he went on, "taking part in the last breaking-in at the Mayfair Crescent flat, and are the two of them one and the same, or are they working together, or what? That feathers business still has to my mind a distinctly feminine touch."

"Ugh," said Olive, and, to prevent him from talking any more, hustled him off to bed as fast as she could.

Next morning the first thing Bobby did, after glancing through his letters, none of pressing importance, was to send for Detective Constable Ford and dispatch him on a tour of the travel agencies.

"What I want," he explained, "is to hear of any agency that makes a point of paying special attention to good food and drink. Quality, remember, not quantity. Sort of gastronomic tour with some slogan like: 'See France and enjoy French cookery.' Something like that. Understand?"

Ford said he did, got the telephone directory, made a list of all the travel agencies, great and small, and started on his round. It was the next day before Bobby heard from him again, and then he laid on Bobby's desk a slip, bearing the address:

Banner Travel Agency,

17a, Up Castle Road,

Seemouth.

"Seemouth?" Bobby repeated. "Oh, yes, of course. Jolly little place. Famous golf links. Half-way between Sidmouth and Bournemouth, and doesn't think much of either place. Had a case break there once. Go ahead, Ford."

"I heard of it from one of the big agencies," Ford continued. "They told me the Banner people had had some bright ideas but not very practical and were said to be in difficulties. 'Please Yourself' yachting cruises were their speciality. Advertised as 'Go where you like in your own yacht at your own choice'. The idea was that you booked for two or three weeks certain, as the case might be, and where you went was decided by a majority vote, subject, of course, to cost, time, and distance—and weather. It was a fair-sized motor yacht, the 'As You Like It', crew of four. What caught my eye, seeing what you told me to look out for, was a paragraph in their circular about using the yacht as an hotel, with special attention paid to provision of best wine and *recherché cuisine*. It was signed 'Kenneth Banner, Member Gourmet Club'. I rang them up to inquire, but all they know about him is that he paid his subscription and turned up sometimes at their dinners, but not very often. They have one every month, very posh affair, with one swell West End chef to plan the menu and another as guest to talk about it and criticize. Lively evenings sometimes, I was told. And if they can turn out a steak-and-kidney pudding any better than my wife can—" and there Ford paused, completing his sentence by a seraphic smile as certain savoury memories surged into his mind.

"Challenge them to a test," Bobby suggested, and not to be outdone in connubial loyalty, added: "And I'll back my wife's omelettes, plain or fancy, against any they can produce—but never mind. Let's see. To-morrow's Sunday. I think a trip to See-mouth on Monday seems indicated. The Banner Agency is still in being, I suppose?"

"Yes, sir. I put a call through to make sure. They're still in business, but said the yachting cruises had been suspended for the time, but would start again soon."

"Well, see your sergeant," Bobby said, "and ask if he can spare you on Monday. If he can, we had better make an early start. Be here by eight o'clock. We'll use my little Bayard—and Government petrol."

"Yes, sir, very good, sir, thank you, sir," said Ford, beaming at the idea of this seaside trip, almost convinced he could have chosen a worse job than the police, and wondering if Mr Owen would want to drive all the way, or was there any chance he would be allowed an occasional turn at the wheel.

This hope, of which Bobby was not wholly unconscious, was amply gratified, for during that Monday-morning drive Bobby seemed content to sit and watch the country-side flowing by while his mind was busy with many thoughts and speculations. Ford, taking full advantage of this, took also full advantage of every opportunity to push the speed up to the sixty or seventy m.p.h. the little Bayard could do, as Ford put it, 'on its head'. So they arrived in good time, parked the Bayard, and found their way to the small and unpretentious office of the Banner Travel Agency.

In the outer office the only occupant was a tall, dark, sullen-looking girl, busy at a typewriter. As they entered she glanced up at them from deep-set, smouldering eyes, more as if viewing them as potential enemies rather than potential clients. She did not speak, but looked at them and waited, her fingers hovering over her machine, her large and somewhat heavy features, her whole attitude indeed, seeming to express an odd latent hostility. At the farther end of the room Bobby noticed a door, marked 'Manager'. He said:

"Oh, good day. Could we see your manager, please?"

"He is very busy," the girl said, this time making her answer sound like a rebuke to a somewhat impertinent suggestion. "I can give you any information you require."

"Thank you," Bobby said. "If you don't mind, I think we should like to see your manager personally."

The girl stared at him in silence. She seemed rather to hope or expect that the steady and unblinking gaze from those sombre, deep-set eyes of hers might make him withdraw his request. As all the effect it had on him was to draw from him the most amiable smile he could produce, she got slowly to her feet, rather with the air of a tragedy queen about to offer a choice of dagger or poisoned bowl. With an odd kind of heavy yet languid grace she went across, knocked at the managerial door, and entered.

"A rum 'un," Ford muttered in Bobby's ear. "I've seen a panther at the Zoo move like that."

The door opened again, and the girl came out and stood silently aside for them to enter. From within boomed a voice:

"Come in, gentlemen, come in."

The room Bobby and Ford entered in response to this invitation was a bare little office, its sole occupant a thick-set, stout, not to say fat, middle-aged man, with a great flat moon-like face now beaming welcome and good fellowship from behind a large desk. But on it Bobby could see no sign of the press of business of which the typist had spoken. The walls were decorated with a number of posters, showing places of interest at home and abroad. A notice proclaiming 'We are agents for all shipping lines', was conspicuous on the wall behind the desk, and there were the usual office accessories—telephone, safe, filing-cabinet, so on, including one rather dilapidated arm-chair and two smaller chairs. A pipe lay on the desk as if it had just been put down, and the general air was one neither of prosperity nor of pressure of affairs. And Bobby noticed that the eyes in that flat, moon-like countenance were small and sharp and cold. He received a sudden impression that the fat, genial, smiling outer aspect of this man concealed a formidable personality.

CHAPTER VI
MISSING PARTNER

Nothing, however, could have been more forthcoming, more welcoming than the greeting now boomed forth in a voice that seemed calculated to shake the very walls of that somewhat ancient building.

"Good day, gentlemen," the man behind the desk was saying or thundering rather. "Do sit down. Anything we can do for you—anything at all—consider it done, gentlemen, consider it done. I do think I can claim the Banner Travel Agency has a reputation for willing, prompt, efficient service. That's our slogan. Service. Service. We put it first, before immediate profit, though I do admit it pays in the long run, pays solid dividends in solid cash. Service—the foundation of every big, successful business in the world. Look at the Quakers. How they've got their reputation. Not honesty. No. Most business men are honest. Have to be, or they go out of business in double quick time. You agree?"

Bobby, who had been wondering when he was going to get a chance to put in a word edgeways, didn't. But, ignoring this question, what he said was:

"Am I speaking to Mr Kenneth Banner?"

"Oh, dear, no," came in quick answer. "I'm Oswald Dow, generally known as Ossy to my friends, and sometimes I think that's all Seemouth. Almost embarrassing at times. Do help yourselves," and he pushed across his desk a box of cigarettes he had suddenly produced. Then his tone changed, as if some quick, unwelcome thought had struck him. "I say," he asked anxiously, "is it about him? Nothing wrong, I hope?"

"Why? Were you expecting there might be?" Bobby asked in his turn.

Dow—or Ossy—sat back in his chair, picked up his pipe thoughtfully, put it down again and said:

"Well, you know, gentlemen, if you don't mind my saying so, you both have a bit of an official air, authority somehow. I didn't notice it at first, but it's there all right." He was regarding them with thoughtful attention, from top to toe, and Bobby had a bitter feeling that he was about to say something about their boots. Ford took tens or thereabouts, even if his own were a comparatively moderate what the shoeshops called an 'outer eight'. But Ossy went on, fiddling still with his pipe and still somewhat hesitatingly: "Well, the fact is, I've been more than a bit worried about Ken. Can't understand it at all. He's just taken himself off without a word of explanation. Left the Agency in the air. Com-pletely in the air. Not a bit like him, not a bit. He rang me up one morning—put through a call from London. Said I wasn't to worry, everything was all right, but he would be away some time. Unexpected circumstances. That was all he said, and that's the last I've heard. Not like him to leave a pal in the lurch. There's the money angle to it, too."

"A deficiency?" Bobby asked quickly.

"No, no, no," Ossy boomed in indignant protest, each separate 'No' louder than its predecessor. "No." This was the loudest 'no' of all, and Ford declared afterwards that it had made the very windows rattle. "One of the best, old Ken," Ossy declared. "He's a partner—a cool two thousand he put in, same as me, and it's still there, the Banner Travel Agency not being bankrupt yet, not by a long chalk."

"You don't know of any other possible explanation?"

Ossy still seemed to hesitate; fiddled with his pipe; pushed the cigarette-box farther across the desk; renewed his invitation to them to help themselves. When they both declined, beamed, and said they must be pipe-smokers, 'same as me', and he had always thought there was something cissy about cigarettes.

"You agree?" he asked anxiously.

"Matter of taste," Bobby answered, and brought him back to a point he seemed to be inclined to boggle over, by reminding him: "I was asking if you knew any other explanation?"

"Yes, you did, didn't you?" Ossy said, still hesitant. "Well, look, I mean to say—confidential? You are police, aren't you?"

"My name is Owen," Bobby said. "I'm from the London C.I.D., and this is Detective Constable Ford, also of the C.I.D. You can see our credentials if you like."

"No, no, not necessary at all," Ossy assured him. "I suppose you're a sergeant or inspector or something," and Ford could hardly contain his indignation at this summary demotion of anyone so important as a commander. "Means it is all confidential?" Bobby nodded assent. "Well, then, I did think just possibly the reason might be sitting out there in the office."

"You mean the typist?" Bobby asked.

"That's right. For the good Lord's sake, don't tell her I said so. Fine girl. Not one of your beauty chorusers, but she's got something—'It'. Only Ken didn't see it. Mind you, I've nothing much to go on. But you couldn't help noticing. You can't wonder. Ken has got 'It' all right too—for the girls. Especially when he takes no notice of 'em, as is general. I've always thought he must have his own girl tucked away somewhere. Only an idea. Ken's a chap keeps himself to himself. Best of pals and all that, but a bit hold-offish. I did rather think it was on the cards that Imra—that's her name, Imra Guire—had managed to put him on the spot. Gave her a kiss or something like that, meaning a kiss and nothing more, same as you or I might kiss a girl just as per usual. But Imra might have taken it it meant buying a ring next morning. Well, there it is. I say, don't forget you promised not to let on to her what I've said. Nice girl, Imra, but a bit of the devil in her. Slung a paper-weight at my head once. Never mind why." He stopped to grin and wink. Receiving no response, he went on: "I've been a good boy ever since. I don't want to lose her. I've always thought it was only because of Ken that she hung on here. Jolly good typist, and they're in short supply. Damn short supply. You agree?"

"Oh, yes," Bobby did agree this time. "Have you known Mr Banner long?"

"Well, not what you might call exactly long," Ossy replied, considering the point as if he wished to be strictly accurate. "We've been running this show together two years, and now another season coming on and no Ken on hand. Can't understand it. We met in a Plymouth pub—I've a lot of friends in Plymouth, half the place, I think sometimes. I was stationed there in an Ack-Ack battery. Sergeant. We had about the worst blitz on record, you know. Ken was an R.N.V.R. bloke. Grouses all the time the whole boiling worked overtime to keep him in a shore job. He's A. 1 at cooking—"

"Oh, yes," Bobby said, remembering that membership of the Gourmet Club. "You mean doing it himself?"

"That's right. A dab at it. Sort of hobby. Could get a job as a chef any time. He says the Navy high-ups always found some excuse for stopping him going to sea, so as to keep him on the cooking job. He did manage to get in on that one-man-torpedo stunt though, and I should have thought those limpets were enough to satisfy any man. You agree?"

"Limpets?" Bobby repeated, puzzled for the moment. "Oh, yes. Automatic mines—to stick on battleships under the waterline."

"That's right," Ossy said. "All unbeknown like, so no one knew anything till the blessed things went off. Ken seemed to have an idea it could be worked in peace-time so as to make a pot of money. Can't think how, and he never said. Seemed to think I mightn't approve. Only thing I have against old Ken—a bit too close with his pals. Well, we got swapping war-time yarns together. At least," he admitted with a broad grin, "I did the yarning, and old Ken did the listening. But he opened up when we got talking peace-time prospects. I was in Plymouth over a job I had been promised. No good. Stank. I'm not fussy, but there are limits, even when you're right on your beam ends, same as I was. You agree?"

"Very much so. My job," Bobby said smilingly.

"That's right," Ossy said. "Sort of professional with you. I forgot. Ken was on the loose, too. He had been skippering a fine steam yacht for an Argentine millionaire. Swell job. Good pay. Good everything. But millionaire had a daughter, and I told you—Ken has 'It' all right. So he got out, thinking the millionaire wouldn't want him for a son-in-law, and him not wanting the girl either. Millionaire grateful, and gave him a jolly good parting bonus. So now he was thinking of buying a yacht for himself if he could get one cheap. You know the Banner Agency speciality?"

"The 'Go as You please' cruises?" Bobby asked.

"That's right," Ossy said. "First idea was 'Mystery Cruises', like the motor-coach 'Mystery Tours' when they drive you round the town and back again. It grew into the 'Choose for Yourself' idea. No bar except time, cost, and weather—Holland, up the Rhine to Switzerland, our own Western Isles, Paris, Norway. Pay your money and take your choice. We specialized in food and wine. My idea, soon as I knew Ken's hobby was cookery. Clients use the yacht as an hotel—de luxe service—and keep your travel allowance in your pocket."

"Did it catch on?" Bobby asked.

"Do hot cakes catch on?" demanded Ossy. "It was overheads turned out the trouble. You always under-estimate overheads. Look at fuel oil. And then I did think Ken went too far when he chucked one of our best clients into the Seine. Of course, he fished him out again—but stories like that get about, and they don't help."

"Probably not," Bobby agreed, this time without being asked. "What was that for?"

"Oh, he had every excuse," Ossy answered. "Never blamed him—would have done the same thing myself very likely. One of the tourist gang got a bit drunk and came on board late with a girl he had picked up somewhere. Ken told her to clear off. Client squared up to him, and well—he went overboard and the girl nearly followed, only she ran off squawking 'murder', and two or three gendarmes—agents they call them in Paris—came on the run. Bit of a fuss before things got sorted out. Unluckily, it all happened in the special Paris yachting port. Did you know Paris provides special facilities for private yachts, to encourage trips up the Seine instead of stopping short at Rouen? And they don't like fusses in their special private yacht preserve. Then the client had to go to hospital for pneumonia or something. He put in a claim for damages and expenses. Ken wanted to fight, but I didn't. We might have won, but rotten publicity, throwing clients into the Seine. You agree?"

"Oh, certainly," Bobby answered. "A mistake to use more violence then necessary. We soon learn that in the Force. Why couldn't he take the chap by the scruff of the neck and run him ashore?"

"That's what I said," Ossy declared. "And then the costs—law costs. No word for 'em. Old Ken's only fault. Hell of a temper when his monkey's up. Half-kill you and then pick you up and be sorry. I've seen him. All about nothing, too."

"Big man?" Bobby asked.

"Oh, no, light weight. Ten stone at the most. But gets in his blow at the top of its carry, and all his weight behind it. To my mind, all boxing's there. You agree?"

"I do," Bobby said, and this time whole-heartedly. He produced a photograph from his pocket. It was that of the dead man known as Hugh Newton, though Bobby suspected he had more names than that. To Ossy he said: "Will you take a look at that and say if you can identify it?"

"Not old Ken," Ossy said at once. He continued staring at the photograph in a puzzled, rather uneasy manner. "Not old Ken," he repeated. "Definitely not. No 'It' about that chap's mug. Seems familiar in a way. No," he decided, "no one I know. Something queer about it some way, don't know what, but there is. Definitely," and now there was even something like fear in his eyes as he flung the photograph down on the desk.

CHAPTER VII
LOST RECORDS

Bobby let the photograph lie for a moment or two where Ossy had thrown it down. Then he picked it up and returned it to his pocket. The whole incident seemed to him significant, though he had no idea what of. Ford, too, had a worried and doubtful look, with a general impression of being prepared for anything, and Ossy was staring at them angrily, he, too, as if prepared for anything.

Nor did Bobby make any attempt to explain that the photograph was of a dead man, touched up to give as near a resemblance to life as might be. Not very successfully though, for even in a photograph the gap between life and death is not easily concealed. This queer momentary tension in which, for its brief period, Bobby had been aware of an impression that from the photograph of a dead man the shadow of death itself had fallen across the three of them, only to fade away again as quickly as it had come. It was in his usual loud, confident tones that Ossy said now:

"I do hope all this doesn't mean there's anything really wrong. One of the best, old Ken. Definitely. Born gambler of course. The risks he took! You ought to have seen him buzzing along on that old motor-cycle thing of his. Only thing I had against him. All these questions though. Upsetting."

"Oh, yes, naturally," Bobby agreed. "We are very anxious to get in touch with Mr Banner. That's all there's to it. We think he might be able to help us. But we don't know. It's all so very vague at present, but I assure you we do appreciate your very helpful attitude." Bobby began to consult his note-book. It was a way he had of securing a few moments delay in which to think out his next line of approach. "Oh, yes," he said again. "Was it always the same crew you had for the 'As You Like It'?"

"Always," Ossy said. "A good lot. Sound rule, never disturb a sound set-up. Now let me see. There was old Ken himself—he was skipper. Stan Foster. Engineer. Bit of a hobby with him. He has a nice little tobacconist business. Doing very well. I've always thought he liked going on these trips to get away from his wife." Ossy paused and chuckled. "But then I'm a bachelor. Still, I have heard Mrs Foster does keep things on the boil. He is the only Seemouth man. The other two are Southampton. There's Herbert Abel, mate, Ken called him. Could lend a hand to anything. And Ted Louis, deck-hand. I don't know much about them. They were never here, Southampton men both of 'em. Ken always operated from Southampton. Much more handy, especially for clients. It didn't take Ken more than an hour to buzz over on his motor-bike if he wanted to see me for anything. His death ride I used to call it—do eighty m.p.h. on the straight and think nothing of it."

"You have records though, I suppose?" Bobby asked. "Addresses, references, so on?"

"Now there you have me," Ossy confessed. "It's this way—a complete clear out. Not a thing left. You could have knocked me flat with a feather—completely flat. Ken must have been here that morning before he 'phoned and taken the lot. Every single scrap of paper dealing with the 'As You Like It'. Everything. And when I say everything, I mean everything. Must have had an outsize suitcase to pack it all in. Unless he had a car of course. Now, tell me, what did he do that for?"

Bobby did not know, so he did not try to answer. Instead he said:

"Mr Banner had a Southampton address, I suppose?"

"Oh, yes," Ossy answered, and wrote it down. "His landlady's as puzzled and worried as I am. He rang them up the same morning. Same thing. Unexpected circumstances. Not to worry. Store everything. Very unexpected circumstances if you ask me. And now all this. Upsetting. Giving me the willies."

"Can you tell me the exact date of the 'phone call?"

"I think so. I expect I noted it down at the time in the office diary. I put everything down as it happens. Only way to keep straight."

Ossy was on his feet now. He went to a cupboard at the other end of the room, and Bobby noticed with some surprise that, fat as he was, he moved with an unexpected lightness and sureness of foot, so much so as to suggest that at one time he had been a first-class dancer or even boxer—two occupations in which speed and sureness of foot are all-important. From the cupboard Ossy took out a book and gave Bobby both date and hour—the latter ten a.m., the former the day of the discovery in London of the death of Hugh Newton.

Bobby thanked him again for the willing help he had given them, hoped everything would turn out all right in the end, remarked that it was long past lunch-time and they mustn't trouble him any longer, though just possibly they might have to pay him another visit. Ossy beamed at this, his face all one crease of good-fellowship, and declared he would always be only too glad to help all he could. He was worried, upset. Very. It wasn't like old Ken. Only thing he had against old Ken was a trick he had of buzzing off on his own without telling his partner as he should.

"You agree?" Ossy asked anxiously.

Bobby said he certainly did, and therewith he and Ford departed, on their way through the outer office, noticing, both of them, that Miss Imra Guire was no longer at her machine. Gone out most likely to a long-overdue lunch, suggested Ford. He made this remark in a somewhat wistful voice, and his spirits sank still lower when Bobby did not even seem to hear. But they rose again with lightning-like rapidity when Bobby wandered abstractedly, almost absent-mindedly, into the first restaurant they came to, picked up a menu, handed it to Ford, a little as if he did not know either what the menu was for or why Ford was there, and sat down at a vacant table; still so deep in thought, Ford did not even dare to ask him what he would have, but ordered for them both on his own responsibility. Still, he supposed it was fairly safe to ask for roast and two veg., with boiled pudding to follow. No one could grumble at that, Ford considered. However, when the food arrived Bobby began to pay more attention, and when the coffee stage was reached, he made Ford fairly jump by ejaculating the one word:

"Phoney!"

"Yes, sir," said Ford, and his eyes strayed to the menu as he wondered uneasily whether the word referred to the coffee, their meal, or their recent interview.

Bobby seemed to wake up. He had noticed Ford's glance at the menu. He said severely:

"Wasn't there mushroom, steak, and kidney pie?" and Ford gasped, for how on earth did Bobby know that when he hadn't seemed even to be aware that the menu was a menu.

"Yes, sir, sorry, sir," Ford said meekly. "But steak and kidney isn't everyone's cup of tea."

"I agree," said Bobby, reminiscent of Ossy. "It certainly isn't."

"And then my missus—she's rather spoilt me for steak and kidney outside, the way she does 'em."

"I shall have to introduce her to Miss Doreen Caine," Bobby remarked, and went on: "Did anything strike you in what Dow said?"

"Well, sir," Ford answered, "I did think he was rather too willing to talk. Not quite natural."

"I know," Bobby said, nodding in agreement. "All the cards on the table, but an ace or two up his sleeve all the same."

"And then," Ford continued, "rather a lot of 'only things' he had against Mr Banner."

Again Bobby nodded in agreement.

"Rather," he said, "as if Dow were trying to put across an idea of Banner that at first you would think wholly favourable and friendly and then afterwards you wouldn't be so sure. That ace up the sleeve again. What about the limpets?"

"Limpets, sir?" Ford asked, puzzled for the moment.

"The automatic mines to stick on ships' bottoms," Bobby reminded him. "I did think he wanted us to take special notice of that, but I can't imagine why. The Italians used them against us during the war, I believe."

"If Mr Banner took on that job," Ford said, "he's not short of guts."

"You may have all the guts in the world," Bobby commented, "and be a thoroughly good soldier in war and a thoroughly bad citizen in peace. Mixed grills, all of us. And why all this cookery business turning up everywhere? We might," he said with irritation, "be running a good-dinner stunt for one of the papers."

"Well, sir, it would help, be an attraction like on a cruise," Ford suggested. "High-class feeding. Especial if there's wine some puts such store by over a good glass of beer." Ford paused for a moment, evidently slightly puzzled by this eccentricity of taste. "It all counts," he said.

"So it does," agreed Bobby. "All the more possibly when it's a small motor yacht you didn't expect much from. Instead of corned beef and that sort of thing, really A. 1 stuff."

"It would depend on the cooking," Ford reflected. "Like—" But there he paused, perhaps warned by a glint in Bobby's eye that enough had been heard of Mrs Ford's steak-and-kidney puddings.

"Butter, wine, and Worcester sauce for the extra kick when required," Bobby asserted. "I've heard that's the secret of all really *recherché* cooking. And I suppose on the Continent Banner could get the wine and butter more easily. But would it pay? Have to leave that for the present. Looks like a dead end, but you never know. Those limpets are still bothering me. I got very much the idea that Dow dragged them in for some reason or another of his own. But I can't for the life of me imagine what."

"Yes, sir," said Ford respectfully, but all the same wondering if this time Bobby were not allowing himself to be side-tracked. "Don't you think, sir, Dow might have been trying to sell us a red herring? They aren't things you can eat, are they?"

"Red herrings? Oh, you mean limpets. I don't know, I don't see why not. I must ask Miss Caine. Limpet sauce or something like that. The chief thing I know about them is they stick. Knew all about a vacuum long before *homo sapiens* did. It was more how Dow looked than what he said started me thinking he intended some sort of obscure hint or another. I may be all wrong about that, of course. We shall have to get Kenneth Banner's record from the Admiralty, and we must try to get hold of the other members of this rather unusual yacht crew and hear what they have to say. Herbert Abel was one name, and Ted Louis the other. We'll have to ask Southampton to look them up. Pity no records available about either of them."

"Just a little bit too convenient, don't you think, sir?" Ford put in.

"I do," Bobby agreed. "Something else to remember. Anyhow, while we are here we can look up the 'As you Like It' engineer. Stanley Foster, tobacconist and engineer in his spare time apparently, and see if he's as talkative a gentleman as Mr Ossy Dow."

He turned to beckon to the waiter, and as he did so the door opened and Imra Guire entered. She saw them, and came straight to their table. She did not speak, but stood for a moment, a brooding, sullen, tormented-looking girl. Then she sat down, still in silence, and Bobby beckoned again to the waiter, who apparently had not noticed Bobby's previous summons.

CHAPTER VIII
DESIGN TO MARRY

THE WAITER, who had seen Imra enter, saw also Bobby's second summons, and came at once. To him, Bobby said:

"A cup of coffee for the lady, please."

Imra, chin cupped in hands, still sat motionless and silent. She might not have been aware of the presence of the two men, and her dark gaze seemed to pass them by to lose itself in distant, unknown depths. The coffee came, but Imra took no notice. The waiter retired, though he remained near by and watchful. He seemed to feel that something unusual was going on, and he was inclined to bring the bill as a hint to the three of them to leave. He didn't want any scene of any kind. If there were one he would probably be blamed, but when he looked again he decided it would be better not to interfere. He suddenly got the idea that Bobby had not much the air of one likely to accept hints from waiters. With her dark and brooding gaze still passing the two men by as if she did not see them, Imra said:

"Why were you asking all that?"

"Were you listening?" Bobby asked.

She seemed a little startled by the question, and even brought back her distant gaze to focus it on him, as though she saw him for the first time. Then she said:

"No need to listen. You can hear Ossy across the street when he shouts, and he generally does. Well, why?"

"If you heard what was said, why ask?" Bobby retorted.

"Is it murder?" she asked, and all her body trembled as she spoke, but her eyes were still steady.

"Why should you think so?" Bobby asked in return. To that she made no reply. She knew none was necessary. Bobby went on: "You know the evening before Mr Banner disappeared there was a murder in London. Mr Dow must have known that, too. But he said nothing."

"Ossy is a fool," she said with contempt. "The worst kind of fool—the clever fool. Do you think Ken Banner has been murdered?"

"There is always a reason when a man disappears," Bobby said. "It may be murder. Not often, but it happens. It may be debts or a love affair gone wrong." He watched Imra closely as he said this, but could see no alteration in her dark impassivity. "It might even be merely a desire for change. Or almost anything. But in this case it seems Mr Banner rang up Mr Dow next morning after the murder. So it doesn't seem likely he was the victim."

"I'm not a fool," she told him in her tone of sullen, repressed anger. "You're thinking all the time there's nothing to show there ever was a 'phone call. Ossy says he took it at the 'Blue Bear'."

"Don't you trust him?" Bobby asked.

"As much as I trust you or anyone else," she retorted.

"Why have you followed us here?" he asked next.

"I want to know what it's all about," she answered. "You come here asking all these questions. Well, why?"

"About Kenneth Banner and a London murder," he told her then.

"What else?" she demanded. "Well, what else?"

"Isn't that enough?" he asked in his turn. "I am here to ask questions, not to answer them. You thought of murder at once. I never mentioned the word. Mr Dow apparently saw no connection. You did immediately. Is that significant? Will you tell me one thing?"

"Why should I?" she said, and now her tone was defiant. Then it changed. "Well, what is it?" she asked.

"Do you sleep well?"

She was silent, staring at him doubtfully. The question had taken her by surprise, so different was it from what she had expected. Perhaps it had even frightened her. Then she laughed, not very naturally, and said:

"Like a top. I never wake till it's time to get up. Why?"

"Because," Bobby said slowly, "I thought you might have something on your mind, and I thought you might sleep better if you told me what it was. Think it over. Another thing, I'm told Mr Banner was a first-class cook?"

"So he was. Yes. It helped a lot. To attract clients, I mean. They used to talk about the meals they got, and it was all his doing. He had a real gift for it. He ought to have gone into the hotel trade. He would have done well at it, but he always said he liked the sea better than kitchens."

"The man who was murdered in London," Bobby said, "seems to have had the same sort of gift. A coincidence? His name was Hugh Newton, but there's some reason to think he may have had other names as well. That's a photograph of him," and as he spoke Bobby took the photograph from his pocket and showed it her.

She looked at it long and steadily, but she showed no trace of recognition, of emotion of any sort. Her voice, too, was unmoved when at last she said:

"I think that was taken after death, wasn't it? Ossy told me. He said he couldn't make out at first what was funny about it, and then afterwards, after you had gone, he began to think." She picked it up then from the table where it was lying and looked at it again. "No one I have ever seen," she said, and added: "Definitely."

"You know the papers called it the Chef Murder and so on? Mr Newton had been preparing a meal for two. It was ready for serving when he was attacked and killed. A very tip-top swell sort of affair apparently, the sort of thing you only expect in high-class expensive restaurants."

"I don't see anything so awfully out of the way about fried chicken and apple fritters," she remarked, apparently a little puzzled. "You could get that anywhere, couldn't you? Smoked salmon costs a lot, but you don't cook it. At least not as a rule. They do in France sometimes. You don't know much about cookery, do you? I heard you say it was all in using plenty of wine and butter—and Worcester sauce. Why not pickled onions? It depends on the cooking and nothing else, and that's a gift like any other. Ken had it."

"Didn't any other of the yacht's crew ever take the job on," Bobby asked.

"Ken would never have let them, not even if it were bacon and eggs for breakfast, and there's more to that than most know."

"I know I'm a bit of an ignoramus when it comes to cooking," Bobby admitted humbly. "Odd how it keeps turning up in this business. Mr Banner and the dead man, and you know about it, too, don't you?"

"It's got to be done," she answered with a shrug of her shoulders. "You may as well know how. But not like Ken. He could take a few left overs and odds and ends and turn out a soufflé like a dream. That's finished now," she said, and stared at Bobby as if offering him some obscure challenge he on his part knew not how to accept. "All over now," she repeated; and the tone of challenge changed, till in it there seemed to echo all the lamentations that all through the ages have risen from the sons and daughters of man.

All at once she laughed. Not a good laugh. She cut it short in the middle and, of all things, began abruptly to polish her fingernails.

"Were you in love with Kenneth Banner?" Bobby asked; and this time he made his tone sharp and abrupt to prevent her from thinking too long before she answered.

The device was not successful. She went on polishing her nails, absorbed in the task, as if she had hardly heard a question that in any case she found uninteresting. Still concentrating her attention on polishing her nails, as if to make sure that the job was being properly done, she said:

"What is being in love? Losing your head for the sake of a kiss? I think there was some poor fool he had on a bit of string somewhere. When I say poor fool, I mean girl. The same thing. He wanted me to marry him. I didn't say I would. I might have. You've got to marry someone. Or have you?" And there came a kind of blaze into those dark, dreaming pools of passion that were her eyes. Bobby saw it and was startled, so much in contradiction did it seem to the light carelessness of her tone. She had paused, but now she was saying in the same light, indifferent, casual way: "I expect I'll marry Ossy now," and Bobby wondered if that were really an intention or merely some kind of bluff or else perhaps—despair.

"I think I remember Mr Dow mentioned he was a bachelor," Bobby remarked.

"So he says," she answered casually. "I'll make sure before I tell him."

"Tell him?" Bobby repeated.

"Tell him I'm going to marry him," she explained. "I haven't yet."

"Oh, I see," Bobby said, though he didn't, for he was wondering if Ossy had asked her, or if her announcement would come to him as a complete surprise. "You are sure none of the rest of the crew ever did any of the cooking."

"I expect I should have heard if they had," she answered. "Mr Banner always said he wouldn't trust anyone else. He thought even one botched meal might spoil our reputation we were trying to build up. 'If you want good feeding, go a cruise with the "As You Like It".' That was the slogan we were trying to put about. But I don't know. I didn't really see much of any of the others. Except for Mr Banner, they hadn't much occasion to come over to the office from Southampton, and I never had any reason to go there. There's Stan Foster of course. He has a tobacconist's shop just off the High Street. I'm sure he doesn't know anything about cooking."

"The other two were Southampton men I understand. Ted Louis—"

"Oh, he's a half-wit," Imra interrupted. "He wouldn't know how to boil an egg. Bert Abel I only saw once or twice. Ken told me once he was more than useful—could turn his hand to anything."

"I must try to have a talk with him," Bobby said. "You couldn't give me his address?"

Imra shook her head.

"I told you," she said. "I hardly ever had anything to do with any of them—except Ken."

"Ken the cook," Bobby mused, "and the dead man a cook, and now there's a girl turned up in town who seems to know all about cooking, too. Always this cookery motive."

Imra said:

"What girl is that?"

"Oh, just a girl," Bobby said, and again he was watching her closely, and again he thought that she knew it.

"Most girls can cook," she said indifferently. "Nothing in that," but Bobby felt she thought that this time there was a good deal in it. She got to her feet. "I must go," she said. "I'll be late at the office." She got up and made a step towards the door, but then turned back, and again there came into her eyes that look so like the black thunder-cloud charged with latent lightning. She said: "You haven't told me what girl. I suppose that means you don't intend to. On the track, aren't you? A keen scent? How long will it be before you shout 'tally-ho' or whatever it is they say when the fox is in sight?"

With that she turned again and went swiftly away, and Ford said with a little gasp as he watched her go:

"That's a queer one."

"A formidable one," Bobby corrected him. "Dangerous."

"What do you think she was driving at?" Ford asked, and he was certainly looking puzzled enough.

"Oh, I think there's no doubt about that," Bobby said. "It came out at the end. Like a woman's postscript. She wanted to know if there was another woman in it anywhere. So I told her there was, and now we shall have to look out for any reaction." He beckoned again to the waiter, who came hurrying with the bill, glad to know these troubling customers were at last departing. Bobby paid it, and said to Ford:

"We'll go along and have a talk with the local lads first, and see if they can tell us anything, and then we'll have a talk with Mr Stanley Foster."

CHAPTER IX
SMALL INFORMATION

TO THE HOME of the 'local lads', as Bobby had called them—otherwise known as the Seemouth Police-station—the two of them now made their way accordingly and in almost complete silence. For though Ford was bubbling with questions, he dared not put them while Bobby seemed so deep in thought.

The 'local lads' had, however, very little information to give. Mr Dow was a well-known inhabitant of the town. Born there, he had left as a young man. He had returned once or twice at long intervals to engage in not generally very successful enterprises, and more recently to start, or rather to continue and extend the already started 'As You Like It' cruises and to combine with them a local travel agency. Recently he had bought a substantial share in the 'Blue Bear'—a 'free' house—and now lived there. He was not the licensee, and he took no part in the daily routine of the establishment. It appeared that it was the striking success of the Banner Travel Agency, described by him as 'a little gold-mine', that had provided the money with which to make this purchase. Nothing was known against him, except a memory of some youthful escapades and a few complaints about a certain laxity in money matters. But these, said the Inspector who was providing this information, had never come into Court.

"Just a little sharp dealing," said the Inspector tolerantly. "Two of 'em each trying to do the other down, and him coming off best. There was one story about an old lady losing all her money through him, but she died, and there was no one to carry it on. Besides, he could show letters of his warning her to be careful and she had better consult a lawyer."

"What did she die of?" Bobby asked.

"I don't think that was ever gone into," the Inspector answered and he looked a little startled. "There was a bit of talk," he admitted. "Before my time," he said, with a faint touch of relief in his voice. "Mrs Fanshaw was her name." He hurried on as if to get away from unwelcome thoughts: "Dow went in for boxing as a youngster, and got to be rather too free with his fists. He was fined twice, I think. I could look that up, if you like. I have an idea that was why he left Seemouth the first time. Of course, he's too fat now for that sort of thing."

"There's a Miss Guire, a typist at the Agency," Bobby said. "You know her?"

"Oh, yes, everyone does," said the Inspector at once, and now a far-away look came into his eyes, that Ford later on was rude enough to compare to that of a 'dying duck in a thunderstorm'. "Fine girl. Fast stepper. No one could help noticing her in a place like Seemouth. Keeps herself to herself, and not her fault if she can't walk down the street without all the women wondering where she gets her clothes and all the men gaping. But none of 'em get any change out of her," and this last was said with such asperity that both Bobby and Ford were inclined to suspect that the Inspector was to be numbered among those who had got no change out of Miss Imra Guire.

"Can you tell us anything about Mr Kenneth Banner, Mr Dow's partner?" Bobby asked next. "We want to get in touch with him. He seems to have vanished about the time a man was found murdered in London."

The Inspector whistled softly.

"That's it, is it?" he said. "I'm afraid we can't help you there. Lived in Southampton, didn't he? Came over sometimes, I believe, but I don't know that any of our chaps ever saw him to notice. I know I never did."

Of Mr Stanley Foster, when Bobby introduced his name, the Inspector seemed to disapprove.

"Good mechanic," he said, "but unreliable. Never holds a job for long, and he's got one or two girls into trouble. Wriggled out himself mostly, except for one maintenance order. He seems to have settled down now though. Came into some money recently and bought a tobacconist's business. His wife runs it, and he's stuck to his job with the Banner Agency longer than he's ever stuck to any job before."

"We must go along and see if he has anything to tell us," Bobby said. "You'll keep a look-out for any developments here, will you? Especially Miss Guire. We've had a talk with her, and I'm not sure what it means. She says Kenneth Banner wanted her to marry him, and it's possible she knows where he is or what's happened to him. Mind your step of course. I don't want her to get the idea that we're watching her—if we can help it," he added, as he saw Ford looking very doubtful. "She's tough, formidable, I should say. So is another girl we know of who may be mixed up in whatever's going on. But tough differently, though every bit as formidable in her own way."

"You think there is something going on?" the Inspector asked.

"I'm sure of it," Bobby said gloomily, "and there's nothing at all to show what. We know nothing about the murdered man and nothing much about Mr Banner. All records concerning the yacht and her crew have disappeared. Mr Dow says Banner took them away the morning after the London murder."

"He can't be the murdered man then," the Inspector said, and added, and as if he were not very sure of it: "That is, if Dow's telling the truth."

"If," Bobby repeated, very much as if he, too, was not very sure of it.

He did not feel either that they had learned a great deal, though he supposed some of the information given might prove helpful later on. Provided, of course, there were any later on, for he was not feeling very sure that Ultimate Authority at Central would think that sufficient had been learned to justify continuing the investigation when the crime wave showed so few signs of decreasing and the police forces everywhere remained so short-handed.

"I hope we shall get something a little more definite from Mr Stanley Foster," Bobby remarked to his companion as, having said good-bye to the Seemouth Inspector, they went on to the Foster establishment.

It proved a well-stocked, well-kept-looking little place, and when Bobby and Ford entered, a severe-looking middle-aged woman behind the counter received them with such evident uneasiness and no surprise that Bobby was instantly certain Ossy Dow had sent a warning over the 'phone of a probable visit. He asked if they could have a word with Mr Foster, and the woman said she would tell her husband and disappeared, and Ford said briefly:

"Scared. Why?"

"Uncomfortable about that legacy probably," Bobby remarked. "Isn't at all sure where it really came from. These yachting trips seem to have brought a lot of good luck to the crew—but not perhaps to Mr Kenneth Banner. I wonder if Bert Abel and Ted Louis have had their share."

Mr Stanley Foster came bustling into the shop from the rear regions. His welcome was almost exuberant. Bobby and Ford might have been old friends he was delighted to see again. He was a pale-faced, narrow-shouldered little man with small pale eyes of indeterminate colour set too closely together and one of those long pointed noses that excited the mistrust of William Blake. 'I don't trust your long-nosed fellows,' the poet had written once, and it was a prejudice Bobby shared to the full, though he did not associate it with criminality.

Foster supposed their visit was about Mr Banner, wasn't it? High time, too, in his humble opinion. An extraordinary business, and the last thing you would have expected from Mr Banner, a real gentleman if ever there was one. Two or three end-of-season cruises, very profitable ones, too, had had to be cancelled at the last minute because there was no Mr Banner. Not like him to let pals down, and Mr Foster could at least say that on the 'As You Like It' they were all good pals. So talking, he swept both Bobby and Ford into the room, half-office, half-living-room, behind the shop, produced cigarettes, offered them drinks, looked disappointed, but said he quite understood, when both offers were declined, and repeated for about the tenth time that he couldn't make it out and would never have believed it. He supposed there must be some reason, but he couldn't imagine what.

"Love affair?" suggested Bobby, but Foster shook his head.

"Mr Banner never seemed to know a girl from a lamp-post," he declared, and grinned broadly. "Some are like that, but not me," he said.

"There's a very attractive young lady at the office," Bobby remarked.

"Imy Guire you mean? She's a Tartar. She laid out one bloke flat with the office ruler when he tried to get fresh with her. The only girl in the world," Foster chuckled, "I've ever taken mighty good care to steer clear of. Once she gets going, there isn't anything I would put past her—knifing you or anything else. Sees red."

"Sounds a dangerous young lady," Bobby remarked, and added: "Formidable."

"Same as a wild cat," said Foster, as a brief and final verdict.

"I understand," Bobby went on, "you made rather a point of serving good food on the yacht?"

"That's right," Foster said. "Mr Banner—well, I wish my old woman could handle grub the way he did. Rather too fancy for my taste though. A cut from the joint and two veg. with a help of plum duff to follow, good enough for me. But most of the tourist blokes went all goggle-eyed."

Bobby remarked that he liked good cooking himself, and Ford looked quite dispirited as he began to realize that there are regions in the culinary world whereto even the best of all possible steak-and-kidney puddings never penetrate. Bobby went on to ask about the other two members of the crew—Bert Abel and Ted Louis. Foster agreed that the latter was something of a half-wit.

"Willing enough," Foster said. "Do anything you told him. It had to be simple and straightforward though, and if he wasn't told he would just sit gaping till you felt you wanted to kick him to wake him up. Only you didn't, because if you did you knew it wasn't safe. If you went too far he might easily flare up all sudden like and half-kill you."

"And Bert Abel—what about him?"

"Oh, him and me, we didn't get on so well," Foster answered, though with more reluctance this time, as if unwilling to confess he didn't 'get on' with any of the crew. "Fact is, I never spoke to him if I could help. But Mr Banner seemed to think a lot of him, and I don't deny he could look after an engine as well as the next man—not an expert, you understand," and in this category Mr Stanley Foster evidently wished it to be understood that he was included. "But good enough. And if Mr Banner had something extra on the go for dinner he would put him in charge of the yacht. Bert used to boast he had never passed an examination in his life and hadn't any certificates, but he could navigate anything anywhere with the best of them."

Bobby produced his photograph, but Foster shook his head.

"No one I know," he said. "Not Mr Banner anyway, if it's him you mean."

"Or anyone else you've ever known?"

"Definitely not," Foster declared. "Queer sort of look about him, too. Something you wouldn't forget in a hurry if you ever saw any bloke looking like he does."

Bobby pressed for a description of Kenneth. It was as vague and as unhelpful as are practically all descriptions given by untrained observers. In the end Bobby and Ford had to depart very little wiser for their visit, and more distrustful than ever.

CHAPTER X
SAILOR'S HOME

THE NEXT thing Bobby did was to get on the 'phone to Central. It being agreed that at any rate further inquiries should be made at Southampton, thither he and Ford drove in a Seemouth police car borrowed for the occasion.

But Southampton, too, proved to have very little information to give. The suggestion was made, however, that on the water-front more could be learned. One of the Southampton men would be detailed to accompany Mr Owen if he so wished, though, said Southampton, with obvious but veiled protest, it would have to be a man only just off duty after a long spell, and probably by this time in bed. They were terribly short-handed, and there was no one else available. So Bobby said it would have to be an emergency indeed to justify calling a tired man from his bed, and if he could be given a few addresses and told where the

'As You Like It' usually berthed, he thought that would be suffi-cient. He already had Kenneth Banner's address, given him by Ossy Dow, but could he have those of Bert Abel and Ted Louis, if known.

That of Bert Abel was not known, nor had Bert Abel him-self ever come under the notice of the Southampton force in any way. Ted Louis, however, they did know. He was a kind of half-wit generally to be found mooning about the water-front and doing odd jobs there. He was regarded with a kind of min-gled contempt, amusement, and respect, this last because of his physical strength and of a certain tendency, if teased or bullied too much, to explode in alarming fits of rage. It was, however, fairly certain that he had never been out of Southampton in his life, except on such short sea excursions as those undertaken by the 'As You Like It'.

The next step therefore was to call at the house where Ken-neth Banner had lodged. But here there were new tenants. The former occupants had left for Australia, somewhat suddenly, a month or two previously. They had, the new tenants understood, been planning to go for long enough, but had been held up by money difficulties. Then in a somewhat mysterious fashion these had been relieved and departure facilitated. 'Unexpected good luck' had been the expression used to the incoming tenants.

"Another dead end," Bobby said, as he and Ford walked away after an interview as brief as unsatisfactory. "Coincidence or careful and expert planning by someone in the background who thought it would be healthier if they were out of the way?"

Ford expressed a guarded opinion that it all smelt worse and worse the more you knew, or, rather, didn't know, and Bobby agreed. They took a short time off to get a cup of tea, since that is a ritual no Englishman is likely to forget, and afterwards went on to find the berth of the 'As You Like It'. The distance was not great, and there was a convenient 'bus, so they were soon on the water-front and soon directed to where the 'As You Like It' was lying. On it was a large notice: 'For Sale'.

A youngish man, who evidently saw in them prospective cus-tomers, made a prompt appearance and began to talk. His name was Walters, he said, and in his opinion the 'As You Like It' was dirt cheap and the best value to be found anywhere. A lovely little boat, and in good condition.

Bobby explained that he was more interested in the crew. One of them had been a man named Bert Abel he was anxious to have a chat with. Then there was another man, Ted Louis by name, but he was said to be not very bright. Could Mr Walters give him Bert Abel's address?

Mr Walters said it was a rum go, but Bert Abel had taken himself off, and no one seemed to know where or why. No doubt he had his reasons, and perhaps those reasons were connected with the visit of a lady who had described herself as his wife, and who had hinted that she had strong financial reasons for wishing to find him.

"Sounded," grinned Mr Walters, "as if she had got an order against him but hadn't got the money, as is always a lot more difficult."

Bobby, growing a little excited now, asked for a description of the lady concerned, but Walters shook his head. He hadn't seen her himself. She had only made the one visit, it was months ago, he didn't suppose anyone would remember much about her. It had merely been a matter for joking and getting ready to chaff Bert when he returned. Only he never had returned. Returned from where, Bobby asked, and was told that Bert, whenever he got the chance, would go up to London, where, he used to explain, his wife had a good job and was always wanting him to give up Southampton and stay in London permanently.

"Two wives?" Bobby asked.

"Sounds like it," Walters agreed, "but there's stories of how sometimes, when in drink, he talked about his girl in London he went to see, and her having pots of money and free with it, and it's a sure thing he had more money than the Banner Agency were ever likely to have paid—even with him being a wizard cook."

"I believe," Bobby observed carelessly, "on the 'As You Like It' they made a point of serving extra good dinners, didn't they? Was Abel the man who did the cooking?"

"That's right. Used to say he had been a chef on board one of the big liners, but never said why he left. Good job too if you can stand up to it. He may have taken it on again perhaps. They might be able to tell you more where he used to stay when he was here."

Bobby asked where that was, and was told it was a lodging-house for seamen and others of the transients common in all big seaports. There, where visits from the police were not uncommon, and where there was every disposition to co-operate with those on whose goodwill so much depended, Abel was clearly remembered. He had not, however, been there for some months. The date was looked up, and proved to be shortly before the occurrence of the London murder. Bobby was beginning to get interested now, and when he produced his photograph it was decided, after some hesitation and general consultation, that a clear resemblance to Abel existed, though hardly one to be sworn to. An odd, pinched, empty, so to say, look about it that the rather full-blooded, boisterous Abel had never shown. Something missing somehow. The visit of a woman calling herself Mrs Abel was also remembered, though only vaguely, and even less vaguely as regarded her person. A brief description Bobby gave first of Imra Guire and then of Doreen Caine brought no response other than a shake of the head and a murmured:

"Couldn't say, I'm sure." And then a further: "We didn't take much notice. We often have that sort of inquiry. A woman gets her order all right, and then she spends all her time and all her money chasing her man to make him pay up. Sort of personal on both sides. He would rather go inside than pay, and she's ready to spend twice what she expects to get out of him."

Bobby, like every other police-officer, knew that well enough, and had often wondered at the triumph of ill will and temper over common sense, the general human weakness in fact to cut off your nose to spite your face. So he let the subject drop, and asked if Abel had left any kit behind, and did they know his London address. No kit, they said, but they had a note of his address. He had left it once when it was possible that the 'As You Like It' might sail sooner than had been arranged. If that happened, he had asked that he should be wired to at once.

On Bobby's request, it was looked for and found, and Bobby read it and asked when the next train for London left. There was one, he was told, leaving very soon. Probably it would be possible to catch it if they hurried. Bobby asked for a taxi to be 'phoned for at once, and to the startled Ford, he said:

"It's the address of Mr Jasper Jordan in West King St."

"The *Freedom's Bugle Call* bloke?" Ford asked incredulously, and added the simple but sufficient comment: "Lummy."

"Back again where we started," Bobby said. "Full circle, and what does that mean?"

The brief interval before the taxi arrived he occupied in announcing in various quarters his immediate return to town. Central was mildly interested, Olive more so, the Southampton and Seemouth police considerably less, though much too polite to express the deep hopes both entertained that they were going to hear no more of bothersome London affairs when they had so many of their own to attend to. Olive, when she heard, had expressed a not too confident hope that when Bobby did get home he would stay there, and not go rushing off somewhere else immediately, for she knew by long experience that that was what generally happened when such investigations were in hand. However, she would have supper waiting, she having, by unexpected good luck, managed to secure some genuine pork sausages, and no doubt he would be quite ready to eat the whole half-pound. Bobby answered that he would certainly do his best to oblige, and then the taxi arrived.

At home Bobby dealt with the sausages as he had promised, while Ford also did as much to the no-less-appetising fish and chips fetched hurriedly from the shop round the corner. Nor were either of the two wives much surprised to hear that their men had to hurry off again immediately that the sausages and the fish and chips had both become no more than an agreeable—and even fragrant—memory. Some consolation to know, however, that it wasn't at all likely to be an all-night job, though of course one never knew how things would turn.

It was just about eleven when Bobby arrived at the West King Street corner where he had told Ford to meet him. Ford was there already, for to be late is a privilege for seniors only, juniors must learn to be punctual. Ford, too, was able to report that a light still showed in the basement where the self-styled 'Enemy of Society' conducted his activities that Bobby was now inclined to take more seriously.

To Bobby's knock when they arrived there was a prompt response. The door was thrown open, and Mr Jasper Jordan appeared, recognizing them instantly.

"What the devil," he bellowed. "Back again are you? Now, who would have thought it? Got a search warrant this time? No? Well, never mind, come in, come in, and we with endless talk— now how the devil does it go?"

CHAPTER XI
THE JORDAN G.P.O.

BOBBY DID not attempt to complete a quotation, which indeed at the moment he could not quite remember. Ford looked suspicious. He thought that 'endless talk' sounded very much as if this queer customer of a Jasper Jordan was giving a very broad hint that he had no intention of providing straight answers to straight questions.

They followed Jasper into the room that seemed to serve him for most purposes. It looked even more squalid and untidy than it had done when they had been there before. More books on the floor, more odds and ends of manuscript scattered about, a little more dust on floor and shelves, on a tray the remnants, not of cocoa and biscuits, but of a bottle of beer and a kipper. On a chair close by was sitting a stout, middle-aged woman, with untidy hair, an unhealthy complexion, a discontented expression giving indeed a general impression of having let herself go to seed and regarding the result as another grievance against life. She favoured the two new-comers with a hostile glance, and then appeared to lose interest in them, and to lose herself in her own uncheerful thoughts. Jasper, taking what seemed to be his favourite position, leaning against the mantelpiece and without troubling to give his visitors any invitation to be seated, roared at them in his usual stentorian tones:

"Well, now then, here's the Enemy of Society visited by the Guardians of Society, and what have they to do with each other?"

Bobby was feeling a little tired with the long day he had had, and since Jasper showed no signs of offering them seats, he saw no reason for standing either on ceremony or on his feet. So he pushed a chair towards Ford, hoping that in spite of its rickety appearance it would bear that young man's fairly substantial weight, chose another and more solid-looking one for himself, since for a Very Senior Officer to see a mere constable go sprawling to the floor on a collapsed chair is one thing, but quite another for the said constable to see the same thing happen to a V.S.O. Then he took out his note-book and examined it with close attention, a manœuvre he had often found effective with difficult or reluctant witnesses. Few, seeing that note-book produced and so closely examined, could help wondering what was there written and feeling an urge to talk themselves, even if only as a kind of preliminary defence or defiance.

"Oh, yes," Bobby said profoundly; and the indifferent woman by the table turned to scowl at him over her shoulder and then turned back to sink again into her own gloomy reverie. Bobby had the fanciful idea that she resembled one of the ancient Daughters of Night, grown old and decrepit and powerless, but still seeing aimless visions of ill to come. "Yes," he said, again in a brisker tone, closing his note-book and looking up at Jasper.

This time, however, the production of the note-book did not seem to have had much effect. Jasper's tone was of undisguised mockery as he said:

"Anything I say may be taken down in writing and used in evidence against me. Is that it?"

"Well, you haven't got it quite right," Bobby explained amiably. "We never say 'against you'. Wouldn't be considered at all proper. And surely you don't feel we've got so far that I feel a warning is required? Not at all, not at all," he protested, returning mockery for mockery as he waved a protesting note-book in the air. "Just a friendly little chat in case you can help us." he went on. "By the way, I was wondering what about it if the Enemy of Society received a visit from those other Enemies of Society, more commonly known as gangsters, with their playful habit of tying up their host in a corner while they have a look round for any hidden valuables available?"

Jasper looked so startled at this that Bobby was almost inclined to think that something of the sort had happened, or that Jasper believed might happen, or that at any rate he had said something Jasper had found disturbing. Though what that might be Bobby had no idea. And, too, he had become aware that the silent woman by the table was not indifferent, not lost in her own private thoughts as he had supposed, but keenly alert, sharply attentive. But now Jasper no longer showed any sign of unease. If he had felt worried in any way, or been disturbed or upset by anything said by Bobby, he had recovered, so completely and so instantaneously, that Bobby could not feel sure his first impression had not been mistaken. That in fact what he had thought to glimpse in Jasper of unease, even of fear, had not been a mere effort of imagination on his part. In his usual loud confident tones, Jasper was saying:

"Gangsters? Criminals? Enemies of Society? Nonsense. The brutal tag Society tries to tie on those it has made its outcasts and its victims. Rationalizing its own profound sense of guilt. Poor devils. Only too glad to climb back into Society if they were allowed half a chance. Never had it. No wonder they react. There are no criminals, only a criminal society. I'm on their side."

"Are they on yours?" Bobby asked.

"They would be if they understood," Jasper retorted. "Some of them do already. Some don't, of course. But: (a) There's nothing here worth taking. Not a thing to fetch more than a shilling or two at a junk shop. They can see that for themselves. (b) I'm ready to tackle anyone who tries to make trouble. I'm no beauty, am I, ma'am?" This last was to the silent but attentive woman on the chair near by. "But I'm no pacifist, either." He grinned formidably and held out those muscular abnormally long arms of his, ending in huge, powerful hands. "It wouldn't be the first time I've thrown would-be jokers out on their ears," and he had very much the air of hoping to get some excuse for trying to do the same to Bobby and to Ford.

"Well, don't forget we're always ready to rush to your assistance," Bobby told him ingratiatingly, and Jasper grunted—disdainfully. Bobby went on: "What I really came to ask though, is what you can tell us about a man called Bert Abel?"

This time it was the woman whose sudden involuntary movement where she sat seemed to suggest that the question meant something to her. But nothing apparently to Jasper, who only seemed surprised and a little puzzled.

"Bert Abel," he repeated. "Who's he, anyhow? I don't remember any Bert Abel. What about him?"

"He gave this address. He said he could be heard of here," Bobby explained.

"Oh, well," Jasper told him, "that's nothing. Complete strangers to me do that sometimes. I'm well known, and people know I'm always willing to take in letters—or even parcels and suitcases for that matter. I get called the Jordan G.P.O. Especially," he grinned defiantly, "if it's some poor devil on the run. Never ask questions. That's my motto."

"Got any now?" Bobby asked.

"And that's my affair," Jasper retorted. "None for any Bert Abel though. Don't know the name."

"I see," Bobby said thoughtfully. "Then you tell us that your address was given without any knowledge on your part by a man you know nothing about and have never heard of, but who seems to have believed that any message left here would reach him immediately. It was a telegram he was expecting by the way."

"You state the case," Jasper informed him, again mockery in his tone, "with a truly remarkable clarity. Any court would find you an admirable witness. Mr Abel—if he really exists, if he isn't a pure invention—could have rung up to ask if there was anything for him. If he did, I don't remember it. I don't expect I should. No reason to."

"Well, thanks very much for what you have told us," Bobby said, getting to his feet, and this polite remark earned no more than an even worse scowl than usual from the Enemy of Society, who plainly suspected irony. "Sorry to have had to trouble you, though just possibly we may have to again. I'm sure we both hope not."

"Always glad to see you," Jasper assured him. "The seldomer the better." By now Ford, too, was on his feet, ready for departure. The woman on the chair by the table twisted round, and stared at them in her hostile, angry way, rather as if relieved to see them going.

"Asking a lot of questions all about nothing," she complained. "Nosey Parkers. What's it all about, anyway?"

It was the first time Bobby had seen her so clearly, for till now she had kept her back turned to him except for occasional glances over her shoulder. Clearly not an educated woman. That was plain. Not, he thought, in business of any kind, too slow and heavy in every way for that. Nor a factory worker either. Her hands, fat and pudgy, were not those of one who did work of that kind. Yet of a fairly prosperous appearance as of one who earned good money. He wondered if he dared make a guess. He said to Jasper:

"Won't you introduce us?"

"Meet, ma'am," said Jasper, grinning as if he thought this request rather a joke, "Mr Owen and Mr Something Else, both of the Snoopers' Own, often known as the Metropolitan Police. Mrs Adam, Mary Ellen Adam, I think. One of my oldest friends," and at that he grinned again.

"Adam?" Bobby repeated. "Interesting coincidence. Biblical too, like Abel, and the same initial. No chance of the two names getting muddled, one for the other, I suppose?"

"He's calling you a liar," the woman said.

"Not at all, not at all," Bobby protested. "Easily confused. Biblical both. Adam, the first man. Abel, the first of us all to be a murderer's victim. No C.I.D. in those days to go snooping round. So Higher Authority intervened. No chance of its going unsolved like the Hugh Newton case—up to the present."

"The gentleman's doubtful," Jasper said; and now his tone was faintly uneasy, as if he felt that perhaps he had gone a little too far in trying to score off his visitor. "Oh, well, let him see your identity card. Satisfy him perhaps. Nothing like obliging the police. Duty of every good citizen—like us."

"I'm sure that would be very kind of you," Bobby said, a trifle surprised though by the suggestion. "If you're sure you wouldn't mind," he added to Mrs Adam.

She hesitated, looked at Jasper as if for advice, then seemed to make up her mind, began to fumble in her handbag, and finally produced it. Bobby gave it a glance, saw the name was Mary Ellen Adam, that the address was that of an hotel in the King's Cross district, and handed it back. He decided to risk a guess—a deduction he himself would have called it—founded partly on the address being that of an hotel, since Mrs Adam had not much the air of one likely to be a resident at even a cheap hotel, partly from her general appearance, which did seem somehow suggestive.

"So kind of you," he had said as he returned her the identity card, and now he added: "Occupation—cook?"

"Well, what about it if it is," she demanded resentfully, suspiciously. "Plain roast and boiled, that's me, and none of your fancy fallals."

"Get to know it all, don't you?" Jasper growled, obviously disconcerted, and blissfully unaware that it was his own suggestion about the identity card and Bobby's consequent knowledge of the hotel address that had caused Bobby to risk a shot that had clearly scored a bull.

CHAPTER XII
THE LARGE SUIT-CASE

"You stay here," Bobby told Ford the moment they reached the street. "When Mrs Adam comes out, trail her. I want to know where she lives. The address on the identity card is probably an old one. I'm ringing up to ask for a plain-clothes man to be sent along to take over. We've been on the job long enough."

Ford was, gratefully, of the same opinion. So he retired into a convenient doorway, from which he could keep an eye on the J. J. habitation, and Bobby hurried away to the call box just round the corner in the next street. There he made known what he wanted, was told the best man available would be sent along at once, expressed his thanks, and went back to tell Ford a relief was on the way and he could go off duty as soon as the relief arrived.

"Warn him to keep a sharp look-out," Bobby added. "Looks to me as if something might break to-night."

However, it was a somewhat crest-fallen Ford who made his appearance in Bobby's room next morning.

It seemed that soon after Ford had gone home, Jasper, the self-styled 'Enemy of Society' had emerged from his basement home, carrying a large and apparently heavy suit-case. As nothing had been said about following him, and as indeed it would not have been possible to do so without giving Mrs Adam full opportunity to leave unseen and untrailed, Jasper was allowed to depart in peace. Later, about midnight, no sign having been seen of Mrs Adam, Jasper returned, carrying with him the same apparently still heavy and well-filled suit-case. This he took down the area steps to his rooms and presently emerged again, proceeding then to walk slowly and deliberately up and down the street. Every dark corner, every shadowy doorway, he came to he examined carefully, obviously searching for a watcher. It did not take him long to find where lurked the C.I.D. man, and this discovery he hailed with tempestuous and delighted laughter. After a series of remarks that but for the C.I.D. man's strong sense of discipline would certainly have resulted in a breach of the peace, Jasper informed him that Mrs Adam had gone off some hours ago, and that he, the C.I.D. man, must have been asleep not to see her. There was also an invitation to visit the basement and make sure for himself with the added promise of a cup of cocoa, just to show there was no ill-feeling, and earnest and grinning advice to go home to bed, which was, after all, the best place for those not fit to be trusted out with no nurse to look after them.

"What probably happened," Ford explained ruefully, "is that Jordan helped Mrs Adam get out over the back-yard wall into the bombed house behind and into the street running parallel."

"I expect so," Bobby agreed, equally ruefully, "we ought to have thought of that," and Ford cheered up a little at this use of the word 'we'. Indeed, Bobby's readiness to take his full share of responsibility when things went wrong, instead of passing all blame on to subordinates, was one reason why he was accorded by them the rare and high praise, seldom awarded to seniors, of being considered 'not such a bad sort at bottom'. And this in spite of the fact that no one could be more severe on any real carelessness or neglect of duty. Bobby went on: "Most likely our Jasper wanted to attract attention and give Mrs Adam her chance to get off unseen. I would like to know what was in that suit-case though."

"Bricks?" suggested Ford.

"Might be," Bobby said thoughtfully. "Only was it?"

"He brought it back seemingly heavy as before," Ford pointed out.

"Yes, I know," Bobby said. "There might have been another smaller suit-case inside the first, and that may have been left somewhere, handed over to Mrs Adam even if they had arranged to meet. Jordan must know he would be easily remembered and identified if he showed himself. Not a face to be forgotten, and if it ever launched a thousand ships it would be from panic more than from anything else. You remember he did mention that he took in parcels sometimes for strangers, and no questions asked. He may have accepted it recently and now be a bit uneasy about its possible contents. He has search warrants on the brain all right, which suggests he's been really afraid we might have one."

"Yes, sir, but—well, that means it would have to be something valuable, wouldn't it?"

"It would," agreed Bobby, "and I thought he didn't like it when I happened to say something about concealed valuables crooks might come after and he had better be prepared. He may have begun to think that that special parcel or dispatch-case would be safer somewhere else—with Mrs Adam, for example, as she was there and handy."

"She could leave it in a cloak-room for him or somewhere like that," Ford said. "She wouldn't be noticed or remembered. Dozens of women like her."

"Or keep it herself for that matter," Bobby said. "When Jordan came back, that might be when the big suit-case had bricks in it or something of the sort. If there was a smaller dispatch-case inside, that could have been taken out and left somewhere. All very difficult. But we do seem to be getting somewhere, goodness only knows where. We know Kenneth Banner disappeared immediately after the murder. Jordan certainly comes in somehow, and other useful connections established. The dead man's chef's cap and apron and the travel-agency advertisements carefully removed from the flat led us to the Banner Travel Agency and to the identification of Hugh Newton and Bert Abel as the same man. Miss Guire may not have known Abel was a first-class cook, but Ossy Dow and Stan Foster must have known, and neither let on. Kept it back for their own reasons, crooked reasons it goes without saying. Now, too, we know there are three women in it—Mrs Adam, Imra Guire, and Doreen Caine. Mrs Adam is a cook. I imagine a jolly bad one. But it means she can get a new job anywhere at any time in any name she likes to take for the time. The perfect background for doing the vanishing trick. From what we got to know at Southampton she must be the woman who was there just before the murder, trying to track down a husband dodging payments due under a maintenance order and hating him as only wives and husbands can hate each other. Brood on your grievances and disappointments, and they can grow bigger than Mount Everest."

"Choking a man with feathers," Ford said, "could be a woman's trick, same as you say, sir. And Jordan could have done the knocking out. He's tough enough."

"It's possible," Bobby agreed. "Or Ossy Dow. He's fat, but he's one of those fat men who have plenty of muscle left. Light on his feet I noticed. Or Kenneth Banner, though Ossy called him a light-weight. Light-weights can hit hard and often, but don't get in smashers like the one that knocked out Abel. Well, there it is. Then there's Imra Guire, a queer, dark, troubled girl who, I think, does not sleep too well. And Doreen Caine, also a cook, and I hope the name's not symbolical."

"Not what, sir?" Ford asked.

"Symbolical," Bobby repeated. "There was a Cain once. Not spelt the same way, but having something to do with an Abel. Adam, Cain, and Abel, all very biblical. We needn't bother about that. She wanted the case re-opened, and has managed that much all right. Why? Because she was in love with Newton-Abel, and means to see his murderer brought to justice? If it's that, is it Kenneth Banner she thinks is guilty?"

"He's done a bunk," Ford said. "Looks that way to me, only you never know. All this cooking though. Beats me. It might all come out of that Mrs Beeton my old woman's always talking about. Sort of a Bible to her. Cooking and murder. I don't get it. And that Imra Guire. A nightmare."

"Not so much a nightmare as lives in one," Bobby said. "Now consider the men we've come across—or haven't, when it's Mr Kenneth Banner; and what's become of him and why? Next Newton-Abel and who killed him and why? and we do know that a wife who hated him was on his trail and perhaps she found him. Anyhow, she doesn't seem inclined to have anything to do with us if she can help it. Then Ossy Dow, Kenneth Banner's partner, and a wrong 'un if ever I met one. Next that little rat of an engineer."

"Stanley Foster?" Ford said.

"Yes. Well, what he knows he means to keep to himself, and it looks as if he had been doing pretty well out of the yachting. He can hardly be the murderer though, as he doesn't seem to have left Seemouth—been there all the time. Last, Jasper Jordan, enemy of society by profession, and where is the thread to bind all that together?"

But this was a rhetorical question, to which no answer was expected or required. Bobby got to his feet and looked sadly at his desk, covered with enough documents of one sort or another to keep him busy for the rest of the day if he gave them the attention they ought to have. Ford observed with some satisfaction that he was putting these papers into two separate piles. He thought this indicated that further action was in contemplation. When Bobby had completed this task, he said, indicating the larger pile:

"Cut across to Mr Sandford with this lot, Ford, will you? Give him my compliments, and ask him if he can please deal with them. Don't tell me what he says. Just dump them on his desk and run for your life. This other lot I'll have to tackle later on. Means I'll have to stop to-night till all hours."

He shook his head sadly and looked round for Ford, hoping for sympathy, but Ford had already departed. He returned unharmed, however, from an errand that had turned out to be quite peaceful, since indignation and a wild surprise had held the unfortunate Mr Sandford spell-bound in silence till Ford was well out of earshot. And if then the flood-gates had been opened wide, what cared Ford? since out of hearing is out of minding. Getting back, he found Bobby at the 'phone, looking rather worried. He hung up and said:

"I rang up to ask if that precise little Mr Pyne had been to see about the certificate for his gun. He has, and they've kept it and told him his application would be dealt with in due course. After that raid on Pyne's flat, which seems as if it had been a kind of bright spot in an otherwise only too well regulated life, all their men know him, and the chap on the beat has reported seeing him with J. J. once or twice and once leaving J. J.'s basement lair. We shall have to ask Pyne about it. Seems a bit odd. But ladies first. Miss Caine now."

"Yes, sir," said Ford doubtfully, "only you wouldn't think a Civil Service gentleman like Mr Pyne, would you?"

"Never think, Ford," Bobby warned him. "Never. Not till you've got enough facts for a foundation. Come on. Time we were off."

"Shall I go for a car, sir?" Ford asked hopefully this time, but Bobby shook his head.

"Economy's your only wear these days," he said. "A 'bus for us, my lad."

So a 'bus it was, and fortunately there was one that brought them close to their destination, a small house in a terrace of small Victorian houses, now, small as they were, all divided into flats that were not so much small as miniature. On the house they were seeking two name-plates showed, the lower one 'Walker', the upper one, 'Caine'. A bell above this last Bobby pressed, and a thin voice from above called:

"Will you come up, please?" and looking up they could see at the top of the stairs a woman in an invalid chair in which apparently she had just propelled herself from one of the upper rooms to the landing.

CHAPTER XIII
COOKERY AND POETRY

THE TWO OF them ascended the stairs accordingly. Waiting for them was the occupant of the invalid chair, which she seemed able to manipulate fairly easily. She had already backed it away from the head of the stairs into the open doorway behind so as to leave more room on the narrow landing. Her wasted appearance, the pallor of her face, the features drawn and thin, all proclaimed the sufferer from long illness. But her eyes bright and alert, her voice brisk, low, and pleasant, both equally proclaimed one who had preserved her strength of character in spite of all that prolonged illness and suffering could do. She was saying now, a little doubtfully:

"Are you from the gas company?"

"No," Bobby said. "We had been hoping for a word with Miss Caine. You will be Mrs Caine?"

"Yes," she answered. "I thought you had come about the gas," she repeated, and Bobby guessed she was beginning to think she had been a little precipitate in asking them up. "My daughter is out. Can you call another time?" Then she said: "Are you the two police gentlemen she met at Mr Jordan's? She told me she had been followed home."

"It was necessary to obtain her address," Bobby explained.

"Why didn't you ask her for it?" Mrs Caine demanded, with more than a touch of severity in her voice. "Would not that have been more straightforward?"

"It would indeed," Bobby agreed, "but I am afraid that in inquiries of this sort we cannot always be as straightforward as we might wish. We are not dealing with straightforward matters or straightforward people. Sometimes if we ask for an address and are given it, we find that it's entirely false."

"My daughter is not like that," Mrs Caine said with dignity, but Bobby reflected that mothers do not always know everything about their daughters.

"We are inquiring about a Mr Kenneth Banner, of the Banner Yachting Cruises," he went on. "We think he might be able to help us. I understand he was a friend?"

"I am afraid there is nothing we can tell you," Mrs Caine answered. "It is a long time since we heard anything—three or four months."

"About the time," Bobby remarked, "that the murder took place in Mayfair Crescent of a Mr Hugh Newton. So far as we know, Mr Banner has not been seen since."

"Good gracious," Mrs Caine exclaimed, "you don't suppose Mr Banner had anything to do with that, do you? That's simply incredible." She began to back her chair into the room behind. "You had better come in and sit down. I suppose you mean you want to ask Doreen about him, though I'm sure there's nothing she can tell you. She won't be long. She is giving a talk on pressure cookery at the Polytechnic near here. She should be back soon."

"I gathered Miss Caine was a teacher of cookery," Bobby said, as he and Ford followed her into a pleasant, comfortable-looking room, though one, from a masculine point of view, with too many cushions, too few arm-chairs, and a superfluity of little china ornaments, some of which, however, looked good.

On the wall, too, with some line engravings, was an enlarged photograph of a young man in Air Force uniform, and this caught Bobby's eye from the strong resemblance it bore to Doreen. It might almost have been herself in masquerade.

"My son," Mrs Caine said proudly, seeing Bobby looking at it.

"I see he was awarded the D.F.C.," Bobby remarked, noticing the ribbon shown.

"He was taken prisoner by the Japanese," Mrs Caine said. "They tortured him dreadfully to make him tell things, and he wouldn't. It's such an inspiration to me when I think the little tiny pains I have are so hard to bear. I still have the pill they gave him to use if he had to. Poison, you know. Instantaneous. But he never did, no matter what those dreadful Japanese did to him. Won't you sit down?"

"Thank you," Bobby said, seating himself accordingly, though with some caution, on one of the fragile-looking chairs in the room. "Do you think it wise to keep a thing like that? There might so easily be an accident."

"Oh, I keep it safe at the back of a drawer," she told him. "I like to know it's there. I like to remember he could bear his pain and so I can mine when it's so much less."

Bobby made no comment. Not that he liked this idea of the potentiality of instant death tucked away at the back of a drawer, but he did not feel it was a matter he could pursue. He went on:

"Mr Newton was interested in cooking. A hobby apparently. The evening he was murdered he had been busy preparing a rather elaborate meal."

"I remember Doreen talking about it," Mrs Caine answered. "She thought it must have been difficult to get ready in a small flat. And there was one dish that was new to her, and she was interested. Of course, that was before we had any idea it was the Mr Newton Doreen had met at her work."

"There were full details in all the papers," Bobby remarked. "Mr Newton's name was given."

"We don't read the papers very much," Mrs Caine said. "Never murders," she added firmly.

Bobby was beginning to notice, or so he thought, that Mrs Caine was showing signs of feeling the strain of answering even these few questions. So he suggested that it might be better to wait till Miss Caine could make an appointment to suit her own convenience.

"Or do you think," he asked, "she would prefer to come and see me at Scotland Yard? I could arrange for almost any time to-day or to-morrow."

But Mrs Caine shook her head.

"It's never any good putting things off, is it?" she said. "I think this is her now," she added, as they heard the front door open and a light, quick step on the stairs. "She is a little earlier than usual. People often stop to talk and ask questions, but I suppose they haven't this time."

A moment later the door opened and Doreen entered quickly, coming, however, to a full stop as she saw who was there.

"Oh, you," she said with evident dismay. "Have they been trying to bully you, mother? I do think—" she flashed, turning upon Bobby, but Mrs Caine interrupted.

"They've been quite nice, dear," she said. "Of course, they must ask questions. It's about that dreadful murder in Mayfair Crescent and Mr Banner. I'm sure he can have had nothing to do with it."

"Mr Banner?" repeated Doreen, and now her dismay was still more evident, as if this, at least, she had not expected. "Why? What about him? We don't know anything. Why should we?" She looked across at Mrs Caine almost imploringly. "Do we, mother?" she asked.

"I've just been saying we hadn't heard of him for a long time," Mrs Caine answered, and plainly she, too, like Bobby had recognized the underlying dismay, even fear, in the girl's voice, and this had both puzzled and alarmed her.

"It's all right," Doreen said quickly, in an obvious attempt to re-assure. She turned sharply to Bobby, all aflame now. "I don't see why you should come to us," she said. "It just happened that I met him, and he walked home with me once or twice and I asked him up to see mother. She hasn't many visitors. Well?"

"It also happens," Bobby reminded her, "that he disappeared without explanation at the same time as the murder of Hugh Newton took place," and as Bobby spoke, rather slowly, those last few words, it seemed as if there came into the room the chill, dark shadow of death itself, and Doreen turned away and occupied herself pulling forward a chair.

She had been standing, but now she seated herself. A change, too, had come over her. Before she had been facing him, alert, defiant, a small flame of anger and of indignation. Now she sat very upright, prim and patient, waiting, her hands folded on her lap, her feet placed precisely side by side, as if she were calling on her essential femininity to protect her against what she felt to be Bobby's hard, male aggressiveness. He had been watching her closely. She remained upright and still, apparently unaware of, or indifferent to, the searching scrutiny of his clear, thoughtful eyes. Mrs Caine was looking on with a kind of puzzled unease. The pause was prolonged. Doreen seemed prepared to wait indefinitely. Her mother evidently feared to speak. Finally Bobby said:

"You have shown a rather curious interest in Hugh Newton's murder. I met you at Mr Jordan's, and he seems to have been trying to get the case re-opened. I am wondering if that was owing to any suggestion made by you. You were also acquainted with both men, with Hugh Newton, who was murdered, and with Kenneth Banner, who has disappeared. Do you care to say anything? To tell me, for example, what it is you really know or fear?"

"Oh, Doreen," Mrs Caine cried.

"Hush, mother," Doreen said. To Bobby she said: "I don't think I have anything to say, and I don't think I quite follow you, or what you mean. Because I had met them both, does it follow that I know all about them now?"

"Well, then," Bobby said, and he had recognized an inflexible determination in that low, soft voice of hers, "would you care to tell me how you first met Mr Banner? You did tell me of your first meeting with Hugh Newton, didn't you?"

"I don't see that it matters," Doreen answered. "We were all three interested in cooking. I teach it. Mr Newton knew about it. Mr Banner's agency made a point of serving first-class meals. When I realized that it was the Mr Newton I had met who had been killed in what the papers talked about as the good-dinner murder, I think it was natural I should be interested as you call it. I knew about Mr Jordan. They talked about him at 'The Rose and Crown'. He often went there in the evening. They used to say he was half-mad, but they were afraid of him, too. They said there wasn't anything he didn't know, especially about people living in the district. So I asked him one evening what he thought about it, and he told me to come and see him, and I did, and he was so interesting I went once or twice again. He said the police had made an awful muddle of it all, and he was going to wake them up. They needed it."

"Oh, Doreen," exclaimed her mother, for those last words had been spoken with a really vicious little stress laid on them.

"You haven't told me," Bobby reminded her, "of how you came to meet Mr Banner?"

"I don't see that that matters," Doreen protested again. "If you must know, he came to one of my private cooking classes. I get men quite often. They may be living alone or want to know how to manage if their wives are out working or sometimes simply so as to be able to help. Or they are just interested or have an idea of taking it up seriously. Some of them are very good. I understood Mr Banner wanted to know about it because of being connected with some travel agency that was trying to serve good meals to its clients."

"Did he strike you as having any turn for it? Could he, for instance, take a few left-overs and odds and ends and produce something really first rate?"

"Good gracious, no," Doreen exclaimed, and smiled faintly. "He had no sort of real gift, if that's what you mean. Only a very few have that. It's exceptional. Of course, anyone can learn to cook. But that's not what one means. You can show anybody there's more to eggs and bacon for breakfast than most people ever bother about, but they could never invent a new dish or blend flavours. Wouldn't know how to set about it."

"Interesting," Bobby remarked. "I mean, that about there being more to bacon and eggs for breakfast than most ever know. Very. And about inventing a new dish. Like the Peach Melba, for instance. That's just to show I do know something after all."

"Doreen always says," Mrs Caine interrupted, as if she hoped the questioning was now going to be diverted to cooking and she would do her best to keep it there, "that there's not one in ten thousand can tell when butter's been used and when it's margarine, or even that awful cooking-fat they give you now."

"Like asking you," said Doreen bitterly, "to do fine embroidery with a darning-needle."

"Was Hugh Newton one of those who can turn left-overs and so on into something first class?" Bobby asked next, and again the mention of that name seemed to bring with it into the room a cloud of darkness and of dread.

"I don't know," Doreen answered. "How could I? He talked about cooking as if he really cared, and so I'm sure he would be good, or else he couldn't. Talk like that, I mean. You can tell. Really caring about a thing is the same as being good at it, isn't it? But you can't tell how good, not till you've worked together. He may have been clumsy or heavy with his hands. I don't know. But he could recognize flavour. He knew I used garlic."

"Garlic," repeated Bobby, surprised, for he only knew garlic as something in the south of France, against the general effects of which the use of a gas-mask was desirable.

"I'm a garlic fan," Doreen explained. "So was Mr Newton. That's why he wanted to meet me. I was rather annoyed at first. The 'Rose and Crown' would probably have lost half its customers if it had got about that I was using garlic. Of course, it has to be used awfully carefully. Just rub a clove of it round a dish you are going to use. Giving garlic to the average cook would be like giving a four-year-old a box of matches to play with."

"Mr Newton spotted it?" Bobby asked.

"It was in a new dish I had thought up and wanted to try out," Doreen explained; she, too, very willing to keep their talk on this comparatively safe level, where, not knowing Bobby, she hoped it would remain. "Cod," she said. "Cod is awfully nutritious, but it hasn't much taste. The dullest fish there is, and the most valuable at the same time."

"Like some men," Bobby suggested.

"All it wants is flavour," Doreen went on, "and it's up to the cook to put it there. Broken-up fillet of cod, with the tiniest ever touch of garlic and other things, like milk now it's not rationed any more. I had several tries before I got it right. When I did, they used to ask to have it again at the 'Rose and Crown'. It was getting so often asked for—they called it the 'Rose and Crown's Special'—I had to promise not to let any other restaurant in the district have it, and I got five shillings extra on my fee. I called it 'Poisson Caine à la Marseillaise'. They loved it, except the people who think any prepared dish is unEnglish and don't want anything but meat and two veg."

"You should patent it," Bobby suggested. "Or copyright it or something. Was it the same thing as something on the menu the papers published after Hugh Newton's murder? Mrs Caine was telling me you said it was new, and you would find out about it?"

"Oh, no," Doreen said, slightly indignant. "Mine was quite original, I thought about it a long time—cod is both so dull and so good, and I wanted to make it more interesting. I only meant about 'caneton pressé' in that menu the paper fussed about being hard to prepare in a small flat. It's a 'Tour d'Argent' speciality. I don't know any restaurant here that serves it."

"It wasn't that, dear," Mrs Caine interposed. "It was the one about oysters, I meant."

"Oh, I remember," Doreen said. "'Huitres Flambées', it was. I couldn't imagine what that meant. I expect really it was oysters served on a bed of hot salt. That," she added severely, "strikes me as just eccentricity for the sake of being eccentric."

"Like modern poetry," Bobby suggested.

She nodded a grave agreement.

"Cooking is like poetry," she said. "The poetry of taste and flavour."

"I'm afraid," Bobby admitted, "all this is getting beyond me—both cooking and poetry. Out of my depth. Eh, Ford?"

"Cooking with butter," Ford murmured in a low, awed tone, and he had the dazed air of one listening to tales of cities not so much paved with, as built of, gold. "My old woman is going to pass out when I tell her."

"One other thing," Bobby said to Doreen, "and then I shan't have to bother you any more just now." He laid the merest touch of emphasis on these last two words. "I gather you brought Mr Banner home sometimes, but not Mr Newton. You only met him in pubs, I think you said. He never told you where he lived. Did you never ask?"

"No," she answered. "He hinted sometimes, but—I think I was afraid. There was something about him. Something—dangerous," she broke out suddenly. "I mean you knew he could easily make you lose your head. I don't know why. No one knew. Everyone felt it. He only had to lift a finger, and you went all watery inside and you hated it and him, but it didn't make any difference. I never knew before there were men like that. It was rather awful and rather frightening, and I knew I had to be careful, and I knew he was waiting for me to ask where he lived and I knew if I did it would be the end, and so I never did and I never would—never."

CHAPTER XIV
NO FIREARMS CERTIFICATE

IT WAS ONLY when they reached the spot where they had to wait for their 'bus back to Central, that Bobby broke the silence by saying abruptly:

"Well, Ford, what do you think of that young woman?"

"She's a deep 'un," Ford said with conviction. "Butter!" he said. "Where's she get it from?"

"She may have learned her cooking in France," Bobby suggested. "She could get it there, I suppose. So could the Banner Agency people. What I would like to know is what she's after?

Hugh Newton's murderer or Kenneth Banner's safety? Or something on her own, something quite different?"

"What about Jordan having left that suit-case of his with her?" Ford asked. "She's a deep 'un," he repeated.

"I shouldn't say that exactly," Bobby said, "it's more being utterly ruthless in pursuing her aims, whatever they are. Not going to let anything turn her aside. Not once she's got going. That sort of thing; and when a woman's like that you might as well try to shift her as shift a stone wall—with anything less than high explosive. Looks as if we were at a dead end for the time."

Their 'bus arrived then to bear them back to Central—three 'buses in fact, touching each other in accord with the convoy system, the first 'bus, of course, crammed to suffocation and the third empty.

For the next day or two indeed no progress was made, no new developments occurred. Bobby himself took little part in what little was done, he had plenty on his desk to keep him busy. Ford, however, kept hard at it, making wholly unsuccessful efforts to discover whether a suit-case had been left on deposit anywhere by anyone answering to the description of Jasper Jordan. Unobtrusive and equally unsuccessful efforts were made to trace the present whereabouts and past history of Mrs Abel-Adam. Discreet watch was kept on Jordan's goings and comings, but of this he was so soon aware, and took such delight in leading his trailers on the most fantastic excursions, that it was soon called off.

"Jordan," Bobby said over the 'phone to the D.D.I. (Divisional Detective Inspector, that is), "has a childish love of showing off. No need to encourage it, he's conceited enough already. I should suggest letting up for the time. Just ask your men to keep their eyes open. Any more visits by Mr Pyne to Jordan I should like to hear about. I have it in mind to pay Pyne another call as soon as I can find time. That flat of his seems of interest to some people. Have you done anything about his application for a licence to possess a pistol?"

"Turned it down," said the D.D.I. with decision. "Wouldn't be safe. He would be shooting himself first thing we knew—or his wife perhaps."

"Quite possible," Bobby agreed, remembering a certain vagueness about the position of a safety catch.

With that he said good-bye and hung up, but soon was called to the 'phone again, this time to be put through to Seemouth.

"Thought you might like to know," said Seemouth, "that Ossy Dow has left for London by the afternoon express. He's been drinking rather freely at the 'Blue Bear' and talking in a wild sort of way. Rambling along and muttering to himself. One bit of gossip is that he has said once or twice that someone might hang soon, but it wouldn't be him. It's since your visit. Upset him quite a lot apparently."

"Well, that's all to the good," Bobby answered. "Nothing like stirring things up. Thanks a lot for letting us know. I'll have the train met and get a man to trail him. He's a cunning bird though, and he'll probably be good at covering up. I wonder if his remark about not being the one to hang comes from optimism or from fear. Too much to hope, I suppose, that he's coming to see us. No such luck. Personally, I think he isn't far from the top of the list in the Hugh Newton case."

"I quite agree," declared Seemouth. "We've always thought him a wrong 'un, though there's never been anything much to lay hold of. Very often there isn't with the worst of 'em."

With which profound reflection Seemouth hung up, only to be on the line again within half an hour.

"Something else now," Seemouth announced. "Can't say we don't give you all the news that is news, can you? There's a 'Closed Temporarily' notice on the door of the Banner Agency office, and Miss Guire went off in a taxi to the Seemouth Aerodrome. She got a charter plane to take her to London. Looks as if she meant to trail Ossy and see what he's up to. Is she in the running, too, do you think? Hope not. A fine girl," and the anxiety in these last few words was quite plain.

"Too soon by long odds to think of that," Bobby said reassuringly. "Thanks again quite a lot for tipping us off so well. I'll arrange to have her trailed—easier job most likely than the Ossy one. That is, if she is there to meet him and if he duly arrives. He may double on his trail, and she may not turn up at the station. But it does look very much as if something were brewing—I should say cooking, the way cookery is all over this business."

"Miss Guire is a real dab at it, too," the Seemouth man observed.

"Oh, Lord," Bobby groaned. "Are you sure? I thought she was just ordinary."

"Well," came the response, "I was told she would take over the kitchen at her digs on a Sunday sometimes, and the oftener the better as far as her landlady was concerned. She seems to have told the neighbours Miss Guire could do it a treat, and any hotel would be glad of a chance to snap her up."

Seemouth rang off then, and Bobby went back to his desk, thinking of all the things he would do to the next person who mentioned cooking to him. However, fortunately there was no reference to cooking in the reports that now began to come in. Imra had duly arrived by air, but had made no attempt to meet Ossy's train. From the aerodrome she had gone direct to a large popular hotel and there booked a room for the night. She had a small suit-case with her which she had left at the hotel when emerging presently on what seemed to be an ordinary shopping expedition. Ossy, too, had gone straight to an hotel, in his case a smaller one near Waterloo station. He had not been seen to leave it, and so presumably was still there.

"Question is," Bobby mused, "whether they will stay put, or whether they will slip off again on the quiet. Too little to go on to justify keeping a full-time watch. But I'll see if Pyne has anything to tell us."

Later on therefore Bobby knocked at the door of the Mayfair Crescent flat. It was opened cautiously by a lady Bobby took to be Mrs Pyne, and when he explained his identity and his errand he was ushered into the room he had seen before. Mr Pyne himself appeared at once.

"I have been seriously considering," he explained in his slow, formal way after he had fulfilled the usual rites of hospitality—

the offering of a chair and a cigarette, both accepted—"the advisability or otherwise of requesting an appointment. In my view, not hastily adopted, the refusal to issue to me a firearms certificate and the confiscation of my means of self-defence—namely, a Browning automatic pistol—is arbitrary and impermissible. Two reasons were advanced, namely: *(a)* Risk of accident. This is entirely hypothetical, and I do not accept its validity. *(b)* The protection given to me and to my family in the ordinary course of the work and duties of the Metropolitan Police. I pointed out, without, I trust, undue asperity, that this vaunted protection had lamentably failed to save me from the criminal assault of which I informed you recently. I protest strongly therefore against any such attempt to deprive me of the means to exercise my natural right to self-protection, means in my view, more especially essential to one who like myself has not been endowed with the physical advantages usually possessed by those engaged in burglary and other avocations of a similar nature."

"Very cogently argued, if I may say so," Bobby agreed. "But the plain fact is that the close season for burglars extends all the year round. I believe the law is that while you have the right, in fact, the duty, to arrest any burglar, you must have satisfactory proof that he is one. It could be argued that his presence in the house at night might have some other explanation. You may use force only if he resists or flies. I imagine that resists would mean that he must be allowed to get his blow in first. After that, you may proceed to use force yourself—if still in a condition to do so."

"And 'flies'?" asked Mr Pyne thoughtfully. "What would you consider the full implication of 'flies' as here used?"

"That the burglar is entitled to a fair start," Bobby answered at once. "You must be sure he is really running away and that he has heard your summons to stop. Then you may use force as before—if he resists. The rights of all citizens, even when burgling, must be respected. And if we in the police forget that, we get it in the neck."

Mr Pyne put his finger-tips together and examined them carefully. Then he said:

"I consider myself a law-abiding citizen, as indeed my position at the Ministry of Priorities demands. But I consider myself also as fully justified in providing myself with such means of self-defence as I can secure. We are not yet a police state—a phrase so often used in protest against the enforcement of the most ordinary and necessary regulations. In fact, I don't care a damn what the law says. I'm jolly well going to defend myself if I'm attacked," and this outburst was accompanied with such a knowing nod of schoolboy self-satisfaction as could hardly have escaped anyone's observation, and certainly did not escape Bobby's. But all he said was:

"Well, of course, I fully agree there's a lot to be said for that point of view. Only it's not the official one. What I really called for was to ask if you had noticed any fresh signs of interest in your flat or anyone else showing a tendency to hang about here. We've been working on the Hugh Newton case, and though we've not made much progress we do seem to have caused some uneasiness in at least one quarter. We are still very much in the dark though with very little idea of what's behind it all. You know Mr Jasper Jordan, I think?"

"I don't exactly know him," Mr Pyne answered, looking, however, rather startled by the sudden introduction of the name. "Why? What makes you think I do?"

"Well, it does seem as if in some way or another he may be involved. We don't know. He calls himself the Enemy of Society, doesn't he?"

"An attractive appellation," Mr Pyne said. "It makes its appeal. One does occasionally become aware of a feeling that there is rather too much society lying around at present. A return possibly to more primitive conditions—one doesn't know."

"Short, nasty, and brutish," Bobby quoted. "You called to see Mr Jordan one evening recently, didn't you?"

"Indeed," Mr Pyne said cautiously. "May I ask what gave you such an impression?"

"Oh, well," Bobby explained, "we've been keeping an eye on Mr Jordan, rather to his amusement apparently, and you were seen paying him a visit. After your adventure with your burglars, all the police in the district know you by sight, and so your visit was noticed and it was mentioned."

"I have met him," Mr Pyne admitted then. "He called here after the incident to which you have just referred. Surely you don't mean you think he may be the murderer?"

"No question of that at present," Bobby answered, and added: "But it has crossed my mind while talking to you that Mr Jordan is very much the sort of person who might be asked to secure a pistol for a gentleman considering he has a right to have one and fully determined to—police regulations or not."

"I have no comment to make," Mr Pyne said after a long pause.

CHAPTER XV
ABOUT LIMPETS

THAT ENDED the interview, and Bobby then went on to West King Street to pay another visit there to Mr Jasper Jordan. It was growing late now, and dusk was falling, for Bobby, before this, had been home for that meal Olive was accustomed to designate as high tea, dinner, or supper, according to the hour at which Bobby arrived to partake of it and the time she had been allowed to give to its preparation.

As now he approached the basement occupied by Jasper, he saw coming up the area steps a young man. He seemed in haste and hurried away, not quite running but very near it, in the opposite direction from that in which Bobby was approaching. Bobby increased his own speed instinctively. He hardly knew why. The young man did the same. Probably he very well knew why. A cruising taxi came up, going the same way. The young man hailed it, jumped on before it had stopped. The taxi drove off. Bobby stood still and watched it go, wondering if he was letting his imagination run away with him, or whether there had been a deliberate and somewhat panicky attempt to avoid him.

"If it was like that, well, why?" Bobby asked himself, half-aloud. "On general principles? An old acquaintance, not anxious for us to meet again? Or—?" He paused to put down the exact time in the note-book he always carried. He said, still half-aloud: "Or does it mean Pyne rang up to give a warning? Coming along very nicely, our Pyne, for a staid, respectable, hidebound Civil Servant, well up in the carpet hierarchy. Repressed tendencies breaking loose? The strong wine of adventure going to his head? He'll be burning his fingers pretty badly if it's that, unless he looks out. He can't surely have anything to do with limpets?"

Bobby made up his mind very firmly that he couldn't believe that, and then decided, equally firmly, that in the world of to-day you can believe anything except the probable. Rather pleased with this reflection, which he considered was worthy of Oscar Wilde, he descended the area steps and knocked. Jordan made a prompt appearance. Bobby noticed that he did not seem unduly surprised. He said:

"Making this your home from home, aren't you?"

"One would think you weren't glad to see me," Bobby protested in the most pained tone he could manage to produce. "I just thought I would like a bit of a chat, that's all."

"Bit of a chat indeed," Jasper growled. "I know your bits of chat. Come in if you want to. Nothing to hide."

He led the way back into the room that seemed to serve him both as living-room and work-room. It looked, Bobby thought, much tidier than when he had seen it before, as if someone had been busy with broom and duster. Indeed, a hand-brush and a dust-pan, well filled, in a corner suggested that this operation had been recently interrupted before completion, and he wondered who had been carrying it out. Not Jasper, he was fairly sure, and a little late for the charwoman he had never heard that Jasper in fact employed. Jasper was now pushing forward a chair with a general air of regretting the necessity. He took up his own favourite position with his back to the mantelpiece and said:

"Well, what is it now?"

"Chiefly," Bobby answered, "about that pistol you got for Mr Pyne he asked you for when he was refused a firearms certificate."

"Has the little rat been squealing?" Jasper demanded angrily.

"Now, now," Bobby said, "you mustn't call a highly respectable Civil Servant a little rat. Most improper. And he hasn't been squealing. It's just that I've been, what some people would call, guessing. What I prefer to call intelligent deduction from observed facts. Putting two and two together and deducing—or guessing—that they may make four."

"What do you mean? Trying to be funny clever, aren't you?"

"Rather a good expression," Bobby applauded. "Funny clever! I must remember it. Admirable. Funny clever! The world's ideal at the moment." He paused, saw that Jasper, so baited, was on the point of losing entirely his self-control, decided that that was not at all desirable, decided that Jasper's self-conceit and belief in his own superiority had now been sufficiently shaken to make him at least a little more amenable to questioning, and went on: "You see when one of the two twos to be put together in case they do make four is (a) a gentleman fully resolved to get hold of a pistol unreasonably denied him by mere red tape, a thing he hates and resents, and the second of the two is *(b)* a gentleman who ranks himself as an enemy of society; and when (a) is seen visiting (b) and when in addition *(a)* smirks—a fair word, I think—in a most marked manner, with a sort of sugary self-satisfaction when the subject of pistols comes up—then guessing is not the word. Definitely not. A gift if you ask me."

"Bluff and balderdash," Jordan grunted, trying to keep his end up. "I suppose you think that's all very smart?"

"Well, I rather hoped you would," Bobby answered wistfully. "The worst of explanations. Explain, and people think nothing of it. Obvious. Wrap it in mystery, and they think you're a wizard."

"Well, what do you think you are going to do about it?" demanded Jasper.

"Nothing at all," Bobby told him. "I can't prove in court all the things I know. Too easy if I could. Pyne may very likely shoot himself. Or even somebody else. I hope it won't be me. He has a way with safety catches I don't find at all attractive. By the way, there was a young man leaving here just as I arrived. I thought he seemed in a hurry. Anyhow, when I rather hurried to catch up he didn't seem to want to wait."

"Why should he? What did you want to 'catch up' for? Can't you leave anyone alone?"

"Not," Bobby answered, and now his voice had again that hard, grim note in it that sometimes it could assume, even without conscious intention on his part, "not if there seems even the smallest possibility that something may be known about—murder. Anyhow, this young man jumped on a passing taxi that came up just then, and was off and away in minutes." Bobby had reverted now to the light, bantering tone he had been using at first and that he felt baffled and bewildered Jasper. "Off and away," he repeated, "and nothing left for me to do but whistle: 'Will ye no' come back again?' Was his name Kenneth Banner?"

"If it was, I wouldn't tell you," Jasper roared, glaring furiously.

"Then I'll be off myself," Bobby said, jumping to his feet, for he was really afraid that soon Jasper's self-control might break down completely. "Oh, by the way," he asked with his hand on the door-knob, "know anything about limpets?"

"Limpets, limpets," Jasper repeated, so surprised he almost forgot to be angry. "What are you talking about now?"

"Limpets," Bobby said again. "A sort of shell-fish. Also the name given during the war to a kind of mine stuck on the bottom of ships by a one-man operation. Not a job I should have been in a hurry to undertake."

"Some more of your being clever, I suppose," Jordan growled, and he seemed genuinely puzzled. "May make sense to you—if anything does," he added doubtfully. "Talking through your hat most of the time, aren't you? Are you trying to make out that poor devil of a Hugh Newton was killed by a bomb?"

"I am sure he wasn't," Bobby answered. "Suffocated by feathers pushed down his throat while he was unconscious after being knocked out. The knocking out done by a man. The feathers—would that be a woman, I wonder? If so, both equally guilty. Well, I'll be off, though I may have to see you again. And I think the moment is appropriate for reminding you again that withholding evidence is a serious offence, especially in a murder case, and may lead even to a charge of being an accessory after the fact."

"I don't need you to teach me the law," Jasper retorted. "I know nothing about it all, and it's no business of mine."

"It might come to be so," Bobby answered. "Yours or anyone's, if whatever led to Newton's death is not stopped. It may spread to others—even to you."

"Rubbish, nonsense," snarled Jasper, but with a little less self-assurance than was generally apparent in all he said; and as soon as he was outside Bobby went running round the next corner, into the badly bombed street, still unrepaired, that ran behind and parallel to West King St.

He had not long to wait. Soon sounds of scrambling, of stumbling, of the fall of displaced bits of stone or rubble became audible. From the shadows in whose shelter he had ensconced himself, Bobby watched. Soon, through what once had been the imposing entrance to a large Victorian mansion, there emerged over a heap of rubble, under a placard announcing 'Danger', the figures of a man and a woman. They halted near a street-lamp. Bobby recognized Jasper and Doreen. Jasper was saying, every word clearly audible in the evening quiet of the deserted street:

"Rough going, worse than I thought. It's getting worse all the time—usual shocking neglect, of course. You'll be all right now though, won't you? I want to go back the same way. I don't want that meddling police fellow to get any idea I've a handy back door."

Doreen made some reply, but Bobby could not catch what she said in her low voice, such a contrast to Jasper's roaring tones. Jasper's reply, however, Bobby could hear distinctly.

"Oh, him," Jasper was saying, and the 'him' Bobby correctly took for a reference to himself. "Oh, yes, Mr Funny Clever. No fear of his trying to follow you. He'll be there, opposite my place in the darkest doorway he can find, waiting to see if anyone comes out. Well, he'll see me come out presently and poke a stick into every corner till I get him, and then I'll have a good laugh—shoving his nose in where it's not wanted."

They parted then, Jasper returning for his none too easy and even slightly dangerous clamber through the ruined house, and Doreen continuing on her way to the nearest point where she could hope to catch her 'bus. Bobby hurried to overtake her. She heard his step close behind, but did not look round. Her work took her out too often late in the evening for her not to have learnt that complete indifference was the best technique for dealing with any unwanted and obtrusive male. Bobby said:

"Good evening, Miss Doreen. Do you mind if I walk along with you?"

CHAPTER XVI
STRIKING A BARGAIN

DOREEN TURNED sharply. That accustomed technique of hers, complete indifference, of no use this time, for she had recognized the voice at once. The dismay in her own voice was undisguised as she stammered out:

"Oh, it's you . . . you . . ."

For a moment indeed Bobby was afraid she was going to take refuge in flight, a manœuvre which would have left him helpless, at any rate for the time.

"Oh, please, Miss Doreen, please," he said. "It's all right, it's only that I've got to ask you a few more questions. Necessary, I'm afraid. Now, if you like, if you will let me walk along with you. Or I can call to see you to-morrow morning. Or you can come and see me at Scotland Yard. Whichever you prefer."

"How did you know . . ."? she began, and paused. "I mean . . ." and again she left the sentence unfinished. "Have you . . . is it anything else besides me?" and this time Bobby guessed what made her voice sound so weak, so terrified.

"We haven't arrested Mr Banner, if that's what you mean," he said. "I saw him leaving Jordan's place, but he was off in a passing taxi before I had time to do anything."

"What made you think it was Mr Banner?" Doreen asked. "Besides, it wasn't," she added, recovering now her shaken self-possession.

"Well, I didn't guess who it was at first," Bobby admitted. "I was only sure when I knew you were at Jordan's too."

Doreen was silent for a moment or two. Bobby felt she was half-inclined to deny that she had been there, but if she really had such an idea she abandoned it. Instead she said:

"I don't see how you did know, I don't believe you did, I think you are just guessing."

"I never guess," Bobby protested. "Never. Deduction from observed facts. What I always tell people. Much the same really, but it sounds a lot better. I've always suspected you were more or less in touch with Mr Banner, and if that had been Mr Banner who was in such a hurry to get off, then it was fairly certain you wouldn't be far away. Obvious there had been a woman visiting Jordan—and of course I had seen you there before, so it was pretty certain that woman was you."

"How could you possibly know that?" she flashed. "I'm sure Mr Jordan wouldn't tell you."

"He wouldn't," Bobby agreed, "and he didn't. How much easier it would all be if people told us things. They don't. Not even nice young ladies. Dumb as destiny, all of them. But you did leave plain evidence that a woman had been there just before I arrived."

"I'm sure I didn't," Doreen protested. "I mean I'm sure I never would if I had been."

"Anyone with half an eye could see the place had just been swept and dusted," Bobby pointed out. "There was even a brush and dust-pan still there in one corner. Fact is, some women don't seem able to keep their fingers off a broom if there's as much as a speck of dust visible."

"Speck of dust indeed," Doreen protested indignantly. "It was inches deep everywhere."

"So it was," Bobby agreed. "I didn't think it would be much good asking for a talk with you there and then. Simpler to wait outside, which is what I did."

"Mr Jordan said you would be," Doreen said. "Waiting. That's why he took me out the way he did. Only you were there, too, weren't you?"

"I was," Bobby agreed again. "Jordan had played that game before, but you don't often take a second trick with the same card." He added, not without satisfaction: "I expect Jordan at this moment is hopefully poking sticks into every doorway in West King Street. An innocent amusement. Well, why is Mr Banner hiding? Till now, I wasn't sure about it. Now I know he is—well, rather suggests he's guilty, doesn't it?"

"He isn't—I know he isn't," Doreen said with passion. She did not raise her voice, but it was vibrant with a strange intensity of feeling. "It doesn't matter what he says, he isn't."

"How do you mean—no matter what he says?" Bobby asked, puzzled by the phrase. "He ought to know."

Doreen only shook her head and walked on in silence, quickening her pace, though more as if she wished to leave her own thoughts behind rather than in the hope of outstripping Bobby. He was silent, too, wondering if she was so certain of Kenneth Banner's innocence because she knew who was in fact the murderer. Doreen said suddenly:

"I expect you think it wasn't true about me not knowing where he was. Well, I didn't. I don't now. He rang up. He said it was to say good-bye. That was a day or two after—after—"

"After the murder?" Bobby asked, seeing that the word troubled her.

"After it happened," she said. "And I didn't want it to be good-bye, not like that. So I put an advertisement one day every week in the personal column of the *Announcer* I knew he used to read. And there was no answer. Nothing happened for weeks and weeks, and then he rang up and said I was to forget him and he was leaving the country, and I said can't we meet, if only for just once more, and we did—at Mr Jordan's. I couldn't ask him to come to the house because it would have upset mother so, and I couldn't think of anywhere else. He said all right and he came, and then the 'phone went, and it was to tell Mr Jordan you were coming, and Kenneth said he must go, and he did."

"If he is not guilty, he is a fool," Bobby remarked, and Doreen said, very angrily:

"All very well for you to talk, you don't know, you don't know anything at all!"

"If I did—know anything at all, I mean," Bobby answered, "I might be able to help you. Sometimes an officer of police can prove that that's one side of his duty—to help those in trouble, to protect them sometimes. Why not give me a chance to know something? By telling the truth, the whole truth. Think it over. In the meantime, are you still in touch with Mr Banner? Can you communicate with him? If you can, will you advise him to come forward at once? It will be necessary now to make it public that we want to hear from him. 'Because we think he may be able to help us over the Hugh Newton murder' is how it will be phrased. It will mean his name and description outside every police-station in the country. There must be plenty of his old shipmates who knew him in the war who could recognize him. And the Naval authorities could tell us a lot, I expect. We shall be sure to get all the information we need before long."

But Bobby spoke with more confidence than he felt, for he knew well how easy it is to disappear in the crowded cities of to-day, where so many busy millions pass each other by every hour and never even think of giving each other a second glance.

They had been walking on all the time they were talking thus, and since the distance was not great, they were now near where Doreen lived with her mother. There had been a long silence. Doreen said:

"If I can get hold of him again and tell him, and if he says I can bring you to meet him somewhere, will you wait for a day or two before—before—"

"Before making it public that we want to find him?" Bobby completed her sentence. "Well, yes, I think I can promise that. But not longer," and he thought to himself that the delay would not be of much importance, since it would take almost the day or two mentioned to prepare such a general and widespread announcement as he contemplated.

"And you must promise," Doreen went on, "that if he says I may and I take you to meet him, you won't try to do anything horrid."

"Well, I'm afraid that would be rather a wide undertaking," Bobby told her smilingly. "So much depends, doesn't it, on what could be called 'horrid'. I can't promise anything at all, except with the plain understanding that what I feel to be my duty must come first."

"I do think you're a most awful prig," Doreen said indignantly.

"Oh, am I?" Bobby asked, considering this accusation and rather depressed by it. "I don't know. Anyhow, we must leave it at that. If you let me know within forty-eight hours that Kenneth Banner is willing to meet me immediately and give me his version of what happened, nothing more will be done till I've seen him."

"You'll come alone?" Doreen interposed.

"Oh, I'll come alone all right," Bobby promised. "Understand though, if I don't hear within the forty-eight hours, the notices will go out."

"Very well," she said, in a small subdued voice, and then, with that sudden suppressed, yet vibrant passion he had heard in her voice before, she added: "I don't care, I know he didn't. It's not—it's not—not him."

"Well, that's a first-class, very good personal reason," Bobby said. "But not much good to judge or jury."

At that Doreen suddenly stood still. She turned to stare at him. It was as if those last two words had startled her, as if they had brought before her a vision of a court, of a judge in wig and robes, of twelve grave-faced men called upon to decide a fellow creature's fate. Bobby thought he knew well who in that picture, if it were really in her mind, stood in the dock. Doreen turned away and hurried to the house. Over her shoulder she said:

"I must go in. Good night."

"One moment," Bobby said, as she was fumbling in her handbag for her key. "Tell me, why did you say you don't care? Care about what?"

"I don't care what anyone says—anyone," she answered, and repeated with emphasis: "Anyone, anyone," and her voice had grown high and shrill.

She had her key in the lock now, but again Bobby checked her.

"One thing more," he said. "Do you know anything about limpets?"

"Limpets," she repeated. "What limpets? Why? Do you mean shell-fish, aren't they? Or those things they used to stick on ships in the war under water so as to blow them up? Do you mean about Kenneth? He was given a medal because of doing it."

"Yes, I've heard that," Bobby told her. "I was thinking of the shell-fish just then, and wondering if they were ever used in cooking. Are they?"

"Not that I ever heard of," she answered curtly, and now she had the door open, and she went in quickly and closed it behind her as if half-afraid he might follow her.

"A poignant little scene," he reflected as he walked slowly away. "And what did she mean by her 'didn't care what anybody said?' Someone been telling her something? Well, who—and what?"

CHAPTER XVII
THE HOVERING SHADOW

THE FOLLOWING morning, when Bobby informed his immediate superior of the arrangements made with Doreen, he did not find the news greeted with any marked approval.

"Seems to me," grumbled Superior Authority, "you are as likely as not heading for trouble. I take it you'll arrange to be followed by another car just in case?"

Bobby shook his head.

"Oh, no," he said. "Put the hat on the whole thing. No good trying to pull off anything like that with Miss Doreen. A very wide-awake young lady. As quiet and yielding and all that as water, and as impossible to stop as flood water when it gets really going. If there was a car following she would spot it in quick time, and that would be the end of the whole show—and the end of the kind of mutual confidence I've been trying to build up between us. Got to play fair, or it's no good."

Superior Authority nodded with complete though somewhat reluctant understanding. There is in fact a strange, in a way, incredible psychological situation that in an investigation can develop between questioner and questioned. In it each grows to know intimately the other, in a sense they come to trust each other, and to know, too, that certain rules and conventions will be observed, though neither one could say what those rules and conventions are, and though each is well aware what hangs upon the outcome of their talks.

"Looks to me," Superior Authority went on, however, "as if this girl of yours may be leading you straight into a trap of some sort. They may be thinking it's time you were stopped before you got any nearer, and the girl may be just a decoy. The cheese for the mouse—you."

"Some mouse, don't you think?" Bobby retorted, remembering a certain famous speech. "It wouldn't be the first time anyhow that that bright idea has occurred to some people. Professional risk, but very small this time."

"Oh, well, have it your way," grumbled the other. "What do you propose to do if the young lady lives up to her word and does produce the chap?"

"Hear what the chap has to say," Bobby answered promptly, "and then bring him back here to say it all over again."

"Taking it for granted that he'll be willing to come?"

"Oh, dear, no," Bobby protested gently. "I never take anything for granted. Except that if he's there he'll come all right—willingly or unwillingly."

"I don't like it," declared the other. "This girl, too. An unknown quantity. Girls always are, of course. No, I don't like it."

"Such a lot of things in life one doesn't like, don't you think, sir?" commented Bobby. "Almost everything in fact—except not getting up in the morning."

"Well, don't blame me if you and your girl friend both come back in your coffins, that's all," was the final comment with which the interview closed.

Returning to his own room, Bobby settled down to the routine work of which there was always plenty needing his attention and to await word either from Doreen or from one or other of his assistants he had working on what was coming to be known officially as the Mayfair Crescent Case (Reopened) and privately and off the record as 'Bobby Owen's special'. Nor was it so very long before reports began to come in.

The first was to the effect that Mrs Adam, traced to the small and rather grubby hotel where she had been working as cook and not giving any great satisfaction, had failed to arrive at her usual time the night before. As a consequence, the proprietor had had to undertake the preparation of the dinner himself, and, as a further consequence, the guests had fared even worse than usual. An urgent message sent to her lodgings had revealed that she had left in a taxi early in the afternoon, taking with her all her possessions in one large suit-case and various bundles; and giving Waterloo Station as her destination. Efforts to trace her farther had so far failed completely. It seemed, however, that shortly after her departure from her lodgings she had been inquired for by a man, the oddity of whose appearance had made him well remembered and whose description made it fairly plain that he was Jasper Jordan. It was added that he had seemed equally annoyed and surprised when told that she had left.

"So Jasper's up and doing, is he?" Bobby commented to himself. "Well, so much the better. So long as things are moving, there's always hope. It's only in a dead calm there's no chance of progress."

With which sage reflection he tried to console himself and to control a growing impatience, till presently there came another report to say that Imra Guire had paid her bill at her hotel and walked off, remarking casually that she was returning to Seemouth, where, however, she had not yet appeared.

Finally, a 'phone call to Doreen's home brought the information that she had gone away on what she had described as urgent private affairs. A cousin had been called in to look after Mrs Caine during Doreen's absence, which she had said would only be for a day or two. She had given to no one, not even to her mother, any hint of what were these private affairs, what was her errand, or where she was going.

"Hope," Bobby said to himself, musing over this last bit of news, "she won't be away longer—possibly longer than she ever dreamed she might be," for indeed he was growing more and more convinced that behind all this lay hidden those already guilty of one murder and not likely to hesitate at another.

It seemed to him to be becoming clear from what he knew already, more especially from the odd little incident of the theft of two wrist-watches, nothing else taken, from the murder flat and of their subsequent return, that large sums of money were at stake and, inevitably, the safety of those concerned.

But if the motive was gradually and doubtfully emerging, from the obscurity that had at first surrounded it, into a somewhat clearer light, the identity of the murderer or murderers still remained as completely hidden as before.

"Might be almost anyone," Bobby told himself gloomily. "Only just the one little tiny straw to show which way the wind might be blowing. And too many cross-currents for one to be sure its drift means anything at all."

He tried to console himself with the reflection that at any rate the two men whose names, up to the present that is, had come most prominently into the affair—Ossy Dow and Jasper Jordan—had, again up to the present, remained comparatively quiescent. And then came fresh word from Seemouth. Stanley Foster, the little tobacconist and spare-time engineer, was missing from his shop, had not been seen for a day or two in the neighbouring public-house he always 'used', was believed to have gone to London, and did the Yard think that was likely to have any connection with the general set-up?

Bobby had to answer that he didn't know, and then he rang off and looked worried.

For here it seemed was a new entrant on the scene, and one who hitherto had been thought of as merely a super, or even a spectator, safely out of the way in the wines. But now perhaps about to step forth to play his part in that last act on which Bobby felt in his bones the curtain was about to rise.

He began absent-mindedly to arrange pens and pencils in a kind of pattern on his desk.

"That," he said aloud, putting one down, "is Doreen the inflexible, and that"—he placed a second in position—"is Imra the unpredictable and here"—'here' was a specially fat pencil stump—"is Mary Ellen Adam the incongruous." He added two more, murmuring: "For Jasper the Enemy of Society and Ossy the wrong 'un." He hesitated whether to include Mr Pyne, but did so finally, choosing for him a nice new blue pencil; "Sick without knowing it," he commented, "of rule, routine, and respectability, the three 'R's' of bureaucracy, and letting a touch of adventure go to his head. Risky. Very. In deep water without having learned how to swim." Now there were no more pens or pencils left, so he added a penknife from his pocket. "For Stanley Foster," he said, "so sharp he may cut himself." As an after-thought he found an odd bit of string, tied it into the form of a noose, and put it with the rest. "Kenneth Banner?" he muttered doubtfully. But then he changed his mind, undid it, and shaped it instead into the resemblance of a question mark.

For some moments he sat staring at the resulting pattern, and found in it nor sense nor significance.

With an impatient gesture he swept them all together again, the penknife falling on the floor. To retrieve it he had to go down on his hands and knees, and in that undignified position he was discovered when his next visitor entered the room.

He had come, however, on a different and comparatively unimportant matter. This disposed of, Bobby returned to his own contemplative act, and more and more found his attention concentrating itself on the three women he had named the Implacable, the Unpredictable, and the Incongruous. But this contemplation might as well, for all the enlightenment it produced, have been concentrated, in the approved Eastern fashion, on his own navel. Unless indeed it may be called enlightenment that more and more it grew into his mind that one of those three knew consciously or unconsciously the answer, and therefore that that one was in imminent and certain danger, since it only needed for that answer to get itself spoken for all immediately to become plain. It seemed to him that a shadow like the shadow of death itself had crept into the room and there was hovering over those three names, but uncertainly, as if not yet were it decided on which one of the three it was to fall.

CHAPTER XVIII
THE MOTOR CYCLIST

FOR A LITTLE more than twenty-four hours the situation re-mained unchanged. Then, late in the evening, when Bobby was already beginning to think of bed after a long—and boring—day at his desk, the 'phone rang.

Bobby said something under his breath. Olive didn't say anything, but what she thought was much worse. Bobby picked up the receiver and answered. A voice he recognized for that of Doreen told him that she was coming in a car to pick him up, and would be there in a few minutes.

"I'm sorry for the short notice," she added, "but I've only just been able to make sure it was all right with Kenneth—Mr Banner."

Bobby told her he would be ready when she came, and to Olive he said:

"The Doreen girl. She'll be here in a few minutes, and wants me to be ready. You had better go to bed. I may be late." He saw Olive was looking uneasy, troubled. He said: "No earthly reason to look like that. There's nothing whatever to worry about."

"I know," said Olive. "You always say that, and then you come home just a battered wreck."

"I don't," Bobby almost shouted in his hot indignation. "Battered wreck indeed. That's the other chap."

"Well, you'll take one of those gun things with you?" Olive urged.

"A gun?" Bobby repeated, more horrified this time than indignant. "A nice sort of example that would be to the rank and file, wouldn't it?" They heard a motor hooting outside. "That'll be the young lady," Bobby said. "I'll be off, and don't worry."

"As if," Olive sighed, "your unfortunate wife ever had a chance to do anything else. Oh, why didn't I marry a nice little Civil Servant in a nice little office with a nice little carpet all to himself?"

"Because," Bobby explained as he made for the door, "you had fallen so passionately head over heels in love with me, you just couldn't help it," and therewith banged the door behind him before Olive had time to get out even one of those words bubbling and boiling on the tip of her tongue.

"Men are such cheats," she told herself crossly. "Get the last word by running away, the mean things."

Down below, drawn up before the entrance to the flats, Doreen was sitting at the wheel of a Bayard Twenty. Bobby walked round it, made a mental note of the number, and then got in beside her.

"Your own car?" he asked.

"Oh, no," she answered. "Hired."

She seemed a competent and careful driver, a little too careful perhaps, if that can be thought possible in these days. At any rate, there were one or two indignant hoots from behind as if her modest, less than thirty m.p.h. was too slow for others anxious to get by on their way home—or elsewhere. Not that Doreen took any notice. As for Bobby, as a police officer he applauded. As a man, his fingers itched to get hold of the wheel. Presently he said:

"Any objection to telling me where you are going?"

"I don't know," she answered.

"Oh, well," he said, slightly taken aback by the simplicity of this reply, which had been delivered quite seriously and gravely. "Oh, well, I hope you'll get there."

She made no reply, but drove on at the same steady pace. Now they were out of the main stream of London traffic, and there were no more indignant hoots from drivers who considered themselves unduly held up. Even when a long straight stretch of road with no sign of other traffic lay before them, there was not the slightest increase of speed. Just the same steady jog trot. Bobby began to wonder if there was a reason for this restraint, as indeed there is for everything. Presently he said:

"There is a motor cyclist behind. I think he is following us." Doreen made no reply. Bobby was a little uneasy lest some too-zealous subordinate had thought it safer that there should be an escort. If it were that, Bobby determined grimly that the too-zealous would hear about it—would hear, in fact, quite a lot about it. He said: "If you'll stop the car, I'll get out and ask him what he's up to."

"He's not following us," Doreen answered, and she slightly increased speed, as if for fear Bobby might do as he had suggested and jump out.

But that the cyclist was in fact following them Bobby was certain, and it was clear that Doreen must be aware of it, in spite of her denial. Now, however, before he could decide what to do or whether to do anything but wait, they came to what was apparently a country club or road-house, to judge from its display of lights and Chinese lanterns. Here Doreen came so nearly to a dead stop that Bobby thought they had reached their destination—but not that of the motor cyclist, for he rode by, emitting a hoot as he did so. Doreen answered with her own hooter and increased speed. The country club was left behind, and Doreen said:

"He is not following us. I'm following him."

"Oh, I see," Bobby said, realizing that that was what she had meant when she said she did not know where they were going. That had been left for the motor cyclist to decide, and the country club had evidently been agreed on as the spot where the cyclist was to take control.

Presently the cyclist turned up a side road and then another. Following this, they came soon to where close-growing trees on either hand made a kind of tunnel of impenetrable darkness through which the headlights of car and cycle threw narrow beams like flying arrows of light. Half-way through this tunnel the cyclist stopped and dismounted. Doreen said to Bobby:

"It's Kenneth. He's going to tell you exactly what happened, and he says you can write it all down if you like."

"Good," Bobby said. "I was hoping that," and to the motor cyclist, who had now propped up his machine against a tree and come to the side of the car, he said: "Glad to meet you, Mr Banner."

"I don't know that I can say the same," Kenneth answered.

His voice was light and pleasant, a tenor voice. But it was none too steady. Highly nervous, Bobby thought, and no great wonder if he were. Bobby began to descend, and Doreen said:

"No. Kenneth, you get in. You and Mr Owen can sit in the back seat while you talk, and don't whisper. I want to hear everything."

"She's been plugging that all the time," Kenneth grumbled.

"Oh, all right," Bobby said, and thought that at any rate this showed there were no accomplices lurking in the dark shade of those trees, waiting their opportunity to attack. Which was the uncomfortable thought that had come into his mind when he realized that this black tunnel was their trysting place. An ominous line, full of sad foreboding, had come into his mind, 'Ronald to the dark tower came', and coming to a dark tunnel had seemed to him for the moment even more ominous for Bobby Owen. So it was with some relief that he ensconced himself next to Kenneth on the car's rear seat. He said: "I see you are wearing a mask, Mr Banner."

"Yes, I know," Kenneth said discontentedly. "Silly, isn't it? Melodramatic, and all that. Doreen would have it."

"I told him he must," Doreen said. "I wasn't going to help you get a description for those horrid notices you talked about."

"I told her goggles would be good enough," Kenneth said. "Nothing else would do but a mask. Once she gets an idea into her head, it's no good saying anything. She doesn't listen."

"I do," Doreen exclaimed angrily, "only when I know I'm right and it's the only sensible thing—well, no good talking about it, is it?"

"We won't argue about that," Bobby interrupted. "Please begin, Mr Banner. Miss Doreen tells me you are willing that I should take notes of what you say. Of course, I needn't remind you that anything you do say may be used in evidence. So now, if you'll make a start, Mr Banner."

But making a start was clearly something that Kenneth was not finding at all easy. He hesitated, began to say something, stopped, began again, then abruptly blurted out:

"I didn't murder him. I don't know what I did do. I suppose it's no good my saying that. You won't believe it."

"That doesn't matter." Bobby answered when Kenneth paused for a reply. "What I am here for is to listen to anything you wish to say. Please go on."

"Well, it's like this," Kenneth continued then, and more calmly. "Doreen says you know all about our 'As You Like It' yacht cruises. I mean about our letting the people who booked with us choose where they wanted to go—Paris mostly. And about our giving them slap-up food. We did, too. Up to the best you would get in any of the swell restaurants, and we didn't try to put them off with second-rate grub by handing round third-class champagne. I got the idea from the Air Lines. More common sense to it with us though. On a yachting cruise you have to have meals, and if you can use the yacht as an hotel in port you've so much more of your travel allowance to spend as you like. You may have seen our ads. They were jolly good. 'Epicurus goes yachting'. That sort of thing."

"Do I understand you did the cooking?" Bobby asked.

"No, I'm coming to that." Kenneth paused and gulped. "That was the chap who was—murdered." He brought out this last word with an obvious effort. "Murdered," he repeated. "If he was. I don't know. God help me, I don't know."

"Take it easy," Bobby said.

"Easy," Kenneth repeated, and he gave something that was between a laugh and a groan. "Well, Abel we called him—Bert

Abel, he must have called himself Hugh Newton as well. That was the name in the papers. I've no idea which was his real name. Neither perhaps. He was wizard with food. He could cook up almost anything, and turn it out so you dreamed about it for days afterwards. I'm not so bad at the job myself, but not like him. He was a sort of genius. He could have made big money as a chef if he had chosen to. I think it was his cooking made our trips go so well. It was the overheads were the trouble. I planned to get more yachts on the go so as to reduce them, but the trouble would have been to find more cooks like Abel. We weren't doing much more than pay ourselves wages and a profit of about one per cent on our capital. All right. But I began to notice that all the others seemed to be splashing money around, and I couldn't make it out. Ossy Dow bought a share in a pub at Seemouth. Stan Foster bought a tobacconist's business, and they pay like winking, so you have to put money down to get one. And I got the idea that Abel was doing himself jolly well in town. He said things that made me think. He said he had been lucky at the dogs. Foster said he had had money left him. Ossy said he had bought his share in the pub with borrowed money, and Imra Guire said I was a fool. She wouldn't say what she meant, but by that time I was beginning to smell a rat."

"Was it a rat you smelt or a limpet?" Bobby asked.

CHAPTER XIX
KENNETH TELLS HIS STORY

KENNETH WAS clearly much taken aback by this remark. He was silent for a moment or two. Then, in a tone of mingled surprise and unease—and with a touch of admiration as well—he said:

"Oh, well, I don't know. I have been wondering. What put you on it? Ossy asked a whole lot of questions about the job and how we stuck the things on, clamping them or what. I thought he was just interested. People are. I've often been asked about it, but I can see now Ossy went into a whole lot of detail. It never struck me there was anything behind. It was only when the others all seemed so flush and I wasn't that I began to worry."

"I don't know how big these limpet mines are," Bobby said, "but I suppose they are a fair size. Anyhow, in the same way something fairly big, big enough to hold quite a lot of valuable stuff, could be fixed to your yacht's bottom?"

"I suppose so," Kenneth agreed. "I daresay you think I ought to have spotted it. I never did."

"Swiss watches," Bobby remarked. "A lot of very valuable watches could be packed away in a very small space."

"I hadn't got as far as that," Kenneth said. "But I did let the others see I thought something was wrong. Then Abel or Newton, or whatever his name really was, hinted he was getting worried and he thought something might be going on we two knew nothing about. He said he really had been making big money betting, and if I would come along to the flat he was running on the strength of it, he would show me how he did it. But it was a bit thick to suppose that Stan Foster had had a fat legacy from an aunt no one had ever heard of before and no details given. And Ossy's story about borrowing money to buy a share in the pub was even thicker. You don't borrow money so easily as all that, unless you have jolly good security to put down. Well, I fell for Abel's story. He played me for a sucker all right. I expect you think I was all sorts of a fool."

He paused for confirmation—or perhaps denial. It was the confirmation he got in the shape of an emphatic nod and an equally emphatic:

"Oh, yes."

"All very well to talk," grumbled Doreen from her driver's seat. "You would have just the same."

"Oh, yes," agreed Bobby once more, and Doreen did not know whether to be still more offended or to be placated.

"He was awfully plausible," Kenneth continued, too absorbed in the telling of his story, in the recollection of those days of dawning doubt and suspicion, to pay much attention to any interpolations. "He wasn't only a first-class cook, a wonder cook. He could jolly you along almost as he pleased. He could talk our tourists into doing any odd job for us on the yacht without their having the least notion it wasn't all their own idea. He could have served up a dried haddock and made you think it was the greatest delicacy on earth. Mind you, what he did serve up was rather more than jolly good—it was superb. I don't know why he wasn't head chef at some swell hotel. Or why he wasn't in Parliament, the way he could talk. I rather think perhaps he just liked doing things the crooked way."

"I know," Bobby agreed. "There are people like that. They think it's clever, and then they won't, or can't, settle down to any regular discipline. A man like that can take a good job for a short time and do well, and then he gets restless, or feels he isn't making money fast enough and starts playing tricks. But please go on with what you were saying."

"All the same," Kenneth went on, "I don't think I was altogether taken in. I still felt uneasy in a way. But I agreed to go to his flat. It never struck me there could be any danger or any sort of trap. Anyhow, I shouldn't have cared. I expect I felt I was quite able to look after myself." Bobby was aware that at this Doreen muttered to herself: "Men always think they can, only they just can't", but Kenneth, unhearing, continued: "But then, just as I was starting out, there was a 'phone call. I couldn't make much of it."

"Did you recognize the voice?"

"No. It was a woman's I think. I didn't notice much. Whoever it was rang off in the middle of what she was saying. It all seemed to add up to telling me not to go out that evening and, if I did, to mind what I had to drink. I said why and what was it all about, and that was when she rang off."

"Do you know where the call came from?"

"From a call box," Kenneth replied. "I did ask that. Well, I didn't feel like taking any notice, and I went to Abel's just the same. He was waiting, and he was very jolly and friendly, and said between us we could soon get to the bottom of what was going on behind our backs. He said we could talk about it while we were having something to eat, and he had done my favourite speciality for me."

"What was that?" Bobby asked quickly.

"Fried chicken and apple fritters," Kenneth answered. "He had some special way of doing it, and I had told him once I thought it jolly good. I didn't know it was my favourite exactly. There was smoked salmon on the table. I remember that. Smoked salmon is a bit of a weakness of mine. I was skippering a big yacht once, and the owner used to have it at almost every meal. Abel kept bustling about and talking, and he mixed cocktails and gave me one, and the moment I had it I knew it was doped. I can't describe the feeling exactly. It was just as if one part of me wasn't there at all, and one part of me was looking on, and one part was still me. It was all awfully muddled and confused like a bad dream, all of it except one thing. Abel's face, looking much larger than it was really and quite close and grinning like hell. Then—I don't know how to describe it—it was damn queer. It was just as if the part of me that was looking on was saying: 'You have been warned, and now you've had it', and the part of me that was still me said: 'Got to do something about it', and then all three of us seemed to rush together again and something else as well from outside, so I became all at once all different and a lot bigger, and I hit that grinning face of Abel's with—I was going to say with all my force. But it was more than that—much more than that. I don't know where it came from— the power I mean. I don't believe any heavy-weight champion ever got in a blow like that. I don't believe any human being could have stood up to it. Poets are supposed to be inspired sometimes, and if a fist can be inspired—well, mine was. That big, outsize grinning face of Abel's seemed just to crumple up, and then there he was, lying flat on his back on the floor, with his face all changed and different and blood all over it, and I was looking down at him, wondering what had happened and hanging on to a chair to keep myself from falling.

"I think all this must have happened in split seconds. I could see Abel's head was hanging half over the fender, and I remember thinking quite coherently that I was too weak on my legs to move him, but I could get a cushion to put under his head. I grabbed one from the couch, and then I went down flat, and the chair and cushion and all, and me, right on top of him where he lay. All at once I felt most awfully sick, and I was beginning to see things that weren't there."

"What sort of things?" Bobby asked when the other was silent for a moment of two, as if finding difficulty in expressing himself.

"Faces mostly," Kenneth said then. "A procession of faces, horrible, grinning faces. I can remember saying out loud: 'You aren't real, you know', and at the same time thinking that of course they were, more real than reality, for that matter, and I was afraid. Besides I didn't want to be sick there, as I felt I was going to be. I managed to get on my feet somehow and to get to the bathroom. The faces weren't there, thank God, I had got away from them, and I wasn't sick either. It just wouldn't come, though I did my best to bring it up. I couldn't, and then I was on the floor again, and I knew I would be unconscious very soon. I could feel it coming in waves, and I still had sense enough to know that if Abel came round first and found me there like that he would kick the inside out of me, and I had better get off, and the sooner the quicker." He paused and looked slightly embarrassed, even shy. He said: "I don't think I put it quite like that at the time, but I daresay what was at the back of my mind was—well, I'm no film star, but I didn't want Doreen to see me next time with a broken nose and all my teeth knocked out or an eye gone perhaps. So I did—got off, I mean. Luckily I didn't meet anyone on the stairs, and I don't think there was anyone in the street, and anyhow it was beginning to grow dark. The house next door has been pretty badly bombed, you remember. I was feeling most awfully ill and muddled, but I just managed to get inside, and then I was sick all right. I don't think there can have been anything at all left inside me. It went on Lord knows how long, and long after I had stopped bringing anything up. That was the worst part of it, trying to bring up what wasn't there. I know I honestly thought I was going to die, and then I suppose I went off again, lost my senses, I mean."

"I suppose I shall have," Bobby remarked, "when I'm giving a talk to our chaps, to stress again they must always make a thorough search all round where there's been any crime committed, especially if it's murder. Excusable in a way perhaps this time. I don't know that I should have thought of doing it. You could hardly expect to find a suspect having a snug little sleep next door. It's got a big 'danger' placard on it, too, hasn't it?"

"Snug little sleep," grunted Kenneth indignantly. "Well, anyhow, when I came round it was morning. I lay for a time trying to remember where I was and what had happened. I simply couldn't get it all clear. My head was going round and round, and I couldn't stand upright at first without hanging on to something. What I felt I had to do was to get back somehow or another to my lodgings. When I'm in town I can generally get an old shipmate of mine—a C.P.O., he's retired now—to put me up, even if it's only on a sofa in their sitting-room. But in the street outside there was a small crowd, all staring as hard as they knew how at next door, where Abel had his flat, and there was a policeman telling them to move on, and none of them taking much notice, except to drift away a few yards and then drift back. They were all too busy gaping to pay me much attention, or notice where I came from, but one man did tell me there had been a murder, and another man next to him said he hoped they would get the man who did it, and hang him, and the other chap said he hoped so too, and they generally got their man, and if they didn't it wasn't for want of trying."

"It certainly isn't," Bobby interposed, much gratified by this spontaneous tribute to the work of the Force, and wondering if he could manage to get it published in the next issue of the *Gazette*.

Probably not. The poet sang of Lord Roberts long ago: "'E don't ever advertise." Nor do the police. Kenneth was continuing:

"I didn't quite take it in at first, but when I did it sent shivers all up and down my back, and I was sure they were eyeing me with a sort of 'Thou art the man' look in their eyes. The policeman was still walking up and down with his: 'Now then, move along there, please.' When he came to where we were, he evidently didn't like my looks, and I don't wonder. I expect I looked like nothing on earth. I hadn't found out then that I had only one shoe left. Anyhow, he gave me a special 'Move on you' all to myself. And then he said: 'Stop gaping and get out of it quick, unless you want to be taken in.' I've thought since that's probably about the only time on record a suspected murderer has been ordered to stop gaping and get out of it quick unless he wanted to be arrested."

"Oh, all things can happen in police work," Bobby observed with resignation.

"Well, anyway," Kenneth resumed, "I thought it good advice. My head was all muzzy, and I couldn't think clearly and couldn't quite take it in about it's having been murder, which it wasn't, but all the same I didn't feel I wanted to stop and argue. I just went."

CHAPTER XX
DOREEN INTERVENES

"SILLIEST THING ever," Bobby commented when Kenneth was silent so long it seemed almost as if he had said all he wished to say. In reality he was lost in memory of that strange, bewildering moment when there had first, as it were, begun to seep into his mind some sense of what had happened. "Very worst thing you could have done," Bobby said, with undiminished severity. "Running away."

"You would have done just the same," Doreen snapped. "So would anyone."

"Very likely, especially me," Bobby agreed. "Doesn't make it any the less silly though."

Unheeding this exchange of side-line talk, which indeed he had hardly heard, Kenneth went on:

"I got a taxi to take me home. The driver didn't want at first. I expect I looked disreputable enough. I told him I had been on the tiles all night, and then he was very jolly and friendly. When I got in I told Mrs Green the same thing. I expect even a C.P.O. had been there when he was younger, and she knew it all. Anyhow, she didn't say much. She got me to bed and got me something from the chemist's, and I went off to sleep and only woke up when I had a nightmare about watching a man being hanged. I tried to tell myself there must be a mistake somewhere, or perhaps someone else had been murdered and it was nothing to do with Abel or me. I just simply couldn't take it in. I had knocked Abel out all right, but that's nothing to kill a man, and I knew he had been alive when I got away. I was sure of that, if of nothing else. But then Mrs Green brought in the evening paper, and there it all was. Great fat letters sprawling all across the front page—'Choked to death by feathers'. That made me remember falling, me and chair and cushion and all, right on top of Abel where he was lying, knocked out. So I had to face it that the cushion might have burst with the fall and the feathers come out, and somehow in breathing he had drawn them into his mouth and died. Could it have happened like that? While he was unconscious, I mean?"

"I don't know," Bobby answered. "That will be for the doctors to say. There was something said about the feathers looking as if they had been deliberately and forcibly pushed down the throat."

"Well, they never were, not by me," Kenneth said. "For one thing, I was in no state to do anything forcibly, or deliberately either. I hardly knew what I was doing. I told you. After that cocktail everything was all a muddle, with my head going round like a top, and that endless procession of grinning beastly faces going on and on round the room just over the picture-rail. It wasn't much different next morning in the bombed house. My head was funny, and I couldn't think straight or make out what had happened or what it all meant. Nothing seemed real, except getting to bed."

"Didn't you realize it was all very real after you had had your sleep? Wasn't your mind clearer then?" Bobby interposed.

"Oh, yes," Kenneth agreed. "All except for a splitting headache. The fact is that then, after that evening paper, I panicked, so I was sweating with fear, and the bed shook under me. It wasn't so much that I was afraid of dying. I knew all about that. Most chaps who served in the war did. You don't crawl along under water trying to fix a mine full of high explosives on a ship's bottom without knowing what it's like to be afraid. It was the

idea of the trial and then being taken out one morning for an
eight-o'clock end, attending your own funeral. I tried to tell myself that if only I kept out of the way for a time it would all come
right somehow. Weak minded, I suppose. I thought they might
find something to show it wasn't murder at all, or if it was, that
I had nothing to do with it. I made up my mind to disappear
till I could see better how things were shaping, and then when
I knew more I could either give myself up—or not. Only then I
saw those advertisements Doreen put in the paper. I knew I had
no business to answer them. I knew I had no right to get Doreen
mixed up in the mess and—"

But at this Doreen—twisted round in her driver's seat, listening intently to every word—could contain her indignation no
longer.

"What do you think is the good of me," she demanded furiously, "if I'm to be kept out of everything?" Both men looked at
her in a startled way. It was evident she was in a highly nervous
condition, and was having difficulty in controlling herself. Not
surprising perhaps. "I'll never forgive you," she threatened, and
this time even more furiously.

"Please," Bobby said, holding up his hand, "please don't inter-
rupt. You can tell Mr Banner all you think about him later—and
I don't wonder you do," and that drew the full glare of her angry,
excited eyes upon him, though his louder voice, as he went on,
drowned what she was beginning to say to him and about him.
"It is important Mr Banner should keep strictly to what he was
saying," Bobby declared. "Please go on, Mr Banner."

"That's about all," Kenneth replied. "I did answer those advertisements all the same, and Doreen got me to say I would
meet you here to-night and tell you the whole thing and be sure
to leave nothing out. Well, so I have, and I don't expect you believe a word of it."

"What I believe," Bobby said, as he had said so often before
in similar circumstances, "doesn't matter in the least. I'm neither judge nor jury nor prosecuting counsel. Our only duty in
the police is to find out as much as we can, and everything that
seems to us to be true and relevant we put before the Public

Prosecutor. Then it is for him to decide if there ought to be a trial, for the jury to decide if guilt is proved or not, for the judge to say what ought to be done about it. In this case, what you've told me is unfortunately entirely your own uncorroborated story. There's rebuilding, you know, going on in the bombed house you mentioned. That means all trace of vomit will have disappeared, so it can't be analysed to see if it shows any sign of a drug having been given you. At the time, if you had come forward and told your story, that could have been done, and would have been a most important corroboration. If that's what the analysis showed, of course. Nor any chance of finding your lost shoe either. Then, again, in none of the reports made at the time—I've read them all—is there any mention of any overturned chair on or even near Abel's body. Can you suggest what Abel's motive could have been for drugging you?"

"Well, I expect they wanted to stop me worrying. They could see I meant to get to the bottom of what was going on."

"Such a lot of other explanations could be suggested," Bobby told him. "I'm afraid I must ask you to come back to the Yard with me so that what you have to say may be taken down in a formal statement you will be asked to sign."

"No," Kenneth said at once, and repeated: "No. Doreen told me it would be all right. You had promised, and she said it would be safe to trust you. I didn't much believe it, but I thought I had better come. I wanted to get it off my chest for one thing. I wanted to pretty badly. And I wanted Doreen to hear. And I thought it would be a good idea to find out if it sounded convincing. Well, jolly plain you don't find it convincing. I'm not complaining about that. I don't expect I should in your place. No," he said once more, and with even more emphasis than before. "I've made up my mind. I'm not going to stand a trial with everything against me and no chance of being believed. I'm not taking any eight-o'clock-in-the-morning walk, I can stand a good deal, but not that. I expect I had a sort of hope you would say it was good enough, that it would stand up O.K. Well, you don't, and most likely no one else would. So I'm not accepting your kind invitation. I've got other ideas. Even if I did get off, I should always be known as the fellow tried for murder, and people would always be saying: 'Jolly lucky to get off', 'Guilty as hell', they would tell each other. 'Wonderful how a smart Q.C. can bamboozle a jury.' And if the trial turned out the other way, then—the gallows. Or possibly life imprisonment. I'm not having that either. There's something else. I expect it'll sound silly. I got a decoration for that limpet-mine job. They would take it away, they always do. I don't see why. What you've done in the past has nothing to do with what you've done or are supposed to have done later on. But they would, and every other chap who had it would feel it had been disgraced and lessened. But if there's no trial and no verdict, that can't be done." He paused. He had been talking quickly and feverishly. He resumed in a calmer, slower tone, choosing his words, it seemed, with greater care: "There's something else. It counts for more. I haven't asked Doreen to marry me. I never will. She says we must, and at once, and nothing must stop it. Well, that's her idea, but I'm not having it. She's not going to be the widow of a man hanged for murder. She's not going to be tied for life to a man serving a life term in gaol. Or even to a man the police would never stop trying to catch. Would you?" he appealed to Bobby.

"Never," Bobby answered.

"You see," Kenneth said to Doreen. "So I'm going to get out of this world altogether. Save the cost of a rope, if nothing else," he said with a twisted grin. "As soon as I feel it's come to that. But Doreen has made me promise to wait a bit. Drowning, I think, the way so many good chaps went during the war. It's a sort of debt I almost feel we owe them. And easy. All you have to do is to swim till you can't any more, and then the sea takes you."

Doreen said in a very low voice.

"Kenneth. Please don't."

They were all three silent then—a strange and heavy silence. Bobby had been trying to watch both her and Kenneth at the same time. A difficult task. He said:

"All that makes it still more necessary you should come back with me. Only cowards despair."

"All right. I'm a coward if you like," retorted Kenneth. "But I'm not giving in, all the same. Not to you, I mean. That's that."

Doreen said:

"I must take an aspirin." She opened her hand-bag and began to fumble in it. In spite of the steadiness of her hands, and the calmness of her voice, Bobby could feel that she was wrought up to the highest pitch of nervous tension. Once more she said: "I must take an aspirin." To Bobby she said: "You promised, and I believed that I could trust you."

"I told you plainly," Bobby replied, "that what I felt to be my duty must be my over—the overriding consideration. I warned you any promise I made was subject to my duty."

Doreen put something in her mouth—apparently the aspirin she must have managed to find at last in her hand-bag, in which she had been fumbling so long. She was trembling violently as she did so, and there seemed to be something of finality and of despair in the gesture that she made.

"Very well," she said. "Now then."

To Kenneth, Bobby was saying:

"If you won't come quietly, I shall have to use force. After all, I'm a bigger man than you."

"I was prepared for that," Kenneth said. He took a small pistol from his pocket, slipped back the safety catch. "If you try that on, if you try to lift a hand, I'll drill you full of holes."

"That, of course," Bobby told him quietly, "will make no difference, it will only mean you'll have another murder to answer for."

"Damn you," Kenneth said, and flung the pistol down. "It wasn't loaded anyhow. You can have it if you like, for all the good it is." Bobby stooped, picked it up, saw it was in fact unloaded. Kenneth was saying: "You may be bigger, but I'm younger, and I know a bit of boxing, and I expect I'm in better training."

"I always keep myself in good training," Bobby said with dignity, and almost afraid that next thing Kenneth would be starting to call him fat.

"Well," Kenneth suggested, "shall we have it out here and now, in the road I mean?"

Bobby had taken a pair of handcuffs from his pocket. They were things he did not often carry. This time he had thought it a wise precaution.

"I'm going to put these on you," he said. "I hope you won't resist. It will only make it worse for you if you do. Oh, Miss Doreen, I'll just warn you, if you try to interfere, I shall have no hesitation in knocking you out. For I think you are getting yourself into a state in which you are hardly responsible any longer."

"Oh, I am," Doreen said, very gently. "Quite responsible as you call it. But do you mind listening for a moment while I tell you about Tom. He's my brother."

CHAPTER XXI
THE PILL OF RELEASE

THE INTERRUPTION was so unexpected, the words so entirely, as it seemed, irrelevant, that the two men entirely forgot each other and only stared in a sort of bewildered silence. Bobby's first thought was that under the strain of that intense internal struggle in Doreen, of which he had been conscious, in which he felt she was only holding her own by an equally intense inner effort, her mind had at last given way, even if only temporarily. But her expression, calm, collected, even serene, as of one who now knew the appointed path and meant to follow it to the end, put that idea out of his mind. Then he thought that perhaps it was all some sort of trap, so that in that first moment of surprise he could be taken unawares. He said sharply to Kenneth:

"Hold out your wrists."

But Kenneth did not seem even to hear him. So far from being prepared and ready to take advantage of Doreen's surprising interpolation, he was still staring at her with every appearance of being even more taken aback than had been Bobby himself. And Doreen was bending forward, stretching out her hand between the two men with a gesture that was at once commanding and beseeching.

"Please listen," she said. She was speaking more directly to
Bobby. She went on: "When I've explained what I mean, if you
still want to make Kenneth go back with you, I'm sure he will.
I promise that for both of us." She paused as if expecting some
answer. Bobby did not speak. Kenneth was still staring at her as
if what she said hardly penetrated his mind; and then it came
to Bobby that what held him so still and silent was an agony of
fear, a terrible and devastating fear. And of that fear Bobby now
began to feel in himself an echo as it were, an infection of terror,
so that he could have believed there had come to sit with them
in the motionless car on that dark and silent and deserted road
running like a tunnel through the night the figure of death itself,
waiting for one of them at least, and perhaps for all. But why he
felt this he had no idea, for Doreen's voice was calm and quiet
as ever, and her hands, which she now held clasped together
between her breasts, were perfectly still, the fingers interlaced
and quiet.

"Please listen," she said again, and she might well—so calm
was her manner, so quiet her voice—have been about to begin a
talk to one of her cookery classes on how to prepare some dish
needing a little more care than usual. "It's about Tom at first.
He's my brother. I told you. He was in the R.A.F. during the war.
After the fall of Singapore he was sent out to the East. By that
time they were beginning to understand what the Japanese did
to their prisoners. So when any airmen were likely to fly over
the Japanese, they were given poison pills, for them to use if
they felt they couldn't stand it any more. When the Japanese got
to know they called it 'The Pill of Release'. Tom was given one
like the others. He was taken prisoner when he was shot down,
and he was tortured like the others. Please, if you don't mind, I
won't tell you how. I've seen his hands. Even after he got back to
England they had to be dressed, and I did it, and sometimes afterwards at night I would hear him screaming, and when I went
and woke him he had been dreaming it was happening all over
again. He would never talk about it if he could help, but in the
dark when I was sitting by him after he had been dreaming, he
did once or twice. He said the poison pill had helped, because

he knew it was there if he had to. A sure refuge he called it. He brought it back to England with him—he kept it, though they didn't want him to—and mother managed to get it from him, and she has always kept it ever since. You see, poor dear, she has an awful lot of pain, and it's often very bad. She says the poison pill helps her just in the same way, because it reminds her if Tom could bear it, then she could."

"Doreen," Kenneth said, and then again, "Doreen." Then he said: "For God's sake," and was silent.

"I don't see," Bobby began, but he did—very plainly. "I don't know why you're telling us all this," he said, but he did—he knew exactly.

Doreen said to him:

"I took the poison pill from where mother had it, and it wasn't an aspirin I put in my mouth, it was the poison pill. I shall swallow it if you try to do anything to Kenneth. Please, Kenneth, don't interfere. Mr Owen, will you agree to let Kenneth go and promise, and never mind duty, not to do anything about him till we've got back to town? Because if you don't promise—"

She left the sentence unfinished. There was no necessity to finish it. No need to put into words what she intended.

Bobby said, trying to impose his authority:

"Don't be a fool. Give it me at once."

She took no notice. She might not have heard. Indeed, there was almost an indifference about her, as if she waited, with patience and tranquillity, a decision for which she was in no way responsible. Bobby wondered wildly if he dared grip her by the throat and force the poison pill out of her mouth before she had time to swallow it. Oddly, perhaps, it never even occurred to him to doubt her will or, for that matter, the fact. He dared not make the least movement, for he knew that even the lifting of a hand she might interpret as a hostile intention. He found himself perspiring slightly. Kenneth was saying:

"Give it him, Doreen, give it him. You can't do that. For God's sake, give it him."

"Please be quiet, Kenneth," Doreen said. "This is between me and Mr Owen. Only please, Mr Owen, could you be quick?

You see, these pills had a sort of protective covering so you could hold them in your mouth, only it's been so long I'm afraid it may have worn off or something."

What it was his duty to do, Bobby was not sure. But he knew very well what he was going to do. Impossible to sit there and watch the girl die before his eyes. He had a vision of her crumpling up where she sat. He knew he could not face it. Sulkily, resentfully, angrily, he said:

"All right. I promise. Only take the damn thing out of your mouth."

Doreen put her hand up and then paused.

"You haven't said, 'Never mind duty or anything'," she reminded him.

"Never mind duty or anything, to hell with duty," Bobby said. "Does that satisfy you?"

She put out the pill between her lips into her hand. Bobby snatched it from her. Viciously he crushed it to dust between his fingers, and the dust he threw out into the road.

"You needn't have done that, Mother will miss it," Doreen said rebuking; and to Kenneth she said: "Please go. Quickly. I can't stand it much longer. I'll write to you at our Post Office, and don't try to do anything silly. You've promised, too, you know."

Kenneth, a dazed, bewildered Kenneth, a Kenneth who even yet had not fully taken in what had happened, looked rather helplessly at Bobby. Bobby fairly shouted at him:

"Get out. Can't you hear? I've had enough, too."

Kenneth obeyed the joint injunction. They heard his machine chugging away into the darkness. They sat in silence listening. Bobby spoke first. He said:

"You little devil."

"If you would like to box my ears. . ." Doreen suggested. "Because you know you sound like it. I rather wish you would. I'm feeling as if I might begin to laugh or scream or something."

"Laugh away," Bobby growled. "It's your laugh. We'll get him all the same. I shall take very extra special care of that. I'm thinking now what I can charge you with. Attempted suicide? What you want is a term in gaol, and I'll see you get it," but he knew very well this was pure bluff and temper—a rather mean effort in fact to get a little of his own back by frightening her. She knew it, too, and took no notice.

"Do you mind driving?" she asked. "I don't think I can, I'm feeling so funny," and then suddenly she slumped over the wheel in a dead faint.

Not too tenderly, for he was in a vile temper, Bobby got her out of her driver's seat and dumped her at the back of the car, there to recover as best she could. Nor was his temper improved by this new complication. A nice position she had got him into, he thought angrily, alone with an unconscious girl in a car in the dark on a lonely and deserted side road. Anyhow—faint or no faint, unconscious girl or none—he meant to get back to the Yard at the earliest possible moment, there to start a nation-wide hunt for Kenneth. He drove fast, hoping he was taking the right direction. Once he thought he heard a bump behind him, as if by the motion of the car Doreen had been jerked off the seat on to the floor of the car. He didn't care. If she got a black eye or so, that was all right as far as he was concerned. Never, he supposed, in all the long history of Scotland Yard had a senior official been so bullied, bluffed, bamboozled—and by the cheekiest little chit of a girl anyone had ever heard of.

As a matter of fact, the chief effect of the bump had been apparently the recovery of Doreen from her faint. For soon he heard a small voice say rebuking from behind:

"You've just jumped traffic lights."

"Mind your own business," growled Bobby, even more ill-temperedly than before, but all the same, began to drive more carefully.

A fitting end it would be to this night of ill-success, he thought, if he were summoned and fined for a traffic offence. But one he had no wish should happen.

The small voice from behind said meditatively:

"You do sound most awfully cross." This time it was Bobby who took no notice. The small voice continued: "You know, I really am most awfully sorry about it all, but I had to, hadn't I?" Bobby still took no notice. "You see," it went on when no answer came. "I told Kenneth it would be all right, and so I had to be sure, hadn't I? and I was afraid you might be stuffy over it, as soon as you began talking about duty." Was there a faint accent of contempt in her pronunciation of this last word? The voice paused, and suddenly, more loudly, with absolute conviction, it said: "You see, I know Kenneth didn't do it."

"How do you know?" Bobby asked.

Doreen was leaning forward now, over the seat next to the driver's. She replied:

"Well, I just know. Someone must have been there afterwards and done it."

"Who?" Bobby asked this time.

"That's what I want you to find out," Doreen explained.

"Oh, do you?" Bobby snapped. "Didn't seem like it to-night."

"There's no need to be beastly," protested Doreen in a very injured tone.

"We'll find out all we can," Bobby assured her, he hoped threateningly.

She sat back then, and before long they had reached the Yard. Bobby stopped the car and alighted. A constable, seeing there was someone in the rear seat, opened the car door and helped Doreen out. Bobby was making for the entrance to the building. The constable called after him: "The young lady, sir," much as if he were saying 'Your umbrella, sir'. Bobby resisted his first impulse to shout back: 'Tell her to go home and stop there.' Instead he called: "Oh, yes. Get someone to drive her home and garage the car. Better get a doctor for her if she wants one."

"Yes, sir," said the constable in a rather more than slightly astonished tone.

Quite distinctly and in a clear and loud tone, Bobby heard, as he was meant to, Doreen's voice saying:

"Doesn't he sound bad-tempered."

CHAPTER XXII
DAMAGED PRESTIGE

BACK AT HIS desk, Bobby first wrote a report of the night's events. He had no illusions about its probable reception. It would be agreed that in the circumstances he could not have acted differently. Responsibility for causing death could not be accepted. It would, however, also be made plain that the circumstances in question should never have been allowed to arise. Unfortunate that an officer of his rank and experience had permitted it. What steps he could have taken to prevent their arising, or how he could have foreseen Doreen's desperate and terrible device, would not be gone into. The fact that he had had a 'wanted' man, a 'suspect', within arm's length and had not 'brought him in' was the bare fact that would be remembered.

Bobby felt that Fate had played him a dirty trick. But then that is a little way that Fate has, and no doubt it is good for the soul. It was some slight consolation that he could add a brief note to the effect that Doreen had at any rate clearly indicated exactly when, where, and how, she and Kenneth planned to remain in communication. If careful watch were kept on the spot so clearly indicated, it might well be there was at least a good chance of Kenneth's arrest being soon effected. Bobby's secret hope was that this cryptic remark would not be understood, and that one of his critics—of whom he was sure there would be several—would have to come and ask for an explanation. This he would give with an air of faint surprise that anything so obvious had not immediately been understood. Which would be a salve to his injured feelings and help to restore his slightly damaged prestige.

This task finished, he remembered his supper he hoped his patient Griselda of a wife was keeping hot for him. So he locked up his desk, filled in his diary, and went home, there to relate the mischances of this woeful night to a duly and properly sympathetic Olive.

"A chit of a girl," he said, still very crossly, "to put me on a spot like that. Had to let my man go for the first time in my life."

"Do you think she would really have swallowed it if it had come to that?" Olive asked.

"I'm jolly sure she would. I knew it then, and I know it now," Bobby answered. "That girl is all softness and sweetness, sugar and spice, on one side, and all burnished steel on the other. It was the burnished-steel side I came up against."

"Well, there's one thing certain," Olive told him. "It means she believes every word of Kenneth Banner's story, or she would never have had the courage. I mean she believes him not by what you call the softness and sweetness side of her but by the burnished-steel side. It's not so much believing as knowing. I think you had better work on the theory that he was telling you just exactly how it happened."

Bobby grunted, considered this, and then admitted reluctantly that there might be something in it.

"Not," he added, "that that'll prevent us going all out to get the young man. But there are parts of his story that do seem to fit. It's been pretty clear for some time that smuggling was going on and that was what the go-as-you-please 'As You Like It' cruises were a cover for. The limpet motif suggested the method. At a guess I expect their best runs were when they had been doing a nice innocent-looking trip round the coast or up among the Scottish isles. It would be easy to send a code message to pals in France to meet them at sea and transfer the stuff. The tourists would be told it was unrationed food for use on the voyage, as most of it would be, and they would be told also to be sure to say nothing about it in case the authorities tried to make a fuss. Quite legal and all right, of course, if eaten at sea, but the Customs might try to pretend that it was eaten in port, and that would mean a lot of bother and possibly calling all of them as witnesses. A bother for everyone, it would be emphasized, especially, it would be added, as just possibly some of it was occasionally served up in port or anyhow in territorial waters. That would serve to keep the tourists quiet, and how were they to know or even suspect that one of the packages handed across contained not caviare or *pate de foie gras,* but a nice consignment of gold wrist-watches from Switzerland.

"When they got back to Southampton at the end of their cruise and it was evident there had only been a wholly innocent trip round the coast, and no smuggling possible, the Customs examination wouldn't be very strict. All very well thought out, but all dependent on a careful avoidance of giving any cause for suspicion.

"What put me first on the idea of smuggling was the odd story of the two searches of the Abel flat and of the taking away—in the second search, when Pyne had his unpleasant experience of being tied up—of two wrist-watches and then of their return. That suggested there was some motive other than theft for the searches, and a pretty strong motive, too. Then there was the fact that of the five chiefly concerned in the 'As You Like It' trips, three—Ossy Dow, Abel, and Stanley Foster—seemed to have suddenly got hold of plenty of money, while the two who apparently hadn't were the half-wit, Louis, and Kenneth Banner himself. It might be then that Kenneth was beginning to sit up and take notice, as he says was the case, and that the other three were equally beginning to think he had to be silenced one way or another."

"Do you mean you think they drugged him because they meant to kill him?" Olive asked, but Bobby shook his head.

"I don't think so," he answered. "In fact, I'm pretty sure not. The difficulty is to find any motive for Abel's murder. Smuggling doesn't generally lead to murder. In this case murder would be the last thing they would want. It would mean the very thing they were doing everything to avoid—starting a general investigation. Murder means an all-out inquiry to dig up everything possible. More likely there was a plan to compromise Kenneth in some way. Not too difficult. He could have been taken to his lodging in his unconscious state with the explanation that he was drunk, put to bed, and the opportunity taken to plant some of the smuggled stuff on him somehow, here or in Southampton. Or even in his name in a suit-case of his in a London left-luggage office. Something like that. Then it would be put to him that he was in it up to the neck. Information would be given to the Customs and all the blame laid on him unless he came in."

"That would have meant just what you say they didn't want," Olive objected. "Once the Customs knew, they would have had no chance of going on with it."

"No, I know," Bobby agreed, "but they saw the game was up for good unless Kenneth could be brought in somehow. To do that was their last throw so to say. It may be there had just been a specially big run or that they had an accumulation of stuff on hand they wanted time to get rid of. The drugging business does rather look like playing for time before inquiries made what they had on hand too hot to handle.

"All that seems to me a fairly logical build-up, assuming that Kenneth's story can be trusted. There's no flagrant contradiction anyhow. Then there's his story that he tripped over a chair and fell with it and the cushion on top of Abel, still unconscious. If that's not true, I don't quite see the point of inventing it. Not a very convincing detail. There is no mention of an overturned chair in any of the reports made at the time, as there certainly would have been if it was there. It does seem to support the idea of someone else having been in and having put the chair back after Kenneth left. Not very strong in itself, but a point to be kept in mind all the same.

"Something else to which I don't think sufficient attention has been paid is the twice-repeated search of Abel's flat, once when empty and once after Pyne moved in. Clearly that means someone is very anxious to find something—well, who? what? why? Not the seven golden whys some theorists talk about, but three very important whys all the same. Who?—doubtful, very. What?—almost certainly a cache of smuggled watches tucked away somewhere. Why?—hidden by Abel in case suspicion had already been roused and his flat was raided. That brings in a fresh 'golden question'—where? Any suggestions?"

"I expect you mean Jasper Jordan?" Olive said, a little doubtfully.

"Full marks," Bobby told her. "You remember he said he was sometimes called a post office—G.P.O. was the expression he used. Abel evidently knew that, since he made use of him sometimes. Quite natural to think of him when a safe hiding-place had to be found in a hurry. That means a possible past 'where', but not, I think, a present 'where'. I don't see Jasper—with his sort of obsession over search warrants he's always talking about—keeping something he must have begun to have his suspicions about. Moreover, we know he went off with a suit-case and then brought it back again. Looks as if he had taken away a smaller suit-case or dispatch-case inside the bigger one and left it somewhere. Any suggestions where?"

"He might know someone to take charge of it, and there are always the left-luggage offices?" suggested Olive.

"A Beta mark only for that," Bobby pronounced. "Full marks for first suggestion if you had mentioned a probable someone. In any case, a mark lost for the left-luggage suggestion."

"Why?" asked Olive belligerently. "I think it was a very good, sensible suggestion."

"Jordan is not the sort to pass unnoticed," Bobby pointed out. "He knows people stare when they see him, and he is sensitive to it. If not a face to launch a thousand ships, at any rate one to be remembered. Any cloak-room attendant would remember him all right, and routine inquiry would soon have him spotted. The obvious someone is Mrs Abel-Adam. Jordan gets rid of the stuff, and has the excuse that he thought it only right to hand it over to Abel's widow. He considered it had become her property, and he hadn't an idea in all the whole wide world what it was or that there was anything wrong about it. Unfortunately she has taken herself off. Which must mean that she's opened it and found what was in it. If I'm right, a whole glittering display of valuable Swiss watches she means to hang on to."

"I suppose you'll have to try to find her," Olive said. "Of course, you've worked it all out very cleverly."

"Thank you," interposed Bobby. "Praise from a wife is rare praise indeed."

"But," Olive continued, unheeding, "it's all built up on a jolly thin foundation of theory. Anyone," she said severely, "can spin ingenious theories put together out of nothing much."

"Only too true," Bobby admitted, "and you might have added that none of it throws any light on who murdered Abel or why?

Which is the main question for us at the Yard. We don't like murderers running round undetected. They are much too apt to think they can bring it off a second time. They have once, so why not twice? Heath went on far too long. That last unhappy woman ought to be alive and well if—but no use talking about 'ifs'. The smuggling business is a headache for the Customs chiefly though of course we shall do all we can. The murder is for us, and there are several possible suspects—three women and five men in all. One or two of them so unlikely we shall have to pay them special attention. Almost certainly the guilty person is one of them. Always excluding the possible, improbable unknown 'X' who might turn up at the last moment, and does sometimes."

CHAPTER XXIII
BELIEFS AND SUSPICIONS

"Hadn't we better be getting to bed?" Olive suggested at this point, but not with much hope of being heard; for when Bobby was, as now, immersed in a spate of theories, possibilities, and ideas, he was as likely as not to sit up half the night considering them, weighing one against another, discarding them for good, and then picking them up again.

As for bed, that became a secondary consideration till he had everything sorted out and put down on paper, all pros and cons duly noted.

Now, as he uncapped his fountain-pen and drew a pad of paper towards him, he was saying:

"First the three women. Mrs Abel-Adam and Imra Guire," and there he stopped to refill his fountain-pen, which was running dry.

"That's only two," Olive interposed, "and there isn't another."

"Doreen Caine," Bobby said, pumping energetically at a nearly empty ink-bottle. "Been talking about her all evening."

"Oh," said Olive. "Well, it just couldn't be her, not when she's in love with Kenneth Banner."

"Might be the reason why," Bobby retorted. "Or it might be she was in love with Abel and then found out he was married. Not a young woman I should much care, myself, to get across, not when you think of the bluff she pulled off on—me." Bobby almost put this last word in capitals, and paused to frown at the memory. "Capable of anything," he pronounced. "Burnished steel all right, and you make knives and daggers out of burnished steel. That girl could work herself up to anything—and no hysteria about it, either. Just calm, cold, calculation. Unfeminine," he concluded disapprovingly.

"Well, I don't believe it," declared Olive.

"Emotion, that, not logic," Bobby told her, and went on, "next, Mrs Abel-Adam, busily engaged on hunting down a husband I think she had come to hate, not only because he had left her, but because he was also cheating her out of her money she was entitled to. Remember it is certain she had got a clue to his London address about the time of the murder. Take it the Kenneth story is true. Take it that she went to the flat that night and found Abel had been living in what would seem to her luxury, while at the same time keeping her maintenance money from her. It could have caused her anger to boil over into active hate. Suppose the cover of the cushion Kenneth talked about had a tear or hole in it—unmended, this was a bachelor flat—and some of the feathers had come out. I can't imagine their doing so in such a way as to cover Abel's mouth and nose so as to stop his breathing. Besides the medical evidence distinctly says 'rammed in'. But I can imagine the woman raging at his refusing her her money while living in such style himself, noticing as she probably would, since she was a cook herself, that expensive food—smoked salmon—was on the table, thinking she would give him something else to eat and cramming a handful of the loose feathers into his mouth. Quite likely without any clear intention to kill."

"Isn't all that rather difficult?" Olive asked doubtfully. "Besides, how did she get in? She can't have had a key?"

"I shouldn't think so," Bobby agreed. "I am working on the idea that Kenneth Banner, when he left the flat, left the door open, either because he was in the state he describes or because he panicked after committing the murder. You remember the murder was discovered first thing next morning when the milk-man told Marks, the caretaker, that the door of the flat wasn't properly closed and that he got no answer when he called that the milk was there. Means that any time during the night anyone could have walked in, and there is one thing that does rather support the idea of somebody having done just that after Kenneth left. I ought to have spotted it before, but it has only just dawned on me. It doesn't amount to much, and anyhow it doesn't prove anything. Even if there was a later visitor, that's no proof that whoever it was killed Abel. But it may be a pointer."

"What do you mean, just dawned on you?" Olive asked.

"It ought to have dawned on you as well," Bobby told her, and went on: "Then there's Imra Guire, the last of the three women we know of. She made an odd impression when we saw her at Seemouth. A dark, unhappy, passionate girl, who looked as if she lived in a perpetual nightmare. She told us she was go-ing to marry Ossy Dow but hadn't told him so far. She may have been in some sort of emotional tangle with either Abel or Ken-neth or with both at once, and now one is dead and the other in hiding she may have decided to make do with Ossy Dow. It all happened too long ago for there to be any chance of finding out if she was in London that night, and anyhow it would be quite easy to leave Seemouth by the early-morning express and get back by the last train without anyone knowing where she had been or whether or no she had been out of Seemouth that day. It may have been her warned Kenneth against going to Abel's flat. He sticks to it it was a woman's voice. Well, there are the three of them: Imra Guire and Doreen Caine, two strange, unpredictable girls with strange depths in them, as perhaps we all have; and Mrs Adam, the wife who had learned to hate where she used to love. Nor is there any greater bitterness than that."

"It doesn't look to me," Olive declared, "that there is really anything much to go on. It's all mights and mays." Bobby looked gloomy and nodded assent. Olive went on: "But I do think I've just seen what you mean about there being one little pointer you've had."

"Good girl," Bobby approved, though rather absently, as though, discouraged, he had lost all interest in this possible but doubtful 'pointer'. "Let's go on to the men we know were mixed up in it one way or another: Ossy Dow, Stanley Foster, Kenneth Banner, all of the 'As You Like It' crew."

"Three," Olive said. "Unless you include the man you call a half-wit."

"I'm leaving him out," answered Bobby. "Safe to eliminate him. No half-wits in this business. But there's Jasper Jordan."

"Oh!" exclaimed Olive, surprised. "I never thought of him."

"I've been thinking of him quite a lot," Bobby told her. "He clearly makes it his business to know all he can about what's going on locally, if only for use in that rag of his—*Freedom's Bugle Call*, isn't it? It is more than likely he knew something, or even quite a lot, about this smuggling business, and even, in his capacity of self-styled 'Enemy of Society', rather approved than not. Or it may go a good deal deeper. I'll come to that soon. Anyhow, we do know it was his address Mrs Adam got from the Southampton lodging-house, and it must have been from him she got to know where Abel was living. We know, too, that that was about the time of the murder, though we can't tie it down to an exact date. Curiosity may very well, indeed almost certainly, make him follow her, and that would mean he would see her hurrying away, running away rather. Frightened? Jordan being what he is, he would, again almost certainly, slip up the stairs, to see if he could find out what had been happening. If Mrs Adam, too, left the door not properly latched, then it is fairly safe to assume that, getting no answer, he went in.

"You may say that's all built up on surmise. I think it is a reasonable and probable reconstruction of what may well have happened, starting from the few facts we do know. If it was like that, taking it as something to work on as a beginning, then he found Abel either dead or unconscious, with, as before, the torn cushion and its feathers close by.

"On the first possibility he must have decided to say nothing and go quietly home. I rather doubt that.

"On the second, if he found Abel, unconscious, then he is the murderer."

"But why?" Olive objected. "Why should he?"

"Remember I said it might go a good deal deeper," Bobby reminded her. "We know so little about him. All that guff about being the Enemy of Society, and running a Nihilist group that doesn't seem to exist at all, may be pure camouflage, meant to conceal his real activities. Those Swiss watches had to be disposed of somehow. Did the 'As You Like It' gang do that themselves? or are we on the track of a receiver? Difficult to smuggle the things into the country, and more difficult still to get a good figure for them. You have to know the ropes.

"The point is that Jasper has already been suspected by our local chaps of being concerned in black-market activities. Disposing of smuggled goods is going only one step farther. You remember Ossy Dow says he put two thousand pounds capital into the Banner Agency? Yet he also told us that when he met Kenneth Banner at Plymouth just before they started he was on his beam ends. Another of those little discrepancies that may or may not mean a lot. Conceivable, then, that Jordan provided the money, and that he was in it from the start, was in fact the mainspring of the whole thing. Not proved again, but conceivable. Conceivable, too, that Jordan had purposely got himself suspected of black marketing he wasn't guilty of, not merely to get a cheap score off our people, but because he calculated it would be a good camouflage. I've met with it before—letting it be suspected that you are what you are not—in this case a black marketeer—in order to hide what you really are—smuggler. Prove then you are innocent of the first, and it will be supposed you are also innocent of the second. Risky, but such sheer cheek often succeeds. As someone said: 'Audacity, first, second, and third'.

"Conceivable, then, that whether Jordan found Abel already dead or only unconscious he had a good look round, knowing what to look for; found the last consignment of Swiss watches, and went off with them. He would tell himself there was nothing to connect him either with Abel's death or the watches, so it was quite safe. They would be worth a lot of money, and murder has been done often enough for a good deal less than they would bring."

"Yes, but," Olive objected, "you were saying he had taken them away to give to Mrs Adam as the widow?"

"That was when I was trying to see if a plausible case could be made out against her," Bobby replied. "I wanted to see if she could be eliminated, and she can't be. Not yet, not by a long way. There's nothing to show he did in fact give them to her. He may, for that matter, have simply brought the stuff back with him. More likely there was some safe hide-out he knew about. The only one thing we can be sure of is that he knew Abel's address, and was therefore to some degree in touch with him, and that he had come under suspicion of black-marketing activities—and that he is a bitter and frustrated man and calls himself 'The Enemy of Society'."

"But," Olive objected again, "if he is guilty, surely he would hardly try to get the inquiry into his own crime re-opened as he was doing by all those nasty articles he published about you?"

"That could be clever camouflage again," Bobby suggested. "You don't suspect the murderer of wanting a re-investigation of a murder he committed himself. But there's the Doreen girl. She was the prime mover, and we know she had begun to visit Jasper. It wouldn't take him long to see that nothing was going to stop her—as impossible to stop her as to stop some force of nature."

His voice was still heavy with rebuke and indignation as he said this. Olive looked at him, a little curiously. He looked back at her, a little uncomfortably.

"My lad," she said, "you've been getting a bit above yourself. Too much of always coming out on top isn't good for anyone, and now you can't forget a mere girl's getting the better of you for once."

Bobby considered this, and the more he considered it, the less he liked it. He decided he would change the subject. But Olive was speaking again:

"There's the same thing about Doreen," she said. "If she was guilty, she wouldn't be doing her best to start up the investigation all over again when her name had never been so much as mentioned at the time."

"There might be two answers to that," Bobby said. "Murderers sometimes feel their secret is too much for them. They can't leave it alone. The Freudian theory is that their unconscious burdens them with too great a sense of guilt, tells them the spilt blood must be atoned for, and that this may even take the form of a repetition, a second murder, as if to appease the angry ghost by showing it it is not alone. Diving a little too deep into the human mind, perhaps, and even getting lost there. Or again, a murderer may only feel safe if and when someone has been convicted. We can leave all that on one side though. The main fact is that Doreen can't be eliminated. That's all I'm trying to do—see if anyone can be ruled out. None so far. Go on to Ossy. He clearly knew all about the plan to implicate Kenneth, if, of course, that story's true. He would certainly be going to Abel's flat to help carry it out, so there's identity of time and place established. Always the first thing we have to think of. After that, almost everything I've said about Jordan can apply to Ossy. It may as well have been the one as the other who found the flat door ajar and Abel dead or unconscious, and who in the second case decided to make sure, 'mak sikker' as Robert Bruce's friends said, so as also to make sure of the Swiss-watch consignment for his own private benefit.

"There is one thing, however, that does point to Ossy rather than to Jordan. Pyne's statement is that when he answered the door and got knocked out and tied up for his pains, his visitors were a man and a woman, possibly Ossy and Imra. We know Ossy was a good boxer at one time, and he would know how to place his blows so as to get a quick K.O. And Jordan wasn't and wouldn't."

"How can you be sure of that?" Olive asked.

"Oh, you can tell—the way a man moves, the way he holds his hands. It shows at once," Bobby answered. "But then Ossy strikes me as the common-crook type, and the common crook seldom or never takes to murder. I don't know why—different psychological make-up, probably. There's a big difference between the crook and the gangster. Anyhow, impossible to rule Ossy out. He stays on the short list. So does Stanley Foster, though much more doubtfully so, just hovering on it so to say. A sly little man, I think. He would have to be well paid to keep him quiet, for he must have known about the smuggling. But I also think he would be careful to keep safely on the side lines."

"That's four," Olive commented. "You said five. Do you mean your Mr X? No other man has ever had anything to with it, has he?"

"Oh, yes," Bobby answered. "My Mr X perhaps, only now I've given him a local habitation and a name. He has been mentioned all right, but nobody has ever given him a second thought. Rather like Edgar Allan Poe's purloined letter or G. K. Chesterton's postman, so inevitably on the spot he was never noticed or remembered."

CHAPTER XXIV
DEAD END REACHED

OLIVE RECEIVED this last remark with a puzzled stare.

"There isn't anyone else," she protested. "You can't mean Mr Pyne, surely?"

"Oh, dear no, he's out of it if no one else is, was never in it for that matter," answered Bobby. "No, I was thinking of Marks, the porter at the flats. His wife looks after the stairs and landings and so on. He does the odd jobs and that sort of thing. They have the basement flat. Porters at flats generally know all about their tenants, and if the Marks couple didn't know that Abel was not the normal more or less respectable tenant, it would be a world's wonder. On Kenneth Banner's story there must have been a good deal on the evening of the murder they could hardly have failed to notice. Odd noises from the flat itself when Abel and Kenneth were fighting, odd-looking people coming and going, quite enough, anyhow, to make them curious. If Mrs Marks

went up to have what she would call a 'dekko' and saw the door
ajar she would be sure to tell her husband, he would go to see if
there was anything wrong, and then—well, as before. The temptation of the watches, if he found them, might be too strong, and
then equally the temptation to 'mak sikker'. He is a small man
in bad health, and he would argue no one would suspect him of
knocking out a man like Abel, a tough customer. But Abel, once
dead, could say nothing about the unCustomed watches, and
there would be nothing to connect him with them."

"I don't know yet," Olive complained, "if you do or don't believe Kenneth Banner's story."

"Well, I don't either," Bobby told her, "so that's quite natural. Sometimes I do, and sometimes I don't, and in between I
don't know. It fits, and it doesn't fit, turn and turn about. Talk
about a kaleidoscope. An entirely fresh pattern every time. I began by wanting to see if there was anyone I could rule out, so as
to be able to concentrate on the rest. No luck. There's the begin-
nings of the making of a plausible case against every man jack—
or woman jill." He paused, and this time Olive offered no comment. They were both silent for a moment or two. Bobby went
on slowly and thoughtfully: "You know, Kenneth is inclined to
suspect himself. He doesn't admit it. I don't suppose he admits
it even to himself. But the doubt is there at the back of his mind.
That rather futile suggestion of his about Abel's being more or
less accidentally choked by the feathers from the torn cushion
shows that all right—an attempt of the unconscious to relieve
deep anxiety. Fear of the truth drove him into hiding, and now
it's put the idea of suicide into his mind. I think he would at once
if he came to be sure. It may happen any moment if the doubt
grows too much to be borne. Good Lord, am I beginning to talk
like one of those awful psychiatrists? Heaven preserve me from
that at least, but the silly stuff's awfully catching, a sort of mental measles."

"If he had really done it, he would know and remember," Olive declared—with conviction. "If you do it, you don't forget it."

"I don't know so much," Bobby answered—with doubt. "Remember he claims he was under the influence of some drug.

One thing he says is that he saw a succession of faces passing by—ugly, threatening faces. Drugs do sometimes have that sort of effect—like seeing pink rats in delirium tremens. I've heard of that procession of faces before. What the explanation is, goodness knows—or badness. The faces always seem evil and angry. Well, there are all the facts as far as I know them, so you can make up your mind for yourself where you think they point."

"All ways at once," answered Olive. "Just like a compass a little boy with a magnet is playing tricks with."

Bobby agreed, and remarked that it was late, nearly two indeed. Long past bedtime anyhow, though he didn't suppose he would sleep a wink all night, for worrying.

Olive smiled secretly. She had never yet known Bobby to stay awake much longer than five minutes after getting into bed. Often and often when she herself was having a bad night, she had been tempted almost beyond endurance to wake him up and tell him how unfair she thought it he could slumber so soundly and she get hardly a wink of sleep.

This time, however, by exception, for almost the first time on record, Bobby did stay awake, staring out into the darkness, and it was he this time who nearly succumbed to the temptation to wake her up to tell her all about one or other of the new theories constantly flooding his mind. It was nearly morning before he did in fact sleep, and late morning before he woke to find Olive shaking him by the arm and offering him a cup of tea.

"I had my breakfast ages ago," she informed him, "and I've rung up to say you had overslept after being up all night nearly on the Mayfair Crescent case."

"What did they say?" Bobby asked, drinking his tea.

"Oh, they were quite nice about it," Olive assured him.

"Sounds bad," Bobby said. "I had better get a move on." He showed no disposition to do so, and instead yawned mightily. "Doesn't look to me," he said with resignation, "as if there's much we can do, except go on trying to find Kenneth and Mrs Adam, and no easy job to pick out two people from forty or fifty million others. And of course keep an eye on Mr Jasper Jordan. Not easy either, he knows all the tricks, the ugly little brute."

"Don't call him that," Olive said. "It isn't right."

"Well, isn't he as ugly as they make 'em?" asked Bobby.

"Of course he is, uglier," Olive agreed as she retired with the empty teacup. "That's why you shouldn't say so—taking a mean advantage of what he can't help."

Bobby at once thought of several crushing retorts to which no possible answer could be given. But as Olive wasn't there now, it didn't seem much use uttering them. So he got up and dressed instead, and after his belated breakfast arrived at the Yard, where he found his view that for the moment they had reached a dead end was already held—even strongly held. The routine search for Kenneth Banner would go on, of course. Kenneth had become one of various other 'wanted' men, though it did still seem a little doubtful what charge could be preferred against him if and when he was found. Unless, of course, he was willing to repeat the story he had told Bobby, and that no one thought likely. Efforts, too, to get in touch with Mrs Adam would be continued, but there again only because it was thought she might be 'able to give useful information', to use the stock phrase. In fact, all that seemed possible was to continue with a kind of watching brief, more especially with regard to Jasper Jordan. And naturally the Customs authorities would be warned again that attempts would probably soon be made to dispose of a large consignment of smuggled Swiss watches.

It was also rather broadly hinted by the Assistant Commissioner, to whom Bobby was talking, that it might be as well for him now to leave the Mayfair Crescent case to others. For the moment a dead end seemed to have been reached. There were plenty of other matters requiring attention. Questions of organization, requests for a new series of lectures from some of the smaller provincial forces, and so on.

"Seem to be quite keen on your talks," remarked the Assistant Commissioner with an air of baffled surprise. "Should have thought they had plenty of their own chaps to do that for them." Bobby coughed modestly, his popularity as a lecturer was in fact always a considerable surprise to himself. "This other thing," the A.C. went on, "is becoming a sort of general paper-chase—

the smuggling gang chasing the watches, the Customs people chasing the smugglers, and us chasing a suspected murderer, and what will come out of that, goodness knows, I don't. No substantial proof even that there is any big consignment of smuggled stuff at all."

"I think," Bobby suggested mildly, "that the consignment, a big valuable consignment, is a logical deduction necessary to make any sense at all of what's been going on."

"Logical deductions are all very well," the A.C. admitted, "but you can't slap 'em down under a jury's nose. That's what counts. Of course, something may turn up at any moment to give a fresh start. You never know. Important clues do drop out of the skies sometimes."

"So they do," agreed Bobby. "The thing is to recognize them when it happens."

"Of course, of course, it's all there," agreed the A.C. in his turn, and somewhat impatiently, for what was this but pointing out the obvious? "By the way, there is a report in from one of our chaps, Sergeant Evans. He is working on the Manton jewel burglary. In one jeweller's shop where he was making some inquiry he was told a young woman had been in offering stuff she wanted to sell."

"Swiss watches?" Bobby asked hopefully.

"Not a bit of it," answered the other, who had in fact been more or less playing for this question so as to be able to squash more effectively any such dawning hopes. "Old-fashioned stuff. Valuable, but hard to sell. The shop bloke said he was suspicious at first because some of the Manton stuff had been listed as old fashioned. But the description didn't agree, and the young woman didn't boggle about waiting while he sent round to the bank for the notes she said she wanted as she hadn't a banking account and needed ready money immediately. So it seemed all right, and he paid up, but thought he would just mention it in case the Manton list wasn't complete and these particular items had been omitted by mistake. But there is one rather odd detail that wasn't noticed at first. It turns out now that the address given was West King Street, Mayfair."

"Jordan's address," exclaimed Bobby. "What on earth—?" and then he was silent.

"Exactly," said the A.C. "Can't say I see any connection with either the murder or the smuggling. Do you?"

"Did Evans get a description of the woman?"

"Young, tall, dark, striking looking, rather sulky expression, silent," the A.C. answered, reading from a slip on his table.

"Sounds as if it might be Imra Guire," Bobby said.

"One of your suspects," the A.C. commented. "She may want the money to make a get-away. I don't see how we can stop her."

"How much did the jeweller pay her?" Bobby asked.

"Two hundred, half in fivers, half in ones. He claimed it was a good price, but he admitted that it was only about breaking-down value. Old-fashioned stuff like that he said he might have to keep for years to sell as it is, and then have to break it down finally."

"Well, I can't see any connection at the moment either," Bobby admitted. "I wonder—"

He paused suddenly. There had come back into his mind a memory of a casual item of information casually mentioned during his talks at Seemouth. The A.C. was watching him curiously.

"Had a flash of inspiration?" he asked, half-teasingly, half-impressed.

"It's only that I've just remembered something," Bobby answered slowly.

CHAPTER XXV
"OUT"

WHEN BOBBY went on to explain what it was he had heard at Seemouth and that he had just remembered as possibly significant, the Assistant Commissioner was not much impressed. He did agree, though doubtfully, that possibly it might give a useful lead. As for its linking up with the other piece of hitherto rather disregarded information Bobby had also picked up during that visit to Seemouth, well, it might, or it might not. Most likely merely an unimportant coincidence.

Bobby never trusted coincidences during an investigation. To him they were never that and nothing more, whatever a primrose might have been to Peter Bell. Often they had their own significance. All the same, it didn't do to attach too much importance to them. But he would have to ask a few questions when he had time to get round to it. No hurry. The proper timing of a question was almost as important as the question itself.

Later on, just as Bobby was going out to lunch, a fresh report came in. It concerned Mrs Adam. Of the others, Ossy Dow, Imra Guire, and Stanley Foster were all three known to be back at Seemouth, where, however, the office of the Banner Agency still had up the sign, 'Temporarily Closed'. Nothing had been heard of Kenneth. Nothing suspicious had been observed in the conduct of Doreen. Jasper Jordan, self-styled Enemy of Society, appeared to be pursuing his usual activities, though it was not too easy to say what these were. But now Mrs Adam, and it was clear from the description given that she was the person referred to, had driven up in a taxi to a City jeweller's establishment, and there had offered for sale a valuable gold wrist-watch. The assistant she was talking to had not thought she looked the sort of person likely to own so valuable a watch, had asked one or two questions, and finally had asked her to wait while he went to fetch the proprietor. Whereon she had snatched back the watch, run out of the shop to the waiting taxi, and driven off in it. The assistant had been alert enough to take a note of the taxi's number and to report the incident to the City Police. They, in their turn, had passed on the information to the Metropolitan Police for action, if thought necessary.

Bobby did think it necessary, since all this seemed to raise a strong presumption that Mrs Adam was in possession of the smuggled watches. So he sent out instructions for the taxi-driver to be found and questioned with as little delay as possible.

This was effected by the middle of the afternoon. The taxi-man had, however, nothing much to say. He had driven his passenger to Liverpool Street, where she had told him she had to catch a train, and there all trace of her was lost.

"All of which means," Bobby decided, talking to the sergeant who had brought him the report, "that she is almost certainly in possession of the stuff. She may have got it on the night of the murder, either after committing the murder herself or by the accident of having arrived after someone else had done the killing." But that involved, apparently, the working once more of the long arm of coincidence, so Bobby felt inclined to put it aside in favour of his earlier theory that Jordan, having had the dispatch-case containing the watches left in his care—in his G.P.O. capacity—and becoming suspicious of its contents, had decided to get rid of it by handing it over to Abel's widow as the rightful owner. "Probably felt that put him on the right side of the law," Bobby decided again. "That is, unless he's really deep in it all. As he may be."

"What about his using Mrs Adam to get rid of the stuff bit by bit?" the sergeant suggested. "Or even handing over one or two watches to sweeten her if she knows too much? Or even to get her more mixed up in it?"

"I don't think Jordan is likely to do anything like that," Bobby said, after reflection. "He is far too fond of playing his own game by himself and far too self-satisfied to want anyone else's help. Plenty of other possibilities. Abel might have given it her himself by way of making up for what he owed her under the maintenance order. She might not want to say so, for fear of coming under suspicion. I don't think I've ever known a case where there were so many possible explanations, all equally suggesting the innocence or the guilt of so many of those concerned. All the same, I think I'll try to have a chat with Jordan to-day. I can see if he is willing to talk, though I don't expect our 'Enemy of Society' bloke to be very helpful. Hard to know how far he may be prepared to go in his self-appointed role. A warped, embittered, first-class mind working on a sense of utter frustration. I expect he feels he ought to be Lord Chief Justice if he had had a fair deal."

"Sounds to me," said the sergeant, "like him being well on the way to going crackers."

"He never strikes me at all like that when I am talking to him," Bobby said, shaking his head. "I should say he was as sane as anyone can be in a world as mad as this one."

The sergeant said politely that no doubt Mr Owen was right, and anyhow there were the MacNaughten rules, and retired, while Bobby, as soon as he had got his desk clear, took a 'bus that ran past the corner of West King St. There he alighted and walked down the street to the house, where in the basement flat dwelt Jasper Jordan, only to find himself faced with a notice on the door, bearing the simple word 'Out'.

Bobby stood looking at it thoughtfully for some moments. It might be, he reflected, merely an indication that Jordan did not want to be disturbed. Or again it might be that Jordan had returned but had not removed the notice. In any case, it seemed worth while to knock, and knock accordingly Bobby did, as loudly as the absence of a knocker and the use of bare knuckles permitted. A good deal to his surprise, he heard footsteps approaching at once, and then the door opened and there appeared Doreen Caine.

Which was the more surprised it would be hard to say, and if Bobby said, 'Oh, you,' the more loudly of the two, certainly Doreen's mouth opened the more widely. Bobby was the first to recover.

"Mr Jordan here?" he asked.

"No, I thought it was him knocking," Doreen answered. "It's funny."

She went back in the flat, and he followed. She turned round then in the passage and repeated: "It's funny. I don't like it somehow."

"Hasn't he been here?" Bobby asked. "Who let you in?"

"The door was open," Doreen said. "Not wide open, just closed. That notice 'Out' was on it. I pushed the door back and called, but there wasn't any answer, and it was so silent I began to be afraid. I kept calling, and then I went in. I thought Mr Jordan must be ill or something. There wasn't a sign of him or anyone anywhere. I can't make it out. I thought perhaps I would wait till Mr Jordan came back, and then I heard your knock and I thought it was him."

"I had better have a look round," Bobby said, a little uneasy now himself, for he did not think it in any way like Jordan to go off leaving the door of his flat open, and now there were stirring in his mind memories of that other flat of which, too, the door had been left unlatched.

Doreen stood aside to allow him to enter. He went into each room in turn. There were three in all. Nowhere could he see the least sign of any disturbance, nothing in any way suspicious or unusual. All the same, his uneasiness increased. There was still the door left open. There was still Jordan's unexplained absence. He remembered the warning he had once given, that the 'Enemy of Society' in the abstract might be receiving a visit from the enemies of society in the concrete, more commonly known as gangsters.

The first of the three rooms, the one Bobby had been in on his previous visits, the former kitchen he imagined, in those Victorian days when from it had issued, if not Kipling's five meat meals a day, at any rate three of them, all sufficiently lavish. Behind it was a second room, at one time the scullery, now evidently used by Jordan for sleeping, eating, cooking. It was dark, lighted only by a small barred window, smelt damp, and Bobby suspected the presence of numerous black beetles, but did not investigate that detail. There was a small truckle bed, table and chairs, shelves for crockery and so on, and a tall, narrow, oaken cupboard, that in this dim light almost resembled a coffin. Probably it was what had given rise to the story current at the 'Rose and Crown' that Jordan kept his coffin in his bedroom. Bobby opened it. It was stuffed full of clothing, mostly old, but some looking new. Bobby made sure there was nothing else, and then shut it again. The third room was smaller, did not seem to be much used, was cluttered up with all kinds of lumber and odds and ends, none of any special interest or value. Bobby guessed that when Jordan found anything in the way he just threw it in here and forgot it. From it opened a back door on what had once been a small walled-in yard but was now a heap of rubble from walls overthrown by the explosion of the bomb that had wrecked the houses in the parallel street at the rear.

Bobby went back to the front room, where Doreen was quietly waiting.

"Were you expecting to meet Kenneth Banner here?" he asked. Doreen looked at him but made no reply, nor did she answer when he repeated the question. She sat still and silent, watching him. He changed the question and asked: "Do you come here every afternoon to see him or to see if there's any message?"

"Kenneth has not been here, if that's what you mean," she answered, then: "And there's been no message that I know of. I come in the afternoon because it's generally my free time. Most of my cookery talks are morning or evening. If I'm helping with anything special, a lunch or a banquet, that's morning or evening, too. A newspaper once called me a free lance of the kitchen."

"Yes, I see," Bobby remarked, "but not quite what I asked. I take it Mr Jordan likes you to come?"

"I think so, I think he's rather lonely really. He's a little morbid about people staring at him, and he thinks they laugh at him when he's not there. He's got no one to look after him," Doreen added, with woman's immemorial conviction that no man can ever do that for himself.

Bobby for his part was fully convinced that Doreen's visits had for their object to get or keep in touch with Kenneth. Probably a meeting-place could easily be arranged by 'phone without Kenneth running the risk of visiting a place he must guess would be more or less under observation. He said:

"Well, I don't know that there's anything to be done. Mr Jordan may be back soon. He may simply have forgotten to lock up. Not like him, but you never know. Shall you wait any longer?"

"I must go soon," she said, looking at her wrist-watch. "I have a demonstration to give for a pressure-cooker firm—a three-course dinner cooked in fifteen minutes," she said with a faint smile.

"An age of speed," Bobby said, conscious that both he and she were talking as much to hide a growing disquiet as for any other reason. "No time to be lost."

"The slower the cooking, the better the flavour," Doreen told him. "Nature always takes her time. It's only people who are in such a hurry."

"I must go," Bobby said. "If you're stopping on, you'll have to make up your mind whether to leave the door the way it was or shut it. I'll tell the man on the beat to keep as close a watch on the place as he can. Can't keep it up all the time, but he'll do his best. Good evening."

He began to move towards the door. She watched him in silence till he had it open. Then abruptly she said:

"I had better tell you. I daresay it's all nonsense. It's Mrs Adam. She's frightened. She's saying she expects she'll be the next to be murdered."

CHAPTER XXVI
AGENCY ERROR

BOBBY TURNED back quickly. He was wondering how this fitted in with the recent report of Mrs Adam's visit to a City jeweller and her rapid flight therefrom. He did not think he liked it very much.

"How do you know?" he asked.

"It's what she been saying to people, she said it to me," Doreen answered.

"When was that?" Bobby asked quickly. "I didn't know you knew her."

"I don't, I've never seen her," Doreen told him. "It was when she rang up yesterday. I went to where she was lodging, but she was out, and I couldn't wait. So I left my address and would she give me a ring, and she did, and that's what she said. She sounded very excited and upset."

"Where was she? Lodging, I mean?"

"Erewhon Street, in Pimlico. Number Seven. But she's not there now, and she didn't ring from there. She left first thing this morning without saying anything about where she was going, and she must have made up her mind in a hurry, because she had paid a week in advance, and she only stopped the one night."

"How did you know where to find her?"

"Well, I asked," Doreen explained simply. "I knew she worked as a cook, so I inquired at one or two employment agencies for hotel and cafe staff if they had her name on their books. The Liddel and Scot Agency had, and they told me the last address she gave them, and so I went there."

"We've been looking for her," Bobby said, rather discontentedly. "I'm sure our men would go to the employment agencies. I think I remember the Liddel and Scot was one. They all said they didn't know."

"Well, of course," Doreen told him, with the patient smile of one explaining things to a very small boy. "What would become of their business if it got about they were giving people's addresses to anyone who came asking for them? Especially policemen. They might have heard you had been buying an egg or two off the ration. Of course, if the agency had known it was something serious like murder, it would be different, but they weren't told that."

"We can't go hinting about people being wanted in a case of murder," Bobby grumbled, eyeing with considerable disapproval this girl who first had put him on the spot so badly, that for the first time in all his long career he had had to let his man go, and who now had succeeded so simply in finding a witness, even a suspect, his men had failed to get any trace of. "What did she say exactly when she rang you?" he asked.

"It was all muddled and confused," Doreen replied. "It was about how she had been stopped in the street by a man who jumped out of a car, and he wanted her to get in, and she wouldn't, so then he tried to hustle her in, and she screamed, and people came, and he said, 'Next time we'll get you, if we have to do you in for it', and then he jumped back into the car and drove off full speed."

"Did the agency people say she had been to them recently?" Bobby asked.

"No, not for a long time," answered Doreen. "They had to go a long way back to find out. They know me, you see. I've sent them business sometimes, so they didn't mind, and they gave me the last address they had. I went there. It was a Mrs Harris. She and Mrs Adam are rather friendly. Mrs Adam told her the same thing about the man and the car. She had wanted to stay at Mrs Harris's, but there wasn't room, and she had gone somewhere else, and she said her room there had been searched while she was out. It looked as if someone had got in through the window, because the door had been fastened by a wedge, and she couldn't open it at first. So then she went to Mrs Harris's again, and Mrs Harris gave her the Pimlico address; she left in a hurry this morning as if something else had frightened her."

"It's rather a disturbing story," Bobby said, and he told himself this made it certain that Mrs Adam either had the smuggled watches or was believed to have them.

Believed by whom, though, threatened by whom? And if she were the holder of these unCustomed watches whose existence seemed more and more certain, though as yet there was no tangible proof that they did so, much less that they were in her possession, how did that fit into theories of complicity in her husband's murder? On these thoughts the voice of Doreen broke in again.

"I told the agency they must let you know, because it was serious, and they promised," she was saying. "They said they would ring up and tell you they had had another look through their card index and found her name this time. It had been overlooked before because it had been filed wrongly."

"They hadn't when I left," Bobby remarked.

"They may be waiting till closing time," Doreen suggested. "It doesn't do an agency any good to have police coming and going. Or they think it doesn't."

"Did Mrs Adam give any description of the man she says tried to get her into a car?"

"I didn't ask. I didn't know what to think. It seemed difficult to think of anyone wanting to run away with Mrs Adam, and then it wasn't easy to make out what she was talking about, it was all so muddled. It wasn't only about the man in the car or the one she says got through her window and searched her things, but about police trying to find her because of her husband's murder, and she didn't care who killed him, but it wasn't her, and she wasn't going to have anything to do with it, or being a witness. She wasn't going to be bullied into saying what she didn't mean and it being twisted against her."

"Afraid of having to tell the truth, she means," commented Bobby. "If she really has managed to get hold of the smuggled watches, she probably means to hang on to them as long as she can. She may have tried to persuade herself she has the best right to them as Abel's widow, and now she has them tucked away in what she thinks is a safe hiding-place. And it's always possible she actually is connected with his death. She seems quite as likely a suspect as any of the rest of you."

"You mean me, too?" Doreen asked, but without any great show of surprise.

"It could be that way," Bobby told her.

"Yes," she said, slowly and musingly. "Yes. It wasn't me, and it wasn't Kenneth, but it's no good my saying so, is it?"

"None at all," agreed Bobby. "In a case like this, 'say so's' don't count."

"I never thought," Doreen went on, in the same musing tone, "I should ever be sitting in a flat belonging to someone else who wasn't there listening to a policeman telling me I'm suspected of murder. You never know, do you?" and now her tone had become one of grave astonishment.

"You never know," repeated Bobby. "Never." He went on, a little viciously, for he had not yet entirely forgiven her: "I wouldn't put it past you, not after your performance the other night."

She was silent for some time, apparently considering this with the same grave attention.

"I must go now," she said after a minute or two, "or I shall be late for my pressure-cookery talk. But I don't think it's very intelligent to suspect Mrs Adam. I'm sure she isn't a bit like a murderer."

"No one ever is like a murderer, not even another murderer," Bobby told her.

"You know," Doreen said, pausing on her way to the door, "you know, I think perhaps you're right. About me, I mean. I think I could. I think so if I had to, if there was no other way. If it's for your own man—or your child—or—or—and all that killing in the war like my brother.. . ." Her voice trailed away into silence. "I wonder," she said, and now she had an air of contemplating herself with surprise, and even fear, as if she had glimpsed depths within herself she had never known before were there.

"Yes," Bobby assented, speaking also very slowly, very thoughtfully. He looked again at her small, strong face, at the small, firm chin below the determined, close-set mouth, at the clear, unflinching eyes. "A Judith in the making—or made?" he said. Again there was a pause before he added, more lightly: "I must be going, too. I mustn't get too far lost in speculation. What an investigator has to look for are facts, not theories. I think I had better shut the door when we go. No sign of Jordan yet, and he'll have his key. I'll leave a message pinned on it to say I would like to see him when convenient. He may know something about Mrs Adam and her story."

"You don't think he was the man with the car, do you?" Doreen asked. "She would have said so, wouldn't she?"

"She might not have wanted to," Bobby answered. "Anyhow, it's no good thinking anything till we know more—blind man's buff at present." He crossed to the table in the middle of the room. On it lay the usual confused litter of papers. He was looking for a spare scrap of blank paper to write on. He noticed a few letters and circulars lying there unopened. "Did you put them here?" he asked, showing them to Doreen.

"They were lying in the passage," she answered. "I picked them up. There's a card from Mr Pyne. I must go."

Bobby had picked the card up and was looking at it. It was Mr Pyne's visiting-card, and it bore a pencilled message to the effect that he had called, that he had got no answer, and would call again some other time. Bobby put it down without comment. He went with Doreen to the door, watched her ascend the area steps. He fastened his own message to the door under the 'Out' notice, and then followed up the steps, after he had made sure that this time the door was securely closed. As he reached the street he saw a uniformed man, standing there, apparently waiting.

"Oh, it's you, sir," he said. "Instructions to keep an eye on that place. There was a young lady just come up. That's why I waited."

"Miss Doreen Caine," Bobby said. "The place seems empty, and there's an 'Out' notice on the door. Miss Caine told me she found the door ajar, so she went in to wait for Mr Jordan if he came back. He must have left the door open when he left. I don't altogether like it, so try to keep as close a watch as you can. Tell your Inspector to let me know at once if Mr Jordan returns. Too many doors left open in this business, too many for my liking anyhow."

CHAPTER XXVII
THE IMPORTANCE OF OPEN DOORS

From West King St., Bobby went on to Mayfair Crescent, close by. There when he knocked the door was opened by Mr Pyne himself, looking as prim and neat as ever.

"Oh, good evening," he said, recognizing Bobby. "Come in, won't you?"

He led Bobby into a small room, which, Mr Pyne explained as he looked round with an air of complacent approval, was known as his 'den'.

"Please be seated," he said, indicating an old and somewhat rickety arm-chair, from which he had first removed, by the simple expedient of sweeping them to the floor, a pile of oddments of one kind and another. "Excuse me for a moment, will you?"

Therewith he disappeared; Bobby suspected to inform his wife of the presence of a visitor. In his absence, Bobby subjected the room to that careful, intent scrutiny he always liked to give to one he had not visited before. He believed that in this way he often obtained valuable indications of the character and disposition of the occupant.

A mere hasty glance around would in this case, however, have been all that was required. Immediately apparent was that what might be called the 'note' of the room was a kind of calculated, even 'planned', disorder. There was a pipe-rack but no pipes in it, they were lying about anywhere. There was a cigarette-box used as an ash-tray. The cigarettes were on the same table, as far away as possible, piled in an untidy heap—except for those that had fallen on the floor. The waste-paper basket seemed to be a kind of combined 'In' and 'Out' tray, and the floor for odd, torn scraps of paper. The same sort of deliberate untidiness was everywhere to be seen. A curious contrast to the sitting-room Bobby had been in on the occasion of his first visit, and no doubt an equally curious contrast to what Bobby supposed would be the carefully regulated, impeccable order of the Pyne office at the Ministry of Priorities.

"Still the Jekyll and Hyde idea," Bobby said, half-aloud. "The careful, orderly, neat, official-minded bureaucrat, and his other self irresistibly drawn to the 'Vie de Bohème'. May explain the attraction Jordan seems to exercise on him. But it hasn't affected the way he talks, at least not in talking to me. Could that official lingo of his be put up by his Dr Jekyll unconscious as a kind of last line of defence against his Mr Hyde unconscious? And how far would that be likely to affect his actions? Away from the office, did his character and disposition entirely change?"

These doubtful speculations came to an end when Mr Pyne returned, bearing with him an hospitable tray, on it, sherry, whisky, soda-water.

Bobby asked if he might choose the sherry, which incidentally was excellent, and merited to the full the appreciation he expressed. He went on to explain, by way of starting the chatty talk he often found more useful in obtaining the information he wanted than would have been any more formal questioning, that he never drank spirits.

"Enough violence comes my way," he said, "without my importing it into my drinks."

"So great a contrast to my own existence," commented Mr Pyne, and there was almost a touch of nostalgia in his voice as he went on: "The one irruption of violence into a career usually far removed from the occurrence of the unexpected, is that with which you are already acquainted. It is still remembered at the Ministry," and his voice now was not so much nostalgic as complacent. "Our commissionaire, a Military Medal man, talks to me now with a comradely air, as much as to say, 'We've both been there, not like those desk-wallahs'."

"Well, we must hope," Bobby said, "that nothing of the sort will happen again."

"Yes, indeed," declared Mr Pyne with emphasis, his Dr Jekyll side now clearly in the ascendant. "I gather that large-scale smuggling of watches from the Continent is supposed to be connected with recent occurrences?"

"You would hear that from Mr Jordan, I expect," Bobby said, and without waiting for an answer, continued: "It's only suspicion as yet, no proof. Practically certain, all the same. We even know the chief method used—an ingenious application of the 'limpet' mine used in the war. It seems likely, too, that the whole consignment was in Abel's hands and is the motive for his murder. We are going on the theory that that is also why this flat was raided twice. Probably the idea was that the watches might be hidden under the floor or something like that. Anyhow, we believe the search for them is still going on, and that means a risk of more violence if we don't know enough to act in time. We have two investigations on hand at once, linked but separate. The search for Abel's murderer, the more important, and the search for the watches. A sort of double search, in fact, a twin search. Oddly, it was the attack on you that gave us the first real lead to a motive. Two wrist-watches were taken, weren't there? and then returned. Now we think that they were taken to see if they were part of the smuggled lot. If they had been identified, of course it would have meant you had the rest as well. They weren't, and so they were returned."

"What an extraordinarily exciting idea," Mr Pyne said, looking very regretful as he thought of what might have been. He finished his sherry and put the glass down with a distinct swagger, as if he already saw himself defying smugglers, police, and custom-house authorities all at once. "I can assure you that no such exciting discovery was made here. I ask myself what my own personal reaction would have been in circumstances of so unprecedented a nature. My wife, I have little doubt, would have immediately rung up the doctor."

"The doctor?" Bobby repeated, puzzled.

"It is always her first thought when anything apart from the customary household routine occurs," Mr Pyne explained. "She rang for him once when we had need of the services of a plumber. My daughter, I fear, would probably have considered herself entitled to choose one of the watches for herself—as a souvenir. She would consider she had 'won it', an expression often used by a cousin who served through the war. Young people of to-day have not the meticulous respect for law and order which characterized my own generation. One much regrets the days when a Victorian young lady would have solved the problem by fainting. But all this is so entirely problematic," and again he sighed gently as regretting one of the great 'might have beens' of life.

"I have just been at West King Street." Bobby said, thinking it time to bring the conversation back from speculation to fact. "Mr Jordan was not there. Have you seen him recently?"

"Not for some days. I called yesterday evening, but there was no response when I knocked. I did so repeatedly and loudly, using the handle of my umbrella. I left my card with a message that I would try again another evening."

"Was there an 'Out' notice pinned on the door when you were there?"

Mr Pyne gave this question careful consideration.

"My answer must be in the negative," he replied presently. "Indeed, I may say I am convinced that such was not the case. Such a notice could not, in the circumstances, have by any possibility escaped my observation."

"Do you mind telling me if there was any special reason why you wished to see him?"

Mr Pyne again hesitated for a moment or two before replying, looking the while so self-consciously conspiratorial that Bobby nearly smiled.

"An entirely private and confidential matter," Mr Pyne announced at last. "One on which I should not feel it proper to communicate the details to you in default of Mr Jordan's full knowledge and consent."

"I understand," Bobby said gravely. "From information we have received, it appears that the door was this evening found left half-open so that anyone could have walked in."

"That is indeed remarkable," Mr Pyne agreed. "If your information is reliable, that is. It would seem to indicate that Mr Jordan had left temporarily in order to post a letter or on some similar errand, his intention being to return immediately, but in fact had not done so. The question then arises: 'Why pin an "Out" notice on the door?'"

"Exactly," Bobby said, approving this bit of deduction. "The same thing seems to have happened here after Abel's murder. We have information that one person certainly here that night may very well have left the door open when going. If it is merely a coincidence, it is a coincidence I don't like."

"You don't mean," Pyne exclaimed, looking really startled for once, "there is any idea Jordan may have been murdered, too?"

"Oh, no," Bobby declared, not quite accurately, for his mind was full of doubtful and uncertain fears. "Suspicions of all sorts, I suppose. That's all. Threats have been made apparently. In fact, there is any amount of suspicion, all of it pointing different ways at once. Generally, when we suspect the motive we get a pretty clear idea of where to look for the criminal. Not this time. It is why I have a worrying, nagging feeling at the back of my mind that there is something behind this business of not properly closed doors I ought to be able to get at. Perhaps not. Was there anything, anything at all, even the smallest thing, that struck you as at all unusual when you were there and didn't get any answer?"

"Nothing at all—" and then Mr Pyne paused, hesitating.

"Yes?" Bobby said questioningly. "Please go on. The merest trifle might help. You never know in an investigation like this what may not give a lead."

"I hardly think it could in this case," Mr Pyne said. "It is merely that a car was waiting outside the house where Jordan has his basement tenement. A somewhat unusual occurrence. Few of the tenants in that locality are likely to be car owners. Some might be, no doubt. It could well have been the property of a visitor to one of them. Or of a doctor. There was a woman, apparently the driver—at any rate she had on a kind of chauffeur's cap. She was standing on the pavement, and she was holding partly open the door of the car. Somehow she gave me the idea of being very much on the alert, tense, waiting."

"Another partly open door," Bobby murmured, "even if this time only of a car. Please go on."

"There is nothing I can add," Mr Pyne said. "Except perhaps that I did receive an impression that when I opened the gate at the top of the area steps and began to descend, she—I don't know how to put it. Startled, almost as if she were about to say something to stop me, as if she were—well, frightened. At the time I thought that she had failed to see clearly and had experienced a momentary impression that I had lost my footing. I don't know. I had almost forgotten the occurrence till now."

"You are sure it was a woman?"

"Certainly. On that point my recollection is absolutely clear, though she was wearing slacks—a deplorable garment I cannot think displays to any advantage the grace and beauty of the female form."

"Would you know her again?"

"I fear not," answered Mr Pyne. "I paid her appearance no particular attention. It was, besides, beginning to grow dusk. All I can say is that, as far as my recollection goes, she was tall and dark."

"Thank you very much," Bobby said, getting to his feet. "I must not keep you any longer. Thank you again for your help. It may prove very valuable."

CHAPTER XXVIII
STRENGTH OF SILENCE

NEXT MORNING, on his desk, Bobby found waiting for him an apologetic letter from the Liddel and Scot agency people, explaining that owing to an error in filing, Mrs Adam's former connection with their agency had been overlooked at first, but had now been established. It continued with all the information Bobby had already received from Doreen. He picked up the 'phone to express his thanks therefor; added a gentle hint that he hoped their filing system would be improved, as otherwise complications might arise, even when their licence came up for renewal; cut short their hurried, voluble, and frightened protests with an assurance that he quite understood it had all been purely accidental and, of course, would never occur again, and so hung up.

"Be a bit more forthcoming if we ever want their help again," he reflected.

Then he sent for Detective Constable Ford. Him he dispatched to see what could be done towards tracing the present whereabouts of Mrs Adam.

"It looks," Bobby told Ford, "as if she were 'on the run'. When it's like that and there are hints about another murder, we've got to take it seriously. On the theory that she has the smuggled watches, and means to keep them because she is Abel's widow and now they are her property, the threats will come from one or other of the Seemouth smugglers—Ossy Dow or Stanley Foster, both or either. I don't expect when they started their little smuggling game they thought it was going to end up in murder. Or it might be our 'Enemy of Society' thinking that smuggled watches are just what an 'Enemy of Society' is entitled to. Or Kenneth Banner. No confirmation of his story, and even if it is true about the attempted drugging and the fight, the reason may really have been a quarrel over the smuggled stuff, how to deal with it or share it out or something. That's the background, Ford, I want you to keep in mind. Anyhow, now you know as much as I do, and that's precious little, but does include the one small lead I picked up at Seemouth. You remember?"

"Oh, yes, sir," Ford assured him. "If I might ask, where would you say Miss Caine might come in?"

"Oh, anywhere, nowhere," answered Bobby, still with that note of disapproval in his voice the mention of her name was apt to call forth. "It may be that she means somehow to clear the name of the man she loves, or it may be—something else entirely. I don't know. In any case, nothing she'll stop at."

"I wouldn't much care," pronounced Ford with some fervour, "to be walking out with a young woman like her."

Therewith he went off on his errand, and before lunch was reporting back.

"I got the Pimlico landlady to let me look round Mrs Adam's bedroom," he said. "It was taken on 'no attendance provided, no cooking allowed' terms. She paid a week's rent in advance, so the room hasn't been touched. The only thing the landlady did was to look in to make sure Mrs Adam hadn't committed suicide or died in her sleep or anything like that. She hadn't left so much as a tooth brush, and the only thing I found to show it had been occupied at all was this"—and he displayed with modest satisfaction a railway circular announcing cheap excursions to Seemouth and other places near.

"Day excursion," Bobby commented. "If she went by it, where did she go when she came back?"

"Something may have prevented her," Ford suggested. "From coming back, I mean."

Bobby frowned at the possibility, which he did not like.

"Ask the canteen for sandwiches for us both," he told Ford, "and have a car ready. Hurry up, I've a feeling that the sooner we get to Seemouth the better. If Mrs Adam has really been there, it may mean just anything or nothing."

Ford vanished, always enchanted with the prospect of any long car trip, especially one during which he felt it entirely probable he would be allowed to drive. As happened. For a driver must concentrate on his job to the exclusion of everything else, and Bobby wanted to concentrate on his investigation to the exclusion of everything else.

Seemouth reached, they drew up outside the police-station, warned by 'phone to expect them. Seemouth had not much to say. A discreet watch had been kept on those concerned, so far as that was possible. There had been a great deal of coming and going. The Banner Travel Agency office was still 'temporarily closed', but Imra went there occasionally, presumably to attend to any letters there might be. Ossy Dow was supposed to be in London, negotiating, it was said, for the sale of the Banner Agency to one of the big travel firms. Imra was also away a good deal, looking for a new job perhaps. At any rate that was what she was reported to have said. There had been some irresponsible gossip about the Stanley Fosters, founded apparently on the alleged fact that Mrs Foster seemed worried and nervous and was said to have been heard more than once in loud argument with her husband.

"The neighbours," the Seemouth inspector explained, "are all telling each other that Foster has picked up a girl somewhere, and it's because he goes to visit her, he's so much away. Don't believe it myself. He had a bit of a name for that sort of thing at one time, but that's a long while ago, and there's been nothing of the sort for years."

Bobby nodded, accepting this, for he was well aware how much local police get to know about even the most law-abiding citizens. More especially in the smaller communities, where indeed not only police but everyone else know all about everyone else.

"More likely," Bobby agreed, "Mrs Foster is worried over possible developments—murder or smuggling. I expect she knows a lot herself, and is afraid we may know more. I'm beginning to think she's the woman sent the warning Kenneth Banner says he received. No one else in fact."

He went on next to Imra's address, taking Ford with him as a chaperon, a precaution it was always wise to observe when about to question an attractive young woman—a dangerous race.

As it happened, they met Imra in the street near her home. She was apparently returning from a shopping expedition, to judge from the laden basket she was carrying.

"I thought you would be the next," she greeted them in her slow, sombre voice Bobby remembered so well.

"Next?" he repeated questioningly.

"Isn't it because of Mrs Adam?" she asked. "She told me she wanted Mr Dow, and she was going straight to the police if she couldn't find him."

"She hasn't as far as I know," Bobby said. "Did she say why?"

"She was so excited and upset I couldn't make out what it was all about," Imra replied. "I told her Mr Dow was in London trying to sell the agency."

"Can you give me his address?"

"No, he rang up to say he had left his hotel because it was too expensive, and he would get a cheap room somewhere if he could find one. He said he would ring up again when he was settled."

Bobby turned to accompany her, as she showed signs of wanting to continue on her way. She did not seem pleased, less pleased still when she noticed Ford was following close behind. Her home was close by, and when they reached it she said 'Good afternoon', and seemed to expect them to depart. Bobby explained there were a few questions he wished to put to her.

"We think you may be able to help us," he said, and she gave him one of those strange, long looks of hers, as of one who saw approaching what she feared indeed but was resolute to face.

"Why should I?" she asked. "Help you, I mean." And then: "Suppose I don't choose to answer questions?"

"I hope you won't do that," Bobby answered. "It would make a very bad impression. Conclusions would be drawn. There is such a thing, too, you know, as being detained for questioning. Wouldn't it be better if we talked somewhere else, not in the street. Would you prefer to come to the police-station? It may be necessary to ask you to make a statement."

"I don't think I've anything to say, even if I wanted to, and I don't think I care if you do draw conclusions," she told him, and now there was a certain lofty and defiant scorn in her voice. "No," she said loudly, and then abruptly, for no apparent reason, she changed her mind. "Well, come in if you want to," she said.

She opened the door and went in. She did not look back, and made no gesture of permission or invitation. They followed her down a long, drab passage. At the end of it she opened a door and stood aside. It was a small, dull room they entered, reflecting in no way Imra's enigmatic, vivid personality. She closed the door on them and went away without speaking.

"Making her get-away?" Ford said.

"I don't think so," Bobby answered.

"Looks like death," Ford said. "Looks like a woman in a picture I once saw—ancient queen it was. Offering a choice of a bowl of poison or a knife. Sort of 'As You Like It' business."

Bobby made no comment on this historical reminiscence. He was not without something of the same feeling himself.

"I think she takes things hard," he said. "A born extremist—puts in all she has, and nothing held back. Dangerous."

The door opened and Imra returned. She stood for a moment in the doorway watching them. Then she came forward, and with her came that breath and atmosphere of tragedy that seemed the natural air she breathed.

"Well, now then," she said, and even those commonplace words she managed somehow to invest with an accent of doom. "Well, now then," she repeated, still standing, still watching.

"You know," Bobby said gently, "if you stand there like that we shall have to stand up as well. Wouldn't we get on better if you sat down?"

"Very well," she said, after a pause, as if considering this suggestion, wishing to ignore it, and yet finding no reason to do so.

"One thing that's giving us a lot of bother," Bobby went on, "is that it seems so difficult to keep in touch with people. Mrs Adam, for instance. She has a way of leaving her lodgings suddenly without saying a word. She might almost be trying to hide. From whom? Not from us obviously, if she told you she was going to ask our help."

"She's a fool," Imra said briefly. "If she means to go to you, why not wait till she does?"

"It might mean waiting till too late," Bobby answered. "You knew probably she was married to Mr Abel?"

"I heard so."

"Were you on friendly terms with Mr Abel?"

"No. He was no friend of mine," she said, and stared hard at Bobby, her gaze fixed, blank, unwavering. He waited, for he felt there was more to come. With a slight relaxation of her tense manner, she went on: "He was hardly ever in Seemouth. He lived in Southampton, where our cruises always started. It suited clients better. Us too. There's no really good anchorage here." Then she paused once more, and once more he waited. Slowly, as if the words came from her against her will, she continued: "They say he had a way with women. I don't know. It's what I heard. I didn't mean to tell you that." And now she was looking at him resentfully, as if she felt it was his calm and patient, intent waiting, the forceful suggestion of his hidden will, that in the end had made her speak. "I don't know why I did," she concluded.

Bobby did not know either. He did not know that deep down within him there was, as it were, some hidden power of the will, some forceful unknown energy that could at times make speech come from those who had resolved that they would remain silent. May be it was this deep silence of his own, as he waited, watchful and attentive, his thoughts unknown, this intent and potent silence, that made imperative a response from theirs. At any rate, whatever the explanation, it had happened before in his experience, and even more than once; this kind of reluctant and unwilling response of speech to the power of silence.

"I was told that once before, about his influence with women," Bobby said thoughtfully. "Hard to understand. Some men have it. The male equivalent to feminine charm—glamour—'It'—I suppose. Have you heard anything, or have you any knowledge of the smuggling we have reason to believe was carried on under cover of the 'As You Like It' cruises?"

"It's all over Seemouth," she answered. "I expect you know that perfectly well. I know nothing about it. I never went on any of the cruises. Watches, people say. From Switzerland. I don't know."

"We have further information," Bobby continued, "that Mrs Adam recently offered a valuable wrist-watch for sale to a jeweller in London, but left at once when he seemed inclined to question her."

"If she did, what has that to do with me?"

"You sold some jewellery recently yourself, didn't you?" Bobby asked.

"That's my business," she retorted. "I suppose you've been following me about, watching? What right have you to go snooping after people?"

"You have been neither followed nor watched," Bobby told her, "beyond the fact that your visits to London have been noticed like those of others in the case."

"What's that mean?" she demanded. "What case?"

"The case of murder committed at Mayfair Crescent," he answered. "That is what we are chiefly concerned with."

"You mean I am what you call 'in it'?" she asked scornfully.

"Like some others," he agreed.

"So that's why you've been watching me. Is my selling some old jewellery my aunt left me considered suspicious? If you weren't watching, how did you know?"

"Jewellers let us know when they are offered valuable jewellery privately. As it happened, we had asked for a look-out to be kept for the Manton jewellery, and one of our people was making inquiries at the shop you went to. There's another question I should like to put to you. You know a Mr Jasper Jordan. He lives in a basement flat near Mayfair Crescent."

"I've heard of him. I've never seen him. A crank, isn't he?"

"He might be called so," Bobby admitted. "He seems to have left his flat with the door slightly open, as if he meant to be back immediately. Apparently he did not return at all. Our information is that a car was seen waiting outside the flat about that time. It was driven by a woman. Was it you?"

"Why should you think so? Many women drive cars."

"The description we have might apply to you."

"I should like to hear it," she said then, a touch of mockery in her voice.

"Tall and dark," Bobby said. "A distinctive bearing."

"Is that all? There must be millions of us tall and dark." She gave one of those smiles of hers that were like no others. "What is a distinctive bearing?" she asked.

"Hard to define, easy to recognize," Bobby told her, and went on immediately: "Do you think you could remember where you were the night Herbert Abel was murdered?"

She gave no least sign that this sudden and abrupt question in any way disturbed her. But it was a long time before she answered. She sat as motionless as before, her hands clasped loosely before her. He noticed that even her feet were still, feet that often betray a nervousness otherwise well concealed. She might not have heard, except for the deep, veiled eyes that were so fixed, so intent.

"No," she said. "It is a question, that. Why do you ask it?"

"I think there was a woman present that night," Bobby said. "Was it you?" he asked for the second time.

"If it were, do you think I should tell you?" she retorted, and then: "Have you asked Doreen Caine? Or Mrs Adam? Or is it only me?"

This time it was Bobby who did not answer for a moment or two. He could see how closely she was watching him, and he was certain she felt that her last two questions had embarrassed him, even if she did not realize why or how deeply. He had been intending to ask her next to explain how it was she had been able to make the reference she had done when he first saw her to the meal Abel had been preparing before his murder. But now he had the impression that it would be better to wait a little longer. Now she was on the alert, defensive, defiant, wary. At any moment she might refuse to say more. If he let further questioning wait, giving her more time for reflection, she might be more willing to tell all that he was certain she was keeping back.

"Well, you know," he answered at last, "you mustn't expect me to give you information about other people. We shouldn't about you, you know. But why do you mention Mrs Adam and Miss Caine in particular? Is it because you know something?"

"I know Mrs Adam was his wife and was telling everyone what she was going to do to him when she found him. And she says Doreen Caine was one of his women. He had plenty, every fool girl he met, I expect, and why not her? Perhaps she hit back? Did she? Something for you to think about," she said, and again came that strange dark smile of hers it was so hard to understand—an enigmatic, Mona Lisa smile. "Or why not try to find the missing Mr Jasper Jordan? If he's not where he lives, he must be somewhere else, mustn't he?"

"Yes," Bobby agreed. "Yes. Somewhere."

CHAPTER XXIX
MR JORDAN'S RETURN

ON THAT doubtful note, their talk ended; and it was in silence, Bobby silent because he had so much to think over, Ford because he did not dare intrude upon the thoughts of a senior so much absorbed in them, that they returned to the police-station, where they had left their car. They were nearly there before Bobby seemed to wake from his abstraction.

"Gives you something to mull over, doesn't it?" he said to Ford. "But takes it out of you, too. I would rather have a good old rough-and-tumble any day than a talk like that, all hints and allusions, and what have you."

"Yes, sir," agreed Ford, though in fact he had felt no such strain, having indeed taken no part in a duel of words of which he had not well understood the significance. He added: "Was she hinting Miss Caine is an A. 1 cook and might have been helping Abel get ready that swell supper of his?"

"Abel seems to have been a swell cook himself," Bobby reminded Ford. "Hardly likely he would want her help. Possible,

I suppose. Garlic seems to have been a sort of bond of brother-hood between them—between him and Miss Caine."

"Garlic, sir?" Ford repeated, for he hardly knew what gar-lic was, except vaguely as something that foreigners had for dinner—and just like them. He ventured—apologetically: "You know, sir, I was half-expecting you would press Miss Guire about the supper Abel had got ready that night. Extra special, wasn't it?"

"I did mean to," Bobby answered. "But then I thought I wouldn't. I got the idea all at once that it wasn't the time. Tim-ing's everything, you know. Ask a cricketer. Ask a boxer. You are both, aren't you? You ought to know. One hit will go to the boundary and another rate a lucky single, though you've put just as much into it. Ripeness is all as someone said, and ripeness means timing. When you are asking questions, timing is just as important as the question itself."

"Yes, sir," agreed Ford. "Difficult though."

"Everything's difficult," Bobby told him. "If it wasn't, it wouldn't be interesting." They had reached the police-station now. "I'll just go in and tell them we're off, and they'll say 'Thank the Lord', but not out loud."

It was a long drive back to town, and late when they reached the Yard. Ford—seniors don't always have the best of it—was sent off home, but Bobby had to set to to write out the notes of the talk with Imra he had been busy making during the drive. These, too, he had to type out himself—a one-finger job for him—as all the typists had gone home. All, that is, except one, and she saw him coming and had time to dodge.

Next morning, however, he found on his desk a memo, marked: "Urgent. In re, Mayfair Crescent Case (re-opened)."

It came from the D.D.I. of the district, and was to the effect that Mr Jasper Jordan, reported 'absent from residence', had returned. He had been seen and spoken to by the constable on the beat, who had noticed him leaning over the area gate, smok-ing a cigarette. Jordan had been aggressively rude. Couldn't, he had demanded, a man go away to the seaside for a day or two if he wanted a change, without all the police in the place running after him? Why didn't the police stick to their job, if indeed they had one, which to him, Jasper Jordan, seemed extremely doubtful. Perhaps they would next be asking to see his hotel bill to make sure he had paid up? Well, if that was what they wanted, they could whistle for it.

But at this point the constable beat a retreat, battered indeed, but still unbowed, though a barrage of invective followed him all down the street.

"Touchy gentleman, our Jasper," Bobby remarked to a colleague who had come into the room to consult him on another matter. "Anyhow, another turn of the kaleidoscope. Why all that about the seaside and the hotel bill? Just possibly means the seaside is where he hasn't been and an hotel is where he hasn't been staying, and he hopes we will waste our time looking for them. Which would also mean he doesn't want us to know where he was. Why? And that hanging about at the top of the area steps looks very much as if he wanted his return to be noticed. I think I had better try to get away in time this afternoon to see if I can get anything out of him."

"You don't expect him to tell you anything, do you?" asked the colleague. "Most likely he's been getting rid of those watches and wants to cover up. Hot stuff, and best got rid of pronto."

"Better than best—put hot stuff in cold storage," Bobby retorted, "and often what a man tells you is as much in what he doesn't say as in what he does."

The colleague put on a doubtful air, said that was too subtle for him, and retired; and Bobby succeeded in getting away in time to reach West King Street shortly before five—that doubtful hour which is neither still afternoon nor yet evening. He had to wait a little and knock twice before at last Jordan came to the door. Seeing Bobby waiting there, he promptly emitted a sort of muffled shout that was at best, however, but a pale reflection of his earlier full-throated roars. Indeed, he looked very much, Bobby told himself, the worse for wear. Pale he was, his features drawn, a dirty patch of sticking-plaster on his neck, his gait most unlike the vigorous, confident stride Bobby remembered, his former swaggering boisterousness much reduced. He was plainly doing his best to recover it though.

"My dear old pal back again with his usual search warrant in his pocket most likely," he was saying. "Never mind showing it. Come along in and tell me what it's all about this time. Or is it only that you can't leave decent people alone, but must always be poking your nose into what doesn't concern you?"

He led the way into the front room Bobby had been in before. There he took up his favourite position with his back to the fireplace, and again Bobby was conscious of an odd impression that somehow the man was oddly shrunken. He seemed to have become a smaller impression of his earlier self, as though he had recently been badly shaken. The room, too, was even untidier than usual, not so much more untidy perhaps as more disorderly. The brand new typewriter Bobby remembered had now become no more than a battered ruin. One of the rickety chairs was in bits in a corner, and in another corner was what remained of the aspidistra Bobby had noticed on his earlier visit. It had apparently been knocked over and trodden on.

"Take a seat," Jordan said, with a vague wave of his hand round the room. "Suit yourself. Well, what's it all about?"

Bobby chose one that seemed the most likely to bear his weight, removed from it some tools—a hammer, a screwdriver, screws, two padlocks, a file, a collection Bobby noticed with some interest, since it was the first time he had seen anything to suggest Jordan ever troubled to do anything in the way of odd jobs needing tools—and said:

"Well, you know, Mr Jordan, really and truly, we have far too much on our hands that does concern us to bother about what doesn't. Item: murder not far from here."

"Well, I didn't do it," Jordan snapped. "I didn't know the poor devil, never so much as set eyes on him for that matter."

"Item," Bobby continued: "smuggled watches of unknown but probably considerable value."

"Well, I haven't got them," Jordan said. "Wish I had. Smuggled indeed. What right have you, has Society, to stop a man buying a watch and selling it again if he wants to?"

"If you really had the watches as you say you wish you had," Bobby countered, without attempting to answer this question of high political philosophy, "what would you do with them? Hand them over to Mrs Adam?"

"I suppose you think that's clever," Jordan snarled, for now his once deep-throated, menacing growl had degenerated into little more than a mere feline snarl.

"Not clever," Bobby assured him mildly. "Just a guess."

"Ask her if you want to know," Jordan said.

"Got to find her first," Bobby pointed out, "and she seems to have gone missing—common form in this case." He waited, hoping for some comment, but got none, though he noticed Jordan showed no sign of surprise. Bobby went on: "Item: a basement flat with its door left open for anyone who wanted to walk in. It's the duty of the Guardians of Society—us—to warn the Enemies of Society—you—that when that happens, other enemies of Society may walk in and make a clean sweep."

"Wouldn't pay the cost of taking the stuff away," Jordan said, "and the Guardians of Society can go to hell for all I care."

"Well, so we do sometimes," Bobby told him. "In the course of our duty—or at any rate to a good imitation. You know, Mr Jordan, you don't look as if the sea air has done you much good. Quite a nasty little scratch on your throat, isn't it? Shaving, I suppose?"

"Is that another item?" Jordan asked, but, Bobby thought, with a touch of uneasiness in his voice, as though he were not best pleased that this had been noted and commented on.

"Oh, I wouldn't say that," Bobby answered. "Well, I'll be going." He got to his feet. He pointed to the ceiling, where conspicuous against the general grime, showed some freshly broken plaster he had only now noticed. "Someone trying to break through to the room above?" he asked.

"Piece of damned carelessness," Jordan said angrily. "Might easily—" and then he stopped short, as if suddenly conscious that he had been about to say too much.

"Exactly," Bobby agreed. "Might easily have killed someone—even Mr Jordan. Shall we see if there's still a bullet there?"

"What's it matter if there is?" Jordan demanded. "It was accidental. Silly ass fooling about with a gun he didn't understand. Thought the safety catch was on, and it wasn't. That's all."

"Quite enough," Bobby said. "I hope whoever it was had a certificate. Astonishing, the number of people who don't seem to know it's an offence to be in possession of a pistol without one. Or who don't care, and hang on to the thing all the same. Don't mind risking a fine. Do you mind telling me who it was?"

"Yes, I do," Jordan retorted. "Why don't you follow up the clue, as you would call it I suppose, and track the scoundrel down? That's your job, isn't it?"

"So it is, and very good advice, too," Bobby agreed. "Let's start. Observed fact: a hole in a ceiling. Deduction: a bullet made it. Problem: track down the man who fired the bullet. Well, well. We'll do our humble best. Well, I must hurry off and get down to it. Evening, Mr Jordan, I may be seeing you again before long."

"Don't trouble," Jordan said. "The less I see of your sort, the better I like it."

"I know, I know," Bobby agreed. "A common sentiment with all the different varieties of the Enemies of Society." Suddenly he changed the bantering tone he had hitherto adopted since he thought it the one most likely to penetrate Jordan's armour of self-importance and self-confidence. "Mr Jordan," he said, "why not drop this rather silly pose of yours? I think it's already taken you farther than you intended. I wish you would believe that you could trust us a little and be sure of getting a fair deal."

Jordan yawned. Then he said:

"I prefer my own fair deals. Don't forget to shut the door as you go, or there'll be more excitement and more wild searches going on—seaside and all."

"Well, think it over," Bobby said. "Good evening," and therewith he went.

THAT SOMETHING very odd had been going on in Jordan's flat, was now sufficiently plain. And when that 'something very odd' was mixed up with an unsolved murder mystery and a consignment of smuggled watches of unknown but probably high value, it was clearly an immediate and pressing duty to find out what that something was.

"Won't be too easy either," Bobby told himself ruefully, as he walked away. "Jordan's not talking. The Guire girl and Miss Caine aren't talking either. Probably all set to protect either themselves or someone else, and all three of them hard nuts to crack in their own private, different ways. Mrs Adam and Kenneth Banner not to be found so far. Stan Foster and Mr Pyne both at present in the wings, but liable to take the centre of the stage any moment." Bobby shook his head still more ruefully at the prospect before him. "And the only clue, if you can call it one, a passing reference to a 'silly ass' who thought a safety catch was on when it wasn't."

He had reached Mayfair Crescent now, and when he knocked at the door of Mr Pyne's flat, it was opened by a sedate-looking elderly lady, nearly as prim in manner and dress as Mr Pyne himself. She might, indeed, have been a replica of him—or he of her—in the other sex. When Bobby asked if he could see Mr Pyne she countered by asking if it was anything she could attend to, as Mr Pyne was unwell and confined to bed.

"Sorry to hear that," Bobby said at his most amiable. "I hope he wasn't really badly knocked about in that nasty little scrimmage."

"Oh, how did you know?" she exclaimed, very much taken aback, and then, when he only smiled at her benevolently, went on in uneasy protest. "I didn't say anything like that."

"Oh, no," Bobby agreed. "Only—well, our job to know things. From information received, that's our stock phrase. I'm afraid it's necessary I should have a talk with your husband. It's really rather serious, what with one thing and another and the murder committed here."

Mrs Pyne was by now thoroughly frightened. She mumbled something indistinct and went off, leaving him standing on the door-mat. He took the precaution of advancing a step or two into the entrance lobby, in case she got the idea of banging the door to and leaving him on the wrong side. Mrs Pyne came back, looking as if she were on the verge of something, Bobby didn't know what, but hoped it wouldn't be tears, hysterics, or fainting, three feminine trump cards to which he knew no answer. In a faltering, unsteady tone, and without apparently even noticing his journey into the interior, she asked him to come this way, please. She introduced him into a fair-sized bedroom as trim and neat and tidy, Bobby was certain, as any office in the whole vast Ministry of Priorities with all its many annexes and all its myriads of employees. In the large double bed lay Mr Pyne, anything but trim and tidy, with a bandaged head, two lovely black eyes, a badly cut and swollen mouth, and a sprouting beard it would evidently not be possible to introduce to a razor for some time yet, all affording strong circumstantial evidence that he had not been entirely a stranger to the unexplained incident Bobby was more than ever certain had recently taken place in Mr Jordan's basement flat.

"Dear, dear," he commiserated. "I had no idea it was as bad as that. Must have been quite a rough house over there in West King Street."

"Has Jordan been telling you about it?" Mr Pyne asked, a new lisp in his voice coming from the fact that two of his front teeth were missing.

"We won't go into that," Bobby said, drawing up to the bedside a chair Mr Pyne was indicating. He saw no reason for explaining that he had acted simply on his memory of how on a previous occasion Mr Pyne had shown himself rather hazy on the subject of safety catches, of how Mr Jordan had expressed an opinion that someone had shown himself equally hazy or more so over their usage, and of how he himself had seen reason to believe that Mr Pyne had obtained, through Jordan's agency, another pistol in place of that taken possession of by the local police. It was indeed to this capacity of his to remember and to correlate detail that he owed his success as an investigator, rather than to any superhuman powers of logical deduction leading, from a footprint to a personality. "Observe and remember, all is there," he was inclined to say at times. Now he was continuing aloud: "'From information received' is the cliché we like to use. I am suggesting that you and Jordan were both concerned in a recent incident taking place at his flat."

"I must consider my position carefully," Mr Pyne said, in his new lisping voice, "before attempting to reply or committing myself in any way. There are others concerned to whom certain undertakings have been given. I can, however, give you my emphatic personal assurance, which I stress, that if—assuming for present purposes that such is indeed the case—anything of an unseemly or even of a regrettably violent nature, lying possibly outside the stricter limits of legality, of which I am in no way convinced, did in fact occur in the locality or habitation you have mentioned, then it was, on the assumption aforesaid, in no way connected with the crime committed in this flat. It might well be that any occurrence of the nature now suggested was in fact"—here Mr Pyne paused and frowned, evidently deep in thought—"a drunken orgie," he brought out at last and lay back on his pillows, exhausted but triumphant.

"Mr Pyne," Bobby said gently, "doesn't it strike you that you may very well find all this turning out very awkwardly? It's got to come out sooner or later. I don't know how you as a Civil Servant will be affected, but there it is."

Mr Pyne put his finger-tips together, regarded them seriously and in silence for some moments, and then spoke even more deliberately than usual.

"It is a contingency to which I have given," he said, "my most careful consideration. In my settled view—one not lightly arrived at—the publicity given to the events you have referred to would probably lead to the termination of my term of service."

"What I was thinking," Bobby observed.

"If such an unfortunate contingency did arise," Mr Pyne continued, "I am unable to express at present any decided opinion as to what course of action I should consider it advisable to adopt, though few indeed would be open to me. I might possibly take to drink."

"Rather hard on your family," Bobby suggested, a little alarmed, for he somehow felt the remark had been made quite seriously in all good faith.

"My daughter," Mr Pyne assured him earnestly, "would be very pleased—at any rate at first. She has informed me on various occasions that you might as well be dead as respectable. 'Dead and buried alive', was the expression she used. When I pointed out that this was in the nature of a contradiction in terms, she became much annoyed, and did not return home till far on in the small hours, even refusing next morning to say where she had been. Indeed, she was not in a condition to do much more than express a strong wish that she was in fact both dead and buried—or at least that her head was. My wife, I think, would thoroughly enjoy the efforts she would undoubtedly make to reform me. She, too, has recently expressed much dissatisfaction with the intolerable tedium of a housewife's life—get up, wash up, clean up, bed. She had not, I think, been so acutely aware of this till her attention was directed to it by a recent 'Mass Observation' report. Fruitless attempts to reform me would be a welcome change, and no doubt you have noticed that no woman is ever so happy as when she is attempting to reform someone—preferably her husband."

Bobby made no comment on this. He felt it was a side issue he had no right to consume official time in discussing, but all the same, for the moment, he and Mr Pyne were one—no longer investigator and investigatee, but just two married men. Then Bobby said, now official again:

"Would you be prepared to make a statement?"

"You must excuse it if I seem to be evasive," Mr Pyne answered, with earnest politeness, "but after thirty years of knowing the future precisely—from to-morrow's task to probable promotion by seniority and presently retirement on pension—I find it intoxicating, bewildering, to contemplate instead a future entirely problematic. It is not indeed wholly without a certain pleasurable excitement—a perverse and unnatural pleasure no doubt, but in its way, enjoyable. I must have time to decide. I have entered into certain obligations, and observing them affects other people. I know my recent conduct must appear highly unbecoming, indeed unpardonable, in anyone connected with the Ministry of Priorities, of which it is not too much to say that on it the smooth working of the whole economy of the country finally depends. Yet, I repeat, I have committed no action of an anti-social nature. The contrary indeed."

There was no more to be got out of Mr Pyne, and Bobby decided to follow his usual plan—that of not pressing witnesses too hard at first, but to allow them time to remember and to reflect. Mr Pyne, Bobby thought, might well feel 'on further consideration', as he himself would have said, that the prospect of dismissal, and of then taking to drink, contained the less of pleasure, and even of excitement, the nearer it drew. It would be merely the exchange of one monotonous routine for another fully as monotonous, and much less agreeable.

So Bobby took himself off home, and there sat in silence, staring hard at the ceiling, till presently Olive came into the room to tell him to get going. Supper was nearly ready, and time he started to lay the table. So he settled himself more comfortably in his chair, transferred his fixed gaze to her, and said:

"Jasper Jordan disappears from his flat, leaving the door open. The flat is much as usual, no sign of any disturbance. Jordan reappears and seems to want his return to be noticed. He says he has been on a trip to the seaside, but his flat now shows a good many signs that things have been happening—including a bullet hole in the ceiling—and Jasper himself appears much the worse for wear. Ditto Mr Pyne, who suggests a drunken orgie in the flat as an explanation. Unconvincing somehow. But what does it all add up to?"

"I don't know," Olive answered, gently impelling him to his feet. "The plates and things are all in their usual places."

"Are they?" said Bobby abstractedly. "Listen—"

"There's something burning," said Olive, and disappeared.

"Mrs Adam," continued Bobby to the vacant air till Olive returned, "claims that an attempt was made to hustle her into a waiting car. Has something of the same sort been tried with our Jasper, and was it more successful? There's that waiting car seen outside his flat to remember. Probably driven by Imra Guire. If so, is it possible Mr Pyne helped and that's how he got damaged? There must have been someone else on the job if it was like that, someone who raked in Pyne. Who?"

"Why should anyone want to run away with Mrs Adam or Mr Jordan either?" demanded Olive. "I'm sure I never should."

"We aren't the only people interested in those smuggled watches," Bobby reminded her. "Secondary with us, priority with them. But how fit in the rough house at Jordan's flat? He can't have been held there? I went all over it with Doreen Caine, and there was no sign of him or anything else out of the way. Or—or—or—"

"Never mind 'or'," said Olive. "Come and get your supper."

"Or," Bobby said, as meekly he followed her to the supper-table, she, and not he, had laid, "does the explanation lie in the door of the flat being left open? As were those other doors."

The 'phone rang. Bobby went to answer it. Olive said:

"Bother the thing. Tell them you haven't got home yet, and you must have your supper, and it's been waiting for ages."

Bobby listened, put back the receiver.

"They say," he told her, "they've had a 'phone message that a lady I know will be waiting in the Embankment garden next to the Houses of Parliament at ten to-morrow, and if I come alone she will have something to tell me. Now which of the three of them will it be? Doreen, Imra, or Mrs Adam?"

"Wait and see," said Olive.

CHAPTER XXXI
RENDEZVOUS

THE NEXT morning therefore Bobby was punctual in his attendance at the spot suggested. He took the precaution, since one never knew what might not be behind this kind of appointment—even pistol shots from a distance, for instance—to get a C.I.D. man who lived near to accompany his wife and their two small children to the same gardens. There the children could play in the sand-pit provided by a benevolent County Council, while father and mother, one with the morning paper, the other with her sewing—for women must work, though men may read—watched the gambols of their offspring. An idyllic picture, in fact, of a family outing when father has a day off, and no one could dream there was anything else in the background. Though Bobby's suggestion that to make the whole set-up even more realistic the day could really be counted as a day off, and deducted from annual leave due, was received with such pained surprise that he had hurriedly withdrawn it.

On one of the seats overlooking the river Bobby, on his arrival, saw at once a solitary woman: Mrs Adam, and when he joined her she wasted no time in preliminaries.

"I'm fed up," she announced. "Chased and chivvied. That's me. From morn to night, and never know what next."

"Too bad," said Bobby sympathetically. "No wonder you're fed up with it."

"That Miss Caine," said Mrs Adam with venom. "Her and her foreign stuff. Muck I call it. No sort of a meal to give a decent, hard-working chap."

"What's Miss Caine been doing?" Bobby asked.

"Poking her nose in where not wanted," Mrs Adam explained succinctly. "Nosing after me as only want to be left alone. What I say is what belonged to him that's passed away, did ought to be mine, him and me being man and wife, decently married in church, and as good as two hundred pounds in the Post Office he had off me and then done a bunk—well, hadn't I a right to what was his, and now it's mine by lawful rights?"

"Suppose you tell me," Bobby suggested, "what it was had been his you are talking about? Smuggled watches?"

"How was I to know as they were smuggled?"

"If you hadn't a pretty good idea, why did you walk out of that jeweller's near Liverpool Street Station in such a hurry?"

"Nosey, he was, and me with a train to catch and all."

"Nosey he was," Bobby agreed, "and nosey, as you call it, I'm afraid you're going to find me. Come, come, Mrs Adam, out with it. Where are they?"

"A-hh," Mrs Adam said thoughtfully. "That's just it. Where? Suppose I gave you a sort of a hint where you might find 'em— at least, supposing it turns out I'm right, not knowing but putting this and that together—would it be all right? None being touched, and all same as they were. And a reward for their recovery, as would be only right?"

"I can't make you any promises," Bobby told her. "Wouldn't be any use if I did. I don't think there will be any question of a reward. I wouldn't try that on if I were you. But I don't at the moment see what charge could be laid against you. Of course, unlawful detention. That sort of thing. But if you hand them over voluntarily, it would hardly be pressed. At least, I don't think so. Not my responsibility of course."

"Oh, well, if I'm not going to get anything out of it, I'm not saying anything," Mrs Adam retorted, "and there's no charge nor nothing you can have me up on if you can't find 'em ever, same as you never will without me."

She made to get up as she spoke, and to walk away. But Bobby made a gesture to her to remain seated, and at the same time waved to the C.I.D. man who had been watching them over the top of his paper, and who at once got up and began to walk towards them.

"One of my men," Bobby explained. "After what you have told me, I shall have to ask you to go with him to Scotland Yard. For further questioning."

"Proper put my head in the lion's jaws," Mrs Adam grumbled. "I might have known. With cops. They're in the left-luggage office at Willesden." She fumbled in her handbag, produced the receipt, and handed it to Bobby. "Left 'em there last night. Got the Manchester train at Willesden in case of being looked for at Euston, and got out there again coming back."

"Where were they at Manchester?" Bobby asked.

"Where you wouldn't never have found them if I had had sense enough to hold my tongue," she retorted. "At a dining-rooms where I worked once. In an old cupboard with some other belongings of mine I was let leave there. Safe as snuff unless that there Doreen came poking around, her being in the profession, too, and knowing too much and where to ask, pretending she had a good job going as was a wicked lie. But I'm not saying I'm so awful sorry to be done with the things."

The C.I.D. man had reached them now. Bobby handed him the receipt, told him to go to the Willesden Junction station, collect the dispatch-case referred to, and bring it to the Yard. He went off accordingly, and Bobby turned again to Mrs Adam.

"How did they come into your possession?" he asked.

"Left where I was lodging," she explained. "A boy brought it. A dispatch-case. Locked. He said a man had given him a shilling to bring it and to say it was left in charge of a friend by my late husband, and him being deceased and me his widow, it was my lawful property, same as it did ought to be," and her wandering and wistful eyes sought the retreating figure of the C.I.D. man on his way to Willesden.

"Mr Jasper Jordan, I take it?" Bobby remarked.

"There wasn't no names mentioned," Mrs Adam answered cautiously.

"Well, never mind," Bobby said. "No evidence, but at this stage I think we can take that for granted. As also that the man who invited you to go for a drive with him was Ossy Dow, and that he meant to try to get you to hand the watches over."

"If it wasn't bloody murder they was meaning," Mrs Adam said; and this time it was the quietly flowing river to which her gaze was turned, as though she were thinking how easily in its swift depths a dead body could be swept out to the sea. "Same as happened to Bert, and him no loss to me or no one, but not murder, which I never meant nor thought, but they was hinting at plain enough."

"What did they say?" Bobby asked.

"As how Bert had had his, and I might get mine if I didn't watch my step, so I said to mind theirs, or I'd tell what I saw that night, and he looked at me something awful with fiery eyes, and it's my belief if he had got me into that car of his I wouldn't ever have left it alive."

"Possibly not," agreed Bobby grimly. "What was it you saw on the night of the murder?" When she hesitated, he added quietly: "You've said too much not to say more."

"It wasn't anything really," she answered uncomfortably. "I was trying to get hold of him for long enough—him doing me down on my maintenance and all—and then I heard where he was and living like a lord. A swanky flat it was, sure enough, and I nipped up the stairs quiet as I could for fear Mr Soclever might hear. The door wasn't close shut, and there was people talking. I couldn't hear what they said, them talking low and hurried and queer like, but one was a woman—I could tell that—and I knew there was funny work going on."

"What made you think so?" Bobby asked, as she paused with a little catch in her voice and a backward glance over her shoulder, as if she feared what might be there, listening.

"I don't know," she answered. "I just knew. I knew no one talked that way except there was something happened to make them. I wanted to slip away, but some way I didn't, because of wanting to know, and I took a peep round the corner of the door. They didn't see me, they didn't hear."

"What did you see—or hear?" Bobby asked, a vivid picture in his mind of this stout, elderly woman trembling on the small, ill-lighted landing, terror urging instant flight, terror holding her there motionless, as she watched the murderers of her husband whispering together by the side of his dead body.

"I saw there was two of them," she told him then. "A man and a woman, but I couldn't see the woman's face, her back being to me, and her stooping."

"And the man?" he asked.

"Not being certain, I don't want to mention names," she said.

"Don't you think you ought to help us to find your husband's murderer?"

"He was no husband to me," she said sullenly. "Run out on me he did, him and my maintenance, too."

"You should at least have let us know what you had seen," Bobby told her. "Why didn't you?"

"I didn't know then what it was," she protested. "I never thought it was murder. I reckoned it was burglars what had laid him out and me too, if they saw me, and I reckoned the best thing was for me to get off while I could, and so I did, and as for Bert, served him right, but not the time to go after him to get him to pay up. It was only when I got a paper that I knew what I had seen that night."

"You could have come to us then," Bobby said sternly.

"I was scared to," she answered. "Of you cops bringing me in. I had been shooting off my mouth. Talking about putting a bullet in him or slipping him a dose of something as he wouldn't ever want any more after it, and him using my maintenance on any fancy woman he could pick up as was more than flesh and blood could stand."

They were both silent then, but the picture in Bobby's mind had changed. It had become that of a woman, her natural feelings for her husband changed to bitter hate, gaining admission to the flat by the unlatched door, finding him lying unconscious on the floor—possibly she had seen the man and woman she talked of hurrying away and had guessed already that something was wrong—and then in an access of rage stuffing those fatal feathers, so strange an instrument of death, into the mouth that once had kissed her and then had betrayed her. If that was how it had happened, then perhaps also without full intention or full realization of what must inevitably happen. He said heavily:

"I put it to you that the man you say you saw was Ossy Dow."

"I don't know as I could swear to it," she answered, still cautiously. "He almost as good as said it when he wanted to get me to go along with him. Not me," she said, shivering as she spoke, though the sun was warm that day.

"And the woman?" he asked next.

"I told you, I didn't see her clear, and me in no state either to take particular notice, but if you ask me, most like it was that Doreen Caine, or why is she so busy meddling? and her one of his fancy women as is plain and clear."

"Why do you say that?" Bobby asked.

"If she wasn't, what was she always meeting him for, pubs and places?"

"They could have been talking about cooking," Bobby suggested.

Mrs Adam snorted contempt and disbelief.

"You don't talk about it once you've done it," she pronounced. "Only too glad to forget it—talking about the moon more like or something else as is more tasty than cooking."

"You may be right," Bobby said. "We'll get a taxi, shall we? I shall have to get all this in writing and then ask you to sign it. It's important."

"Proper fool, I've been, haven't I?" she lamented. "Telling you all, instead of keeping my mouth shut same as I meant." She looked at him resentfully. "Led me on," she complained. "One thing and another. Not what I call fair does."

"Perhaps your husband might have thought he hadn't had altogether fair does," Bobby suggested, but she only looked contemptuous.

"Him and fair does," she said, "they didn't never go together."

CHAPTER XXXII
SECOND RENDEZVOUS

MRS ADAM'S statement, taken down, finally approved, signed, she was allowed to depart with stern injunctions not to try to stage any more disappearances and assurances that every precaution would be taken to see that no more attempts were made to molest her or to invite her to go for a drive.

All of which meant, Bobby reflected, that enough was now known fully to justify holding Mr Ossy Dow, if and when he could be found. Not that that was apparently going to be easy, any more than it had been easy to find Kenneth Banner. Probably Doreen Caine knew his whereabouts, but not much hope that she would tell. Again, Imra Guire most likely knew where Ossy was, but she, too, would certainly keep that information to herself.

"It's the very devil dealing with two women like those two," Bobby moodily informed Olive, who retorted that it was nothing like so bad as having to deal with any two men like nothing on earth, except two other men, and all of them past human understanding.

Thus crushed, Bobby subsided into silence and then offered to take Olive to the cinema, since that was a nice quiet place where you could shut your eyes and think undisturbed and uninterrupted, free from the insistent clamour of the telephone. The offer was promptly accepted.

"A lovely film, wasn't it?" Olive said enthusiastically as they left. "I did enjoy it—awfully exciting, and so sad."

"Splendid," agreed Bobby. "If all of them were like that, I wouldn't mind going every evening almost."

"What was it about?" Olive asked, dark suspicion in every tone of her voice.

"Eh?" said Bobby. "Why—er—you know. Boy and girl, and in the end she gets him good and tight."

"I don't believe," Olive said sternly, "you ever looked once, and I paid for us both out of housekeeping because you said you had no change, and you'll please give it me back as soon as we get home."

"Not me," Bobby said firmly, but he had to, all the same, and when he had discharged this debt he uttered a gloomy prophecy that anything either Imra or Doreen knew they would keep to themselves, and no way he knew of making them speak.

"Mum as the Sphinx, both of 'em, if I know anything," he announced, and only had to wait twenty-four hours to have it proved that at any rate he didn't know everything, for then there was a long-distance call from one of the ladies in question.

Answering it, the small, distant voice announced that Imra Guire was speaking, that she was coming to town on the morrow, and that she would like to meet him. When he suggested that he would be very glad to see her in his room at Scotland Yard any time she liked, the prompt answer came that she certainly wasn't going there. She would be in Hyde Park, however, about two in the afternoon, next day, near the Marble Arch. There were always deck-chairs on the Park Lane side, near the Arch, and she would be sitting there. But he was to come alone. If he didn't, if any of his private 'snoopers', man or woman, were near, then she wouldn't say a word. Did he clearly understand that? Bobby replied meekly that he did, and before she rang off Imra added:

"I can tell you, for one thing, where Mr Dow got a room when he left his hotel."

"And what the dickens does that mean?" Bobby demanded, both looking and feeling very bewildered. "She can't be meaning to give him away surely?"

"Of course not," Olive said. "Something's happened to frighten her, and she wants help, and so she's thought of you. Almost sounds as if you had made a good impression on her. I can't think why."

"Trouble is," Bobby said, "people only come to us for help when things have gone so far no help is possible. I hope it doesn't mean Ossy has been bumped off. I don't see why he should be, now the smuggled stuff has been recovered." He relapsed into silence then, and only when Olive made some tentative suggestions about bed did he rouse himself sufficiently to say: "That open door—what did that mean? Why?"

"Why what?" Olive asked. "Which open door? There've been such a lot. What a door left open generally means is that anyone can walk in."

"Police or crook," Bobby agreed. "Anyhow, first thing to do is to hear what Miss Imra means to tell us—if anything."

He took care to be punctual at the suggested meeting-place. Imra was there, waiting in one of the deck-chairs she had mentioned. She got up as soon as she saw him and came to meet him.

"There's an open space just beyond the tea-house, overlooking the Serpentine," she said, without preliminary greeting.

"We can sit down there and talk without anyone being able to listen. That's just in case you've got some of your men here to follow us."

"None at all," Bobby assured her, walking by her side as she crossed the road to the paths leading to the tea-house. "I got the idea that this time it wasn't necessary, and, anyhow, if I did you would soon notice it and dry up. When Mrs Adam made the same sort of suggestion, I did take my precautions. But then I don't think she would be so quick to notice things, and I do think she could easily be made use of for—well, for other purposes. And I don't think you could be."

"Don't you?" she said, with some bitterness. "I'm not so sure." Then she asked: "Mrs Adam? what did she want?"

"Well, you know," Bobby answered smilingly. "I thought you were going to tell me things, not ask me questions."

They walked on in silence till, on that pleasant, sunny slope overlooking the Serpentine, they found two chairs sufficiently far from others, from any path, to make it certain nothing they said could by any possibility be overheard. When they had settled themselves Bobby said:

"Well, now then. You were going to give me Mr Dow's address?"

"The address where he got a room after he left his hotel," Imra corrected him. She gave him a street and number in Finchley. "But he's not there now," she said, "though all his things are. He went out last Monday evening to get a drink at a public-house near, the 'George and Dragon'. His landlady saw him there just before closing-time. She spoke to him, and he said he wanted to finish a game of darts, and then he would follow her, and not to lock up till he came. He said he wouldn't be more than a few minutes. He seemed rather jolly and excited, as if he had had a good deal more than only a drink. She waited for him till nearly twelve, and then she went to bed. She hasn't seen or heard anything since, and all his things are there still, everything, toothbrush, razor, everything. It's an electric razor he bought only the other day. A new toy—he would never leave it behind like that unless—"

"Unless?"

"Unless he had to," she answered steadily.

"What do you want us to do?"

"Find him. Find out what's happened. Find out why he rang me on Monday to tell me it was going well and to expect him first thing Tuesday and then didn't come or 'phone or anything."

"What was going well?" Bobby asked. "Why should you think something may have happened?"

"You know very well," she answered impatiently. "that some of them on the 'As You Like It' were smuggling as a side-line. Ossy had an idea of what was going on, and he told me earlier that he thought he knew what it was being brought in and where to find it."

"What was he going to do if he did find it?" Bobby asked. She made no answer. He asked again: "What you mean, isn't it? is that looking for valuable stuff of that nature, no appeal for police help possible, has its dangers, and that Dow may have found that out too late?"

"You can put it that way if you like," she told him. "Well?"

"I can assure you," Bobby went on, "we are already doing our best to find him. And Kenneth Banner, too. Always difficult, though, to find those who don't want to be found. England's an outsize haystack for needles to hide themselves in. If you can give us any help, we shall be very glad. Is there anyone, anything you suspect?"

"A man called Jordan. You know him, don't you? He's mixed up in it somehow. Mrs Adam may know something. I asked Ossy's landlady at Finchley if she had ever seen anyone like them or like Kenneth Banner either. She wasn't very sure, but she did say she thought there was a young man like I said in the 'George and Dragon' Monday evening."

"Miss Guire," Bobby said, "are you sure you have told us all you know? I think you are keeping a good deal back."

"Why should I?"

"There's such a thing as laying false trails, red herrings in the vernacular," Bobby answered. "Or telling part of the truth to hide the whole truth more effectively. You want me to believe you knew nothing about the smuggling that was going on. My suggestion is that, on the contrary, it was you who started it, who was behind it all."

"Oh," she said. She turned in her chair and stared at him long and intently, trying, he knew, to probe his inmost thoughts. "No," she said abruptly. "Why?"

"I've talked to all of you of the Banner Travel Agency," he told her slowly, "and I've got the clear impression that only you have the necessary brains, energy, initiative, to put through a scheme of this sort. Dow I take to be a bully, apt for violence if it seems safe, otherwise a small-time crook, but not the man to plan long-term crime."

"Is smuggling a crime?" she asked. "What harm is there in buying honestly a watch in Switzerland and selling it here at a fair rate of profit?"

"We won't discuss the ethics of defrauding the revenue, that is, the nation, either in income tax or smuggling," Bobby answered. "I'm not at the moment so much concerned with smuggling as with murder. That, at least, is a crime—the worst of crimes, even though murderers are not always the worst of criminals. It is a thing that can so easily be done."

CHAPTER XXXIII
IN HYDE PARK

FOR A TIME there was silence. It might almost have been thought that Imra had not heard those words Bobby had spoken so slowly, so quietly. Then she stood up. She did not attempt to walk away, but stood there entirely motionless, nor did she even look at Bobby. But he, watching her closely, felt that for once those dark and hidden depths of memory in which her spirit so often hid itself had been profoundly troubled, as though upon its surface a passing wind had blown. She sat down again.

"Herbert Abel?" she said. "Yes. Yes. Well?"

"I don't think," Bobby went on then, "from what I know of him, that he, any more than Dow, had the initiative or the capacity to plan any such elaborate fraud. I credit Kenneth Banner with both—brains and initiative—but not with the temperament. He might, in my judgment, very well let his temper run away with him, even betray him into violence. Stanley Foster has nothing to make him a leader in any way. His place would always be on the side-line. Though willing to pick up anything that came his way without too much risk. That leaves only you."

"Then you credit me," Imra asked, "with both—with intelligence and initiative? It is always interesting to know what other people think of you." She had recovered that composure which for a moment had seemed shaken, and her tone was light enough, though Bobby thought he could recognize the tense, underlying strain. She was still not looking at him. She seemed to be concentrating her attention on the scene before them, the long, grassy southern slope studded with people taking their ease in the afternoon sun and farther on the Serpentine, where the boats went to and fro, rowed by cheerful, unskilled oarsmen. She said, still not looking at him: "Do top-rank policemen often say things like this without anything to back it up, reasons, evidence? Or have you?"

"Evidence?" Bobby asked. "Not enough to satisfy me. We are talking confidentially—off the record as they say now. By your wish, not mine. May I ask you another question? You told me once you were thinking of marrying Mr Dow. If you have, and if you have a child, whose will that child be?"

"You ask too many things," she told him, her voice now slow and level. "I suppose you've noticed. I didn't expect you to. You are good at noticing. You are quite right. I am going to have a baby. At least, that's what the doctor thinks. Perhaps he's wrong. Time will show. The father—" She paused, and once again it seemed as if that cold dark reserve, so characteristic of her, was about to break down. Then: "My affair, not yours," she said.

"An investigating officer's job," Bobby told her, "is to find a pattern, the pattern, there is only one, into which every detail fits. Even selling jewellery and asking to be paid in cash, half in one-pound notes, suggests that you had pressing need of ready money for some special purpose. Apparently a cheque wouldn't do. Why?" She made no answer when he paused to allow her to reply if she wished. Already she was drawing back into the deep, hidden silence in which so often she sought refuge with her own thoughts and, Bobby thought, her own memories. He resumed: "There's one more question I must ask. You remember, perhaps, you told me once, and there is information that you made the same remark to a third person, that all the newspaper talk about an extremely elaborate meal Abel was said to have been preparing for his expected guest was all nonsense. That is correct. The menu the papers got hold of was picked up in the flat by one of our men. The reporters saw it, and jumped to the conclusion—through some misunderstanding perhaps, something said—that it referred to that night's supper. So the twopenny Sundays splashed it in the headlines. 'Death and the Banquet'. 'Lucullus at the fatal feast'. That sort of thing. But you knew that what was prepared and was ready on the table was something quite different. Smoked salmon. Fried chicken and apple fritters. How did you know that?"

"I suppose someone told me," she answered carelessly. "I don't remember. There was a lot of talk about it. No, I don't remember," she repeated. "Well!" and with this last word both challenge and defiance had come into her voice.

"Were you in the flat at any time on the night of the murder?"

"If I said 'Yes', you would call it a confession. If I said 'No', you wouldn't believe me."

"I have information now to the effect that a man and a woman were seen there that evening."

"Have you?" she said, as if not much interested, but watching him warily all the time. "Kenneth Banner and that girl of his—Doreen something? Was it?"

"There is nothing else you care to say?"

"I have said too much already," she retorted. "You won't get me to say more. Are you going to try to find out what's become of Mr Dow?"

"You may rest assured," Bobby told her formally, "that every possible step is being taken to find both him and Kenneth Banner. Sooner or later, of course, they will both be found. One or the other—or both—will then almost certainly be charged. If the Public Prosecutor agrees. If there is not enough evidence to connect them with Abel's death, then one of them may talk on the smuggling issue. It may happen that, even when the evidence seems at first too weak to support a verdict of guilty, what does come to light during the trial turns out to be enough. There is a starting point now in the information we have about the two people seen that night."

"I don't believe anyone saw anything," she retorted. "No one was there."

"Shall I ask you why you are so sure of that?"

"Because, of course," she answered readily, "if anyone had seen anything they would have done something, called for help, come forward long ago."

"Yet someone was there," Bobby repeated. "On the landing outside. Peeping through the door that wasn't quite shut."

"I don't believe it," she said loudly. "You are trying to bluff. Aren't you? All right. All right." Quite suddenly she began to talk in a low, rapid voice, at times running her words together as if she could not get them out fast enough, as though at last the flood-gates were open and the waters freed. "That door," she was saying, "it was open when we got there, just a little. A crack. Not latched. The latch hadn't caught. When we noticed we went in. Bert was there. He was lying on the ground all over blood, and his mouth was wide open, his mouth he had kissed me with and lied as he kissed. The day before Mrs Adam had come to see me, and she told me she was his wife and she wanted to find him to get her maintenance money. I thought I was his wife. We were married at a Registry Office. He gave a false name—Abel, not Adam. Still Biblical. I had let him have all my money my aunt left me. The usual trusting female fool. I mortgaged the house, too, and all the furniture. He had everything. You are wrong about it being all my idea. It was his in the first place—the smuggling, I mean. What I did was to go to France and make contacts with people there, get the thing into running order. I know French almost as well as English. Don't try to take notes of what I'm saying. If you do, I shan't say another word. I shall say you invented it all. We were making a lot of money, smuggling. Bert said when we had enough we would go to America. South America perhaps. But I found out there wasn't any. Money, I mean. He had spent it. One thing and another. In the West End. You can spend a lot of money there—night clubs and things. He had been betting, too. So then he told me he had done with me. The discarded glove. He said that, those very words. He said he had got a new girl. He wouldn't say who it was. I asked him, and he told me to shut up, and he kicked me out. I mean literally. He turned me round and pushed me to the door and kicked me so that I fell down on the landing, and I heard him laughing as I lay there, because I couldn't get up just at first. He banged the door and I went away. It was the time when Kenneth was beginning to be troublesome. I knew there was a plan fixed up between them—him and Ossy—to make Kenneth keep quiet. I didn't know exactly what it was, I didn't care. I kept thinking about Herbert and who it was he called his new girl. I believe now it was that Doreen Caine. It was her knowing about cooking that made him interested in her. She hasn't any looks or anything like that. But cooking was almost the only thing he cared about. He had a passion for it. Did you ever hear before of a man with a passion for cooking? He told me once there was a man cook who committed suicide because the fish was late for the dinner he was getting ready. I don't know if it's true, but he said he could quite understand it, he said he could feel like that himself. He tried to teach me. I can cook, but not what he meant by cooking. Cooking was to him what politics, power, money, music is for other people. Ossy was going to his flat—the one I was kicked out of—to fix it up about Kenneth. I went with him. He didn't want me to. I told him Herbert was meaning to keep the last lot we had got through for himself, and I had to be there because I knew what he meant to do and I could stop it. I don't know if Ossy believed me, but he let me come. I had a pistol I bought in France when I went there to make arrangements. I had to visit some queer places, and I got the pistol just in case. I never needed even to show it. I took it with me that night. I don't know what I meant to do. I didn't think about that. But I didn't mean to be kicked out again, and I meant to try to get some of my money back. I wasn't going to have him spending any more of it on Doreen Caine or whoever it was, and inside me I was all frozen up. I told you. On the way I told Ossy I was going to make Bert give me his share of the watches. It was by far the most valuable lot we had ever got through. When we got there the door wasn't properly fastened, and we went in. Ossy said: 'They've been fighting. Where's Kenneth?' There was a chair overturned, and the cushion had been torn open and the feathers all over everything, and he was lying there with his mouth open, and I picked up a handful of the feathers and I crammed them into his mouth, and I remember saying out loud: 'That'll stop you telling any more lies', and Ossy called to me to come and help him look for the watches, because he thought Kenneth must have taken them, but he would get them back. Afterwards he didn't think so. He told me Herbert had them hidden for fear the flat might be searched. Ossy went back to look at Herbert, and he said he was dead, and we must get away at once before anyone saw us, and I don't believe anyone ever did. Ossy said to leave the door open, and as soon as we had got away he would ring up and go on ringing and that would be an alibi. I don't know if he did."

"Most likely he changed his mind," Bobby said. "Wouldn't have been much of an alibi anyhow."

Imra got up again, and for a moment or two stood in silence by the side of her chair, staring absently before her. She said:

"If you tell anyone, I shall say you invented it all. Remember that."

"I'll remember," Bobby promised. Something, some obscure foreboding made him add: "At any rate, you have your child to live for."

"Or to die for?" she said.

Without waiting for a reply, she began to walk away while Bobby watched. She turned back. She said in a strange, wondering voice:

"Why have I told you what I did? I never meant to. I thought that I could fight you off. Why couldn't I?"

"There are some things that must be told," he answered. "Sooner or later, they must be told."

CHAPTER XXXIV
NO CORROBORATION

LONG AFTER Imra had vanished from his sight over the brow of the hill, on her way to the Marble Arch, Bobby remained sitting there, a sense of frustration and defeat heavy upon him.

For he felt that he knew well what Imra intended, and he could see no way to stop her. Doreen had defeated him by leaving him no alternative but either to watch her die before his eyes or allow Kenneth to go free. Now Imra had told him all he wanted to know, and to his mind at least had made it equally clear what she planned. But of what she had told him he could make no use, since at present anyhow, there was no corroboration, either of fact or word. What she had said to him could easily be denied, and certainly would be. For now that she had obtained relief from the intolerable burden of her secret, any new denial that she had to make would undoubtedly be given with force and conviction.

"Women," he told himself bitterly, "never play fair—stick the responsibility on you. 'Hit me if you dare, you great brute.' That sort of thing. Or else tell you all about it after making sure you can't use it."

Very discontentedly he went back to the Yard. There he dictated a full account of his talk with Imra, unnecessarily pointing out that in default of supporting evidence or other corroboration, it could not be used. Then he sent for Ford, to whom he gave a brief explanation of what his plans were.

"Altogether too many doors in this case," he said. "Kenneth Banner says if he left the door of Abel's flat open, it was because he didn't know what he was doing. According to Miss Guire—or Mrs Dow if they are really married—Dow wanted it left open because he meant to go on ringing up till he attracted attention with the idea that when the murder was discovered, he would have an alibi. Not a very good alibi, if you ask me, and most likely he began to think so himself, as he didn't carry it out. But why was the door of Jasper Jordan's flat left open the time I found Miss Caine in possession?"

"Well, sir," Ford answered, rather doubtfully, "all I can think of is that Jordan was expecting her and left the door like that when he went out, meaning to be back soon. Only he wasn't."

"Ye'es," Bobby said with hesitation. "It's an idea. But there are two things to remember. A car was seen waiting outside, and if it was waiting for Jordan, he can hardly have expected to be back at once to meet Miss Caine, and if it was for someone else—well, who? Then again, it's clear there was a bad scrap in Jordan's flat later on and that hardly fits in with the kidnapping theory. If anything of that sort happened, and then he escaped or was rescued the scrap should have been where he was held."

"There's another thing, sir, if I might say so," Ford put in rather hesitatingly, "there's only Miss Doreen's word for it that the flat door was open. My own idea is she's a young lady would lie the hind leg off a mule if she thought it would help her boy."

Bobby nodded in complete agreement.

"Women have no scruples," he pronounced. "Always put the particular before the general."

"Yes, sir," agreed Ford, wondering very much what this meant.

"The thing is," Bobby continued, "we've grounds now on which to charge Dow, but we've got to find him first. A slippery fish. And until we do find him and question him I don't see how we can hold Imra Guire, which is rather more than urgent. Because unless we can act quickly with her, I doubt whether we shall ever be able to. I shan't feel comfortable till we have her safely in our hands. The only way to save her life is to arrest her and charge her with murder. Queer, but there it is."

"Yes, sir," agreed Ford, still wondering what Bobby meant.

They talked a little longer, Bobby explaining in more detail what was in his mind, aware, too, that he had been expecting a little too much in thinking that Ford, who had not been present at the Hyde Park talk, would understand what it was he feared. So then Ford went off, and Bobby rang up Mr Pyne at his flat to ask if he might pay him a brief visit at once for another little chat. Mr Pyne, in his new lisping voice, agreed, though without any marked enthusiasm. So Bobby departed to find a convenient 'bus, and on arrival the door was opened to him by Mr Pyne himself, still showing signs of wear, but with repairs evidently making good progress.

Bobby expressed his gratitude to Mr Pyne for being always so ready to co-operate, and Mr Pyne looked equally pleased by this compliment and doubtful of it. As soon as they were seated and Bobby had accepted a cigarette and declined a drink, he began.

"You remember," he said, "that when we had our last talk you told me you must think things over before saying more. I had been rather hoping to hear from you."

Mr Pyne did not respond to this opening. He remained silent, placed his finger-tips together, and regarded Bobby thoughtfully. Finally, he said:

"The conclusion I eventually arrived at is that substantial reasons, but I hope not entirely unworthy reasons, compel me to remain silent for probably another twenty-four hours. That period of time elapsed, I shall be at your service." He gave a little regretful sigh. "I am commencing to look back," he admitted, "with a certain nostalgia on an earlier daily routine in which one was seldom confronted with such contingencies as seem inseparable from visits by officers of police. Even my daughter appears now to be inclined to believe that respectability has advantages, hitherto perhaps too lightly regarded. A—tip is, I think, the usual word—a tip to her that I may soon be relieved of my responsibilities at the Ministry and consequently take to drink seems, paradoxically, to have had a sobering effect."

"Oh, I hope it won't come to that," Bobby said. "I don't see why it should. But I'm afraid I can't wait that long—or at all for that matter. I have information now that seems to implicate a man named Dow—Ossy Dow. He may be married to a Miss Imra Guire. I don't know about that, but if he is she won't be able to give evidence against him unless she wants to, which isn't likely. Complicates things, and makes it all the more urgent to find Dow as soon as possible."

"Am I to understand that in your opinion he may be the murderer?"

"I said 'implicated'," Bobby reminded him. "The way we like to put it is that we think he may be able to help. A really large-scale search has been going on. Without much success, so far. I am hoping that to-night—but I mustn't go into that. May be all wrong, what I'm working on. There's something else I wanted to ask. You remember telling me that after the attack on you here, you got yourself a pistol as a protection against anything of the sort happening again. I believe our people here didn't think that necessary, refused to issue you a certificate, and kept the pistol?"

"Officialdom and red tape at its worst," Mr Pyne pronounced.

"That's the worst of a uniformed body," Bobby admitted sadly. "Goes to the head somehow—a uniform. So different when everyone wears civvies to remind them they are just citizens like the rest of us. Human nature no doubt. Never mind. And I seem to remember I suggested that possibly you had provided yourself with one through the help of a gentleman who likes to call himself an enemy of society and likes, I think, to give a helping hand at times to rather different enemies of society?"

"You were very perspicuous," Mr Pyne complained. "All the same a mere hypothesis. I consider it irregular in the extreme to formulate hypotheses so insecurely based."

"Hypothesis indeed," Bobby protested indignantly. "A logical deduction from observed facts. No guesswork about it."

"Guesswork," repeated Mr Pyne with unexpected firmness. "I have no such weapon in my possession. I give you my full and free permission to search every room here. You will find nothing."

"Because, after what happened at Jordan's flat, you thought it just as well to throw it into the river from Westminster bridge?"

This time Mr Pyne fairly jumped.

"How did you—?" he began, and then paused. "More hypothesis," he said. "Guesswork," he insisted, feeling apparently now that he must not apply so dignified a word to a process so irregular.

"Never mind that," Bobby said, and did not stop to explain that this time it was neither guessing nor deduction from fact, but merely the knowledge born of experience that those in London who want to get rid of compromising possessions generally drop them into the Thames from a handy bridge, and that Westminster bridge, as the one nearest to Whitehall, that home—or fortress rather—of officialdom was the one most likely to be familiar to Mr Pyne.

Wise of him not to explain, for this last display of unexpected knowledge had shaken Mr Pyne badly, as was indeed the whole object of Bobby's visit.

"I suppose," Mr Pyne was saying now, not without a faint trace of complacence in his voice, "you have had me trailed, as is, I apprehend, your custom with the more dangerous gangsters. My colleagues, if they knew—" He left that remark unfinished.

"I have heard," Bobby remarked—and knew he shouldn't, but simply couldn't help—"of objects thrown over bridges into the river falling plump into boats passing underneath and then being handed over to the police."

With that parting shot he went away, leaving Mr Pyne still more shaken, contemplating with ever-rising dismay the ever-rising waters into which he had so rashly ventured. And outside Bobby was saying to himself.

"Now, will it work? Is Pyne busy at the 'phone? If only they weren't so sticky in this country about tapping 'phones, what an awful lot we should get to know. But sticky's the word, sticky to the last state of stickiness and beyond."

CHAPTER XXXV
SEARCH WARRANT

LATER ON that evening, once more Bobby, Ford in attendance, descended the area steps to Jordan's flat, that now it seemed—

though Bobby was as yet by no means sure how or to what extent—had become the focus of all that followed upon the smuggling activities of the crew of the 'As You Like It'.

"A misnomer to call their yacht the 'As You Like It'," Bobby had commented to Ford earlier that evening. "Not at all as they or anyone else likes it. I don't suppose any of them ever expected it was going to lead to all this."

"If we are able to pick up Miss Guire," Ford asked doubtfully, "have we enough to hold her on?"

"I'm jolly well going to make it enough," Bobby declared with all the emphasis at his command. "Short of committing perjury or too bare-faced faking of evidence, I intend to be as devoid of scruple as any female woman that ever lived."

"Yes, sir," said Ford, turning pale at such deliberate defiance of all he had been taught and trained to regard as sacrosanct.

"When it's a case of saving a damn-fool woman's life or trying to—" said Bobby, and lapsed into a silence Ford did not dare disturb.

Now Ford was banging at the door of Jordan's flat. Bobby was close behind, urging him to greater and ever-greater efforts. No result, except for a small crowd beginning to gather on the pavement above and at once moved on by a uniform man suddenly and unexpectedly emerging from the unknown. All the same, Bobby knew well enough there were people behind that so obstinately closed door, for a careful watch had been kept, and two figures seen slipping through the evening shades, disappearing down those area steps to be at once admitted, and not seen to leave again. So he did not feel inclined to continue too long this contest of endurance between hammering at a door and a determination to lie low. He took his card from his pocket, wrote on it: 'I have a search warrant. If the door is not opened at once, it will be broken in', signed it, and poked it through the letter-slit provided when the basement qualified as a flat.

"We'll give them five minutes," Bobby said, fairly certain the dropping of the card on the stone floor of the passage within would be heard in the silence following the sudden cessation of

Ford's knocking, and that one of those present would come to see what had been left.

Nor had more than a minute or two elapsed when they heard cautious footsteps approaching and then retreating.

"Considering it," Bobby commented. "Well, we'll give them the full five minutes. Then one final knock, and after that we shall have to take it they mean to go on playing the fool."

But the final knock was not required, for the door opened and appeared a scowling, angry and—or so Bobby thought—a very uncomfortable and disturbed Jordan.

"What is it now?" he growled with a not too successful attempt to regain his earlier defiant truculence. "I've not been well, not at all well. The doctor says I must have peace and quiet, and then you come hammering and banging all the time. What do you want?"

"Well, for one thing," Bobby answered, "I want Kenneth Banner." He raised his voice: "I think you are here, Mr Banner, aren't you?"

Jordan grumbled something inaudible, turned, and trailed dispiritedly up the passage. Bobby followed into that front room, former kitchen, he and Ford had visited before. Jordan said:

"He knows you're here, Banner. Spotted it somehow—all ears and eyes that fellow."

"Mr Pyne, too, I expect," Bobby said, and in fact both of them were standing there like two schoolboys caught smoking by the unexpected visit of the headmaster. "Good evening, Mr Banner. Mr Pyne I've seen before to-night. I've been looking for Mr Banner a very long time and for a certain young lady I was rather hoping might be here, too."

"Well, she isn't," Kenneth said. "Thank heaven," he added. "You can leave her out of it."

"Oh, I meant the other one," Bobby explained, and Kenneth looked blank, as if he could not very well conceive the idea of there being anyone in all the world but Doreen. "I knew Miss Caine wasn't here," Bobby added. "Doing a lecture on the right way to boil eggs or something of the sort. And thankful I am she's not here to do any more of her blackmailing tricks, if you remember."

"Remember," Kenneth almost shouted, a whole battery of exclamation marks following the word. "Good God, I dream of it still. I always shall, I think. She would have done it, too. If she had . . ." He paused, the memory of that awful moment still strong upon him. He said: "If she had, I should have killed you."

"Well, I'm glad it didn't come to that," Bobby remarked. "Don't see what good that would have done, though. You want to keep that temper of yours more under control. If you had, that night at Mayfair Crescent, none of this would have happened."

"How did you know we were here?" put in Pyne, who was looking very uneasy and depressed. "You always know it all, don't you?"

"My job would be a lot easier if I did," Bobby retorted. "Just a matter of trying to—to frame a suitable hypothesis to cover probable reaction. To guess, that is, what you would be likely to do when I had let you see I was getting near the bone. Fairly certain your first idea would be to tell your—shall I say pals, accomplices, or colleagues?—about it, and what had you all better do? So we just came along to sit in at the conference."

"Simple, the way you put it," Mr Pyne commented resentfully.

"My greatest fault," Bobby admitted. "Explaining. Takes all the glamour away, the credit, too. Never explain. The last words of Solomon on his death-bed, I'm told."

"It's one of his little tricks," Kenneth remarked from behind. "Makes you feel a fool for not seeing it before. Gets you down, so you'll talk. Doreen put me on."

"I'm getting," Bobby confessed, "to dislike that girl more and more day by day. I'm sorry for any man who marries her." Kenneth scowled, but didn't quite know what to say, and Bobby was already continuing: "But just at the moment I'm not so much interested in her as in another young woman—Imra Guire. Tell me. Do you want me to take the three of you into custody to be held for questioning on suspicion of being concerned in smuggling, or are you willing to talk?"

"Depends entirely on what you mean by talking," answered Kenneth, who seemed now to have constituted himself the spokesman and leader of the party.

"I want to know what you can tell me about Miss Guire," Bobby said. "I am more than anxious to get in touch with her. I believe it's urgent I should."

All three of them looked blank. Kenneth waited for a moment, as if to give either of the others a chance to speak, and then said:

"I don't think any of us know anything about her. I'm sure I don't. Why should you think we do?"

"You're on the wrong track this time," Jordan put in. "It was Mrs Adam I gave the dispatch-case to. A boy left it here. Abel sent him. With a message it belonged to a friend who might want it soon, and he couldn't leave it where he lived, because he was often away. I had no idea the thing was stuffed with smuggled watches. How could I? It was only after you came poking about I began to think it was all a bit fishy. I didn't want to get mixed up in it if it was, so I gave it to Abel's widow. That's all. Anything wrong in that?"

"I knew all that," Bobby said. "Mrs Adam has handed the dispatch-case over to us. She also offered some useful information. She claims to have been an eye-witness of part, at least, of what happened on the night of the murder. She saw a man and a woman. There are two women concerned that I know of—Miss Guire and Miss Caine. Two young ladies remarkably like each other, and at the same time remarkably unlike. If it was the first of those two Mrs Adam saw, then probably the man with her would be Ossy Dow. If it was Miss Caine, her companion would presumably be Mr Banner."

"Doreen was never near the place," Kenneth asserted emphatically. "I can swear to that."

"A partial witness, I'm afraid," Bobby said, "and without complete knowledge. On his own showing in no fit state for accurate observation. None of you can tell me more? No. Well, then, tell me, what was it happened here, and why. I mean on the evening when Mr Pyne let a pistol off by accident or design"—as he spoke Bobby was pointing to the bullet hole still visible in the ceiling—"and incidentally lost two front teeth."

"Nothing happened," Jordan said, "except that Mr Pyne was showing me his pistol—small automatic it was—and I was telling him to put the damn thing away because he didn't know how to handle it, when he managed to trip up over that hole in the linoleum. The pistol went off, and in trying to recover himself he hit himself such a smack against the table he was clean knocked out. And lost two teeth."

"A most convincing tale," Bobby said drily. "I wonder if Mr Pyne and Mr Banner would be willing to confirm it on oath. There are still some people who rather jib at perjury. Old fashioned no doubt. Well, what about Mr Dow? Was he present when Mr Pyne had that unlucky accident? If so, is there any connection with Mr Jordan's recent visit to an unnamed seaside resort?"

"Why should there be?" Jordan growled. "No friend of mine. Never heard of him till the other day."

"I think," Bobby said. "I must have a look round—to satisfy myself as we like to say. Any of you care to say anything?"

There was no attempt to answer that directly. Kenneth said: "I knew that was coming."

"It'll all come out now," said Pyne. "The termination of my career, but I shan't take to drink."

"Oh, all right, all right," Jordan said. "Poke about as much as you like."

"I may as well tell you," Bobby said. "I have two of my men at the head of the area steps, and two more at the back door."

CHAPTER XXXVI
INCREDIBLE SCENE

WHATEVER BOBBY had expected to see, whatever dark thoughts had been lurking at the back of his mind, however fearful his misgivings, he was absolutely and totally unprepared for what he now saw as—leaving the front room of this basement flat, where so far his keenest scrutiny had been able to detect nothing in any way suspicious—he, Ford following him, entered the second, the back room.

For in the common phrase, this time almost literally true, they could hardly believe their own eyes. It is a moot point indeed who stared the hardest—he or Ford; whose eyes were opened the widest; who looked the most utterly and helplessly taken aback.

"Just a practical joke," announced Jordan from behind.

"Oh," said Bobby, and that was all that for the moment he felt able to get out.

"Prac—prac—practical joke," gasped Ford, and that was all he managed to get out for his part before he, too, subsided into silence.

For what they saw was that the tall narrow oaken cupboard Bobby remembered having seen before was now lying flat on the floor, the clothing it had previously contained heaped in a nearby corner. The top of the cupboard had been hinged, re-moved, replaced, a hole had been cut in it, and through this hole protruded, supported on a dirty pillow, the head of a man, of Ossy Dow, his mouth covered by a strip of surgical tape so that he could utter no sound.

"Practical joke," Bobby repeated angrily, recovering quick-ly from his momentarily dazed condition. "We'll see about that. Get him out of there at once. And hurry." As he spoke he crossed to the helpless victim and removed the surgical tape. He said: "It won't be my fault if you three don't get a few months in gaol to correct your sense of humour. Ford, 'phone for an ambu-lance and a doctor."

"My 'phone's not working," Jordan said. "Got damaged when Mr Pyne had his accident, and they haven't sent to repair it yet."

"There's a call box quite near," Ford said, and disappeared.

"Practical joke," Jordan repeated as he and Kenneth began to obey Bobby's order of release. "Wasn't it?" he appealed to the hapless Ossy.

"That's right," came Ossy's response—rather feebly uttered, but clear enough. "Practical joke—pushed it too far, that's all."

"We'll see what they think of that in court," Bobby retorted.

"I'm not prosecuting," Ossy said, by now removed from his strait and narrow prison and helped to lie down on the truckle bed by the window. "I'm all right. I don't want an ambulance. I don't want a doctor. I don't want police nosing round. All friends here." He glared at Jordan, at Kenneth, at Mr Pyne, and it would be impossible to say at which of them he glared with the deepest fiercest hate and rage and fury: "I want a drink."

"Yes, of course you do," Jordan said hospitably. "Sorry," and he bustled off accordingly to get one. "That's right," he said over his shoulder as he went. "All friends together." He was back again almost at once, while Bobby was still endeavouring to adjust his thoughts to this new development, these unexpected declarations of amity. Jordan was bringing a bottle of whisky and a syphon of soda-water. He poured out a generous portion of whisky, added a little soda, gave it to Ossy and said: "Score even, and no hard feelings on either side. Eh?"

"None," agreed Ossy, putting down his empty glass and looking more than ever charged to explosion point with fury, rage, and hate.

"It was him began it, fixed me that way, he did, just the same," Jordan explained to Bobby, still slightly bewildered by this incredible scene. "Me first, and then him, and it was him fixed the cupboard, hinged lid and all, so your head went through and nothing you could do, held in a vice, and his surgical tape I used as they did on me. Turn and turn about so to say, and that's fair all the world over. And," Jordan added, "for all the help you were, Mr Clever Detective, I might have stayed there till I rotted."

"That's right," said Ossy, viciously as ever. "Till he rotted."

"Was it part of the practical joke that he should?" Bobby asked. He produced his note-book. "I want full details," he said.

"You can put that thing away," Ossy growled. He seemed better now, stronger and apparently little the worse for his confinement. "You'll get nothing in writing."

"You've no witnesses," Jordan put in. "We aren't saying anything. All over and done with. And you can't make us. Nobody can be forced to answer questions tending to incriminate him.

And if we don't speak we can't be cross-examined. If there's anything in this smuggling story of yours—I don't know—go and talk to Mrs Adam, Abel, whatever she calls herself."

Bobby meekly put his note-book back in his pocket. Not the first time he had known its production scare witnesses into stolid silence.

"Suppose you tell me what really happened," he suggested. "Then I shall know better what to do. At present my idea is to take all of you—including Miss Caine—into custody on a charge of complicity in murder, in smuggling, and I expect a few other little things."

"No magistrate would commit, no evidence," Jordan declared. "I'll undertake the defence of us all. I'll knock your evidence endways out of hand. Not that you've got any. None of us will say a word, and you can't make us I told you. No one can be asked to reply to questions tending to incriminate himself. None of us knew anything about the smuggling, and you can't show we did. All Abel's doing. I was an innocent bailee of the dispatch-case. I had, and could have had, no knowledge of what was in it. Same with Abel's murder. If you got Mrs Adam into the box, she couldn't identify anyone, and in half a minute's cross-examination I could get her so tied up she wouldn't know what she was saying, and the jury would be thinking it was her who was really guilty."

"Tell him," Kenneth urged, "what really happened about Dow. We don't want any publicity," and it was clear he was thinking of Doreen. "If you don't, I will."

"Publicity," observed Mr Pyne in this thin, dispassionate way, "would mean the immediate end of my connection with the Ministry," and in that last word there was a note such as a man might use in speaking of his lost love. "Serve me right for not knowing when I was well off."

"O.K.," growled Jordan. "I have noticed in Mr Owen from time to time rare gleams of decency and common sense such as are most unusual in anyone connected with the police, puppets of the law that they are."

"And it won't do any harm," Bobby informed him tartly, "if you try for once to keep a decently civil tongue in your head. Persistent rudeness is such a give away, don't you think? Bad inferiority complex and all that."

"Jargon," Jordan retorted. "The day's jargon, that's all. Inferiority nothing." All the same, the remark had its effect, for it was in a much less truculent tone that he continued: "As for Dow. Thick headed, poor chap. Can't help it. He got it into his thick, thickest head I had those watches he was chasing around. So he took me for a ride. I went on my own without a word of protest, just as if I had been sandbagged. As if, remember. I'm not saying I was. It might have been when I turned my back for a moment. Left the door open when we went off in the car Dow had waiting, and then you came along as usual—you always do, don't you? always come along as and when not wanted."

"Part of my job," Bobby explained. "Especially as and when not wanted."

"'Conducted a thorough examination of flat, found nothing in any way suspicious'. That's what you wrote in your report, wasn't it?" Jordan went on. "So Dow had the idea to come back, me and all, tied up I was, and surgical tape over my mouth. Got that cupboard ready the way it is and popped me in. I could move, wriggle a bit, but not enough to get any leverage. Quite helpless, and two nails fixed so if I wriggled too much they ran into my neck, the more the wriggle the deeper they ran. So I didn't much. Ossy's idea was to starve me out till I told him what I didn't know—where the watches were—and what I did with the dispatch-case. Told me I wouldn't get anything to eat or drink till I talked. Well, I didn't and I didn't—didn't talk and didn't get any food or drink. Dirty trick, though, to cook sausages in the same room so I could smell 'em."

"Dirty trick indeed," Bobby agreed. "I'm beginning to wish I hadn't been in such a hurry to let Mr Dow out of this contraption of his, if it was all his own invention."

"We never meant to keep it up," Dow protested. "I was just going to let him out when those three set on me. And all the time he only had to say who had them. Kidding himself he was protecting a woman as likely as not. Showing off."

"I have no feeling about women," Jordan almost shouted. "Mantraps. That's all they are. Walking man-traps. I didn't choose. That's all. Fixed me up safe as in my coffin, they had. Smart idea, though, to put me back in my own flat when they knew it had been looked through and seen empty."

"Oh, all the brains aren't in the police," boasted Ossy. "You agree?" he asked Bobby, with something of his old impudence.

"Were the brains yours or Imra Guire's?" Bobby asked him, and turning to Jordan, he added: "You've said 'they' and 'we'. Dow and Miss Guire, I suppose?"

"Suppose 'As You Like It', same as their yacht," Jordan retorted. "Banner and the Caine man-trap that's got him, have brains, too—not so much Banner. It's the other half—nine-tenths I mean—has them."

"Doreen thought it out where he might be," Kenneth confirmed. "When we started to wonder what had become of him. I said to leave him where he was. Why hurry? But she would have it for us to come along here at once to see. Beat you by a short head, Mr Owen. I suppose you had been thinking it out on the same lines. Half an hour later, and there wouldn't have been a trace of us. Mr Pyne insisted on joining in the show. Rigged himself up as a postman. Our trouble was how to get the door open. Easy for you, but no search warrants for us. If Jordan were still fixed up in that box thing, he couldn't, and if Ossy were there, as we thought likely, he mightn't want. So we worked the postman idea. Shouted through the letter-box there was a registered letter. We didn't want Mr Pyne to come in, but he jolly well would. Great old sport, Pyne."

Mr Pyne blushed as never he had blushed before, nor ever dreamed he could.

"My daughter procured me the postman's uniform," he explained hurriedly, as if anxious no more should be said on the subject of his alleged sportsmanship. "She is a member of an Amateur Dramatic Society."

207 | STRANGE ENDING

"Dow fell for the registered-letter stunt," Kenneth went on. "When he opened the door we rushed him. He dodged back into the front room. Quite a lively little do while it lasted. Pyne got the worst of it. Laid out flat, and his damn pistol went off. As near as possible got me. Then Dow and I had a set-to. He has a good idea of boxing, but out of training, out of practice. Left himself wide open, and I got home. A K.O. By the time he came round we had found Mr Jordan in that contraption Dow had rigged up. So we shoved Dow in instead, just to let him see what it was like. But we fed him all right. Slops," said Kenneth, with a faint reminiscent smile. "Through a straw. You ought to have heard him curse. A liberal education in itself."

"All highly irregular," Mr Pyne admitted. "But we were all averse from prosecuting. We felt it would lead to unnecessary and indeed most regrettable publicity. In my considered view, so long as we adhere to the extremely plausible story we have— er—concocted, there is no charge that can be formulated with any prospect of its being accepted. This, of course, implies that we shall enjoy the co-operation of Mr Dow, whose not unnatural resentment over recent occurrences may be modified by the fact that he has probably more to apprehend from the operation of the law than have we."

"Yah," said Mr Dow, or words to that effect. But having finished saying it, he added: "O.K. That goes with me, too."

Bobby was inclined to agree that with no direct evidence available, with indeed all those concerned having only one desire—to keep out of court—there was not much chance of a successful prosecution. Nor did he feel there was any reason for bothering too much about what Jordan and Dow had been doing to each other. If they were ready to leave things as they were—well all right. For his part, he did not see why the law should wish to intervene. But of course it would all be carefully considered on the basis of the full report he would submit, and the final decision would rest with the lawyers, not with the police.

His meditations were interrupted by the sudden return of Ford with a doctor and two ambulance men.

"Not wanted," roared Jordan indignantly.

"I'm all right," said Dow, who, however, hardly looked it.

"Never again," said Mr Pyne, waking from meditation as profound as Bobby's, "never again anything for me but the Ministry in the morning and back home at night, and thank God for it. A secure, tranquil, and regular way of life has many overwhelming advantages not invariably fully realized by those whose privilege it is to enjoy them."

"Oh, stow it," Jordan interrupted.

"There's still one little matter of murder you seem to have forgotten," Bobby observed. He turned to Dow. "Where is Imra Guire? She's not been home since I saw her last."

CHAPTER XXXVII
CONCLUSION

THERE WAS a long pause. Ossy was clearly very reluctant to answer. He was trying, as it were, to stare Bobby down. Not an easy task. For Bobby was waiting—not so much with unending patience, as with determination, that silent, unending determination, which, before this, more than once, by sheer force of will, had made reluctant witnesses speak. Then Ossy muttered:

"How should I know?"

"You and she are married, aren't you?"

"Well, suppose we are?"

"I'm not supposing anything," Bobby told him quietly. "Except that a husband generally has some knowledge of his wife's movements."

"Not when it's Imra," Ossy muttered sullenly. "You never know where you are with her. There's a devil in her. Doesn't give a damn what you say. Lets you talk as if you weren't worth even listening to. And if you make so much as to lift a hand—knife you as soon as look at you. If it's one, why not two?"

"What does that mean?" Bobby asked.

"Nothing," Ossy said, and repeated: "Nothing at all." Then he said: "Married we are, and can't be made give evidence against each other."

"Is that why you married her?" Bobby asked, but Ossy only scowled and did not reply. Bobby said again: "Where is she?"

"No idea, I told you," Ossy muttered, and then, when Bobby still waited, he said reluctantly: "I did hear her say something about Birmingham."

"Birmingham?" Bobby repeated, surprised. "Why? Has she friends there?"

"She got to hear about a first-class doctor there. She had an idea she might go and consult him. I don't know why." He paused, and when he saw how Bobby was looking at him, he said hurriedly: "A psychiatrist."

It was what Bobby had feared ever since the talk in Hyde Park, but what also he had seen no way to prevent or even hinder. He turned to Ford and said:

"Carry on here. I must get busy. Too late, I expect."

Therewith he hurried away.

But by now it was too late in the evening for any effective action to be taken. An urgent call to Birmingham was answered however by a promise that everything possible would be done.

"Not much to go on," Birmingham said. "Of course, we know places like you say where she might be. But even if by good luck we hit on the right one, they've only got to deny it, and we're stuck. Have to be careful, too. Some of them as soon as they saw us would be quite equal to dumping her somewhere handy out of the way. Know nothing about it if she's picked up dead. Even if we traced her there—well, she insisted on leaving, and they couldn't stop her. That would be their story. We've had one case like that. Can we say we are acting on the request of the husband, who is extremely anxious?"

"Oh, yes," Bobby answered at once. "Certainly. You can certainly say that," and as he hung up he reflected that if Ossy wasn't anxious, he ought to be—and probably was for that matter, though not on Imra's account.

News of success in the Birmingham search came, however, more quickly than Bobby had dared to anticipate, for in the middle of the morning next day he was rung up with the information that a woman answering to the description given had been admitted to hospital late the previous evening. Those who brought her had managed to slip away in the bustle of admission at that time of night without leaving name or address. The car in which they came had been identified as taken from outside a night club and returned without the owner knowing anything about it. The patient had been put at once on the danger list. Though conscious, she was maintaining an obstinate silence, nor was she in any condition to be pressed to answer questions.

As soon as train and car could take him there, Bobby reached the hospital, where a doctor told him at once that there was little hope.

"These illegal operations are tantamount to suicide," the doctor added. "Or murder if you like. Make 'em legal and let us do them in proper conditions, and a good many lives would be saved. As it is, well, almost sentence of death."

"There may be other considerations," Bobby said. "Two lives involved, and who is the judge? whose the responsibility? But in this case I think death was probably hoped for and expected."

"Well, that's what it is this time anyhow," the doctor grumbled, as he handed Bobby over to a nurse who had been sent for, and who took him to the ward where Imra was lying. She was awake and fully conscious, and she even managed a faint, fleeting smile when she saw who it was. But a smile in which there was now no trace of those dark secret meanings, known only to herself—even if fully to herself—at which before they had seemed to hint.

"I half-expected you," she said, "as soon as I knew those people had let me down, brought me here. Was that you, too? Did they know you might have guessed? I suppose you did after Hyde Park?"

"I was afraid that was what you wanted your £200 for," Bobby said.

"Not too much to pay for death," she told him. "Most get death free. I had to pay."

"You may still recover," he told her, but she shook her head, though so feebly it seemed she had hardly the strength to move it.

"None of us ever meant all this," she went on reflectively, he having to bend nearer to catch what she was saying. "I suppose people never do. Things just happen once they have begun. Bert wasn't bad, not really bad bad. He never meant it either. Things just got all mixed up, and he had to do something. It wasn't his fault he was born so women couldn't keep their heads with him. There was something about him—God knows what. Or the devil. You went all weak inside, and you knew you had to go to him. You didn't know why, but you just had. It wasn't love. Was it hate? It turned to that. What's the good of talking? It's all over now."

"You are young enough to have lived," Bobby said, a little sadly. "Perhaps you will. You should have lived."

But at that her strength seemed to come back to her, to return for one brief and vivid moment. With a fierce, sudden, unexpected effort, she sat upright in bed.

"Do you think," she cried, and her voice was loud and clear and strong, so that all could hear, "I wanted to live to bear the child of the man I killed?"

They were her last spoken words.

THE END

GOOD BEGINNING

Originally published in the Evening Standard, *1 August, 1950*

"CASE OF suicide, name of Ben Allen, 19, Whippet Buildings," said the Station Sergeant as Constable Bobby Owen came in that evening to report off duty. "Cut along and relieve Jenkins. Inspector Morris will be there presently to give it the once over."

"Body's been removed so all you have to do is to see nothing's touched or moved. I'll send a relief as soon as I can, but with all this influenza going about I don't know where I'm going to get one. Hurry along."

Bobby went off obediently. Hard lines after an eight hour tour of duty when supper and bed had been shining so brightly on the distant horizon of his thoughts. But there it was. Things were like that in the police. It was the first piece of really serious police work that had come Owen's way in his total of six months' service. It had been early closing day to-day and so walking his beat was even a more dull occupation than usual.

He knew Whippet Buildings well. Very respectable tenants on the whole, most of them in good employment. He had never had any trouble there. At No. 19 Constable Jenkins was waiting for him.

"All you have to do is to sit tight till the Inspector turns up," Jenkins explained again, for Bobby was a new man and new men have to be told things. "Tell the Inspector that's the list of all articles found on deceased's person. He'll want to check it probably."

Bobby glanced carelessly at the table where lay the dead man's belongings: a bunch of keys, a pen-knife, a folding 2ft. rule, two one pound notes, three half-crowns, four florins, one shilling, five sixpenny pieces, and some coppers, a handkerchief, two railway tickets, singles, to Sheffield, a few used tramcar and bus tickets, other odds and ends of one sort and another.

"Was it gas?" Bobby asked, sniffing the air.

"That's right," Jenkins answered. "Head in oven. His wife found him when she got back from work. Seems Allen had been carrying on with a Mrs. Clements and Mrs. Allen told him he had to choose and now was his chance because of being offered a good job at Sheffield. Upset him, not knowing which, so he took the easy way out."

"Not so easy as all that," Bobby commented.

"Well, he filled himself up with gin first," Jenkins explained, nodding towards a nearly empty bottle on the mantelpiece. "Smelt nearly as strong as the gas when we got in here."

"No glass," Bobby remarked.

"In the sink." Jenkins explained. "Rinsed it out seemingly and left it there to dry. Wanted to leave everything nice and tidy. Funny the things suicides do. Cheery-oh for now."

With that not altogether appropriate farewell, Jenkins departed and Bobby, left alone the little flat, went into the kitchen.

In the sink a glass was standing. Rinsed and left there to dry apparently, as Jenkins had said.

Near by stood unwashed tea things. The unhappy man had evidently had a solitary tea, before priming himself with gin. Bobby's nose assured him that gin had not been taken with the tea, and for some minutes he stood there, thinking, vaguely uneasy.

He went back into the sitting-room, and looked again at the collection of articles taken from the dead man's pockets. His vague, faint feeling of uneasiness increased.

From the landing outside came the sound of angry voices raised in dispute. Women quarrelling apparently. He opened the door and when the little group of flushed and angry-looking women saw him standing there, they dispersed. One, he noticed, let herself into the opposite flat.

When they had all gone, Bobby retired, but soon a knock came. He went to answer it and saw standing there the woman he had noticed going back into the flat opposite. She was holding out a handbag.

"It's Mrs. Clements's," she said. "You had better have it. I don't want to have anything to do with her."

"Mrs. Clements?" Bobby repeated. "Oh, yes. It's because of leaving her Mr. Allen got so depressed, wasn't it?"

The woman snorted indignantly.

"If you ask me," she said, "he was only too glad of a chance to get away from her."

"Well, then, what made him commit suicide?" Bobby asked.

"Because of being so ashamed of the way he treated his wife," she answered promptly, "and her as good a wife as any man ever had, and I don't mind who hears me say so, if she is my sister."

"I'm sorry," Bobby said. "Didn't they get on well together?"

"They did till that Clements slut got her claws into him," she answered with dark anger in her voice and eyes. "That was when he took to drink and her encouraging him all the time at the Red Lion where they met because she knew it was the only way she could keep him, drinking together.

"A wicked, wicked shame, and him with a good wife and home waiting. No wonder he put his head in a gas oven and if it had been me I would have put it there for him long ago."

And then she saw how he was looking at her for she had spoken with a sudden fierce energy that startled him. For a moment they were both silent. But not surprising, Bobby reflected, that she spoke with such heat.

"Had they been drinking together to-day, do you think?" he asked.

"He was sober enough, and not a smell of drink on him," she answered, "last time I saw him. He knocked to ask if I could give him a shilling for two sixpences to put in the gas ready to boil some water for tea for Carrie—that's my sister—when she got back. He had had his, he said."

"I noticed that," Bobby said. "The tea things are there." He was still holding the handbag she had given him. "How did you come to have it?" he asked.

"She had the impudence to say she wanted to tell me how sorry she was about it all. Came knocking at the door, the cheek of her, and walked in before I could say a word. If you ask me, she wanted to get round me the way she gets round people, so I wouldn't say anything about her and how she had been carrying on. We got to having words and I told her to get out and she must have forgot her bag answering back."

"Do you think she was really fond of him?" Bobby asked.

"She wanted him awful bad, if that's being fond of him," the woman retorted. "She was one as couldn't get on without a man. Well, that's natural. You couldn't blame her for that. Only it didn't ought to be another woman's man, lawful wedded for years, as she tried to get."

"No, it oughtn't," Bobby agreed, and the conversation ended.

But he was more thoughtful than ever as he went back into the little sitting-room, standing there, staring alternately at the nearly empty bottle of gin and at the things spread out on the table.

A loud knocking came at the door. He went to answer it. A tall woman was there, well built, good looking, rather flushed and a little untidy.

"You've got my handbag," she said. "I want it."

"You are Mrs. Clements?" Bobby asked.

"Yes," she said. "I forgot it and the lady opposite says she gave it you. Like her cheek and I only hope my money's all right. It's got my pay packet in it."

What made Bobby hesitate, he hardly knew. No harm surely in returning a handbag to its owner. Yet some vague feeling of dissatisfaction made him say:

"Sorry, madam, I am afraid I must ask you to wait till the Inspector comes. He won't be long."

"What for?" she asked angrily. "It's my handbag, isn't it? You've no right to keep it."

"Regulations," Bobby explained amiably. "Lost property."

"It's got my money in it," she protested. "My pay packet. I want it. Four pound notes and four shillings except for one shilling I spent after I got home, and now I want another for the gas."

"I could lend you one for that," Bobby offered, "till the Inspector comes."

She still protested and with vigour. Bobby remained firm. Finally she accepted his shilling though with bad grace and went off muttering threats of complaints to be made to the Inspector when he arrived.

Nor was it long before that gentleman was knocking at the door of the flat. He did not look too pleased as he came in.

"New to the job, Owen, aren't you?" he said. "Well, don't start chucking your weight about too much. The public won't stand for it. What's all this about refusing to give back her handbag to a lady?"

"Well, sir," Bobby explained, "in a case of suspected murder, I thought I couldn't be too careful."

"Murder?" the Inspector almost shouted. "What do you mean? It's suicide, isn't it?"

"I thought," began Bobby, but the Inspector cut him short.

"Don't you get thinking, my lad," he said. "Learn your job first and leave thinking to your seniors."

"Yes, sir," said Bobby.

"And if it's murder," the Inspector went on, "who is the murderer? Has your thinking got you that far?"

"Oh, yes, sir," Bobby answered. "I think I can hear the murderer coming now."

"Eh?" said the Inspector, startled. There came a knock at the door. The Inspector looked doubtfully at Bobby and then went to the door and opened it. "Oh," he said in a relieved tone, "it's you, Mrs. Clements. Come for your handbag. Where is it, Owen?"

"Here, sir," Bobby answered, showing it. "Mrs. Clements says her pay packet is in it—four pound notes, three shillings. Her pay is four pound four a week and she says she spent a shilling after she got home this evening leaving four pound three."

"That's right," Mrs. Clements said resentfully. "What about it? Any objection?"

"Only wondering," Bobby answered, "how you managed to spend a shilling after getting home when it's early closing day and all the shops shut since one?"

"I didn't come here to be insulted," Mrs. Clements said, but she had become a little pale. "What's it to do with you? Give me my bag and I'll be going."

"Mrs. Allen's sister who has the flat opposite," Bobby went on, "states that she gave Mr. Allen a shilling for two sixpences as he hadn't a shilling for the slot meter and wanted one. But he didn't use it, because there is still a one-shilling piece with the other money found in his pockets. I suggest that the shilling used was the missing shilling from Mrs. Clements's pay packet."

"Lies, nonsense, it never was. I'm going," Mrs. Clements said and turned towards the door but Bobby was standing now between her and it.

"I think," Bobby went on, "that taking care no one saw you, you slipped up here so as to have what you told Mr. Allen was to be a farewell drink with him, so you could part friends and no ill feeling. You got him fuddled with the gin you brought—was it doped, I wonder?—and when he was unconscious with it you got him with his head in the gas oven and turned on the gas. Is that the way it was?"

"Good Lord," the Inspector said softly.

"I didn't, never, never, never," Mrs. Clements cried. "What should I for when he was the only man I ever loved?"

"Perhaps," Bobby said softly, "because you could not bear to lose him again to the woman from whom you had taken him."

"And if I did," she screamed, "was I to stand being chucked away like that and him running back to her after all I had done for him and all the neighbours sneering?"

"I think you had better say no more just now," the Inspector told her, "but I'll have to ask you to come with us." Later on, he said to Bobby: "What put you on it in the first place?"

"Well, sir, I think first of all it was that glass in the sink so carefully rinsed out but the tea things left unwashed. It didn't seem to fit in, not even with a man full of gin and meaning to commit suicide.

"And then when I saw the shilling hadn't been used. I began to ask myself whose shilling it was. Mrs. Clements went out of her way to tell me that."

"I see," said the Inspector, approvingly this time. He added: "New to the job, Owen, aren't you? Well, I don't say but that you've made a good beginning."

Lightning Source UK Ltd.
Milton Keynes UK
UKOW01f1017200617
303734UK00001B/22/P

9 781911 579052